Praise f

"The mysterious past and the suspenseful present flow together in Cass Dalglish's literary thriller about nefarious happenings within and below the Alhambra in Spain. If *The Name of the Rose* or *The Club Dumas* kept you up late reading, so will *Ring of Lions*."

– Jack El-Hai, Author of *The Nazi and the Psychiatrist* and *The Lobotomist*

"I am in awe of the meticulous scholarship and research that went into writing Cass Dalglish's *Ring of Lions*. And that's in addition to the great cast of characters and the very unique murder mystery that is at the heart of the novel. This is armchair travel at its best. *Ring of Lions* has something for everyone!"

–Poet and Writer Cary Waterman, Author of *Book of Fire*

"To read Cass Dalglish's *Ring of Lions* is to walk through Córdoba and Granada, to become intimate with the Alhambra and its secrets, and to witness the legacy of pivotal events in Spain's history—the conversion and expulsion of Jews and Muslims, the reign of Torquemada and the Inquisition, and the concomitant rise of Spain as a world power. Reminiscent of Arturo Pérez-Reverte, A. S. Byatt, and Umberto Eco, Dalglish brings together history, architecture, and myth in a murder mystery peopled by transatlantic characters, including two young Americans, one from Cuba and one from New York, tracing their heritage back to southern Spain. In this compelling novel, their personal investment in Spanish history drives our own fascination with its complexities and its far-reaching legacy."

–Becky Boling & D. E. Green, Co-Poets Laureate of Northfield (2023-2024)

"Ring of Lions kept me guessing until the end, more or less sus-pecting everyone, and with less and less breath to spare as the sto-ry remorselessly tightened its grip in its closing chapters. Cass's knowledge of the Alhambra, and of the sweep of Spanish Moor-ish-Jewish-Christian history, of its myths, rumors and fantasies, is a rich mix indeed. The way in which she maneuvers such a large, eclectic cosmopolitan cast, moving them in and out of the action, on and off stage, is truly adroit. The locations, the action movement, the tower-climbing and the chases at the end – *Ring of Lions* is a novel that hinges on historical mysteries and the phantom lure of buried treasure!"

–Jonathon Hill, Professor Emeritus of English, St. Olaf College

The magical Alhambra, Muslim Spain's magnificent medieval pal-ace becomes in Dalglish's spell, the setting for a beguiling mystery. A mix of characters ranging from archeologists, forensic specialists, academics and young lovers all collaborate on the unraveling of a puzzle involving lion number nine in the circle of lions fountain. Along the way, the reader will encounter romance, betrayal, and murder. A heady soup indeed!"

–George Rabasa, author of *The Exile Zone*

"Cass Dalglish's writing of this book — and our reading of it — enacts a ritual of healing, one that digs deep historically and has a broad geographic scope."

–Deb Dale Jones, Scholar of Languages and Mythology

RING OF
LIONS

CASS DALGLISH

**CALUMET
EDITIONS**

Minneapolis

Accept the truth from whatever source it comes...

–Maimonides

Their colors are many, but the light itself is one...

–Ibn Zamrak

For Louis Branca, 1934 - 2015

FOREWORD

BY DEVONEY LOOSER

Cass Dalglish's *Ring of Lions* is a gripping, propulsive thriller that wears its learning lightly. Readers could certainly devour this beautiful novel's story without delving into its historical, geographical, and literary allusions. If you do so, however, you'll greatly enrich your experience. From its epigraphs to its last lines, *Ring of Lions* invites us into a multi-lingual, multi-faith, and old-new world, centered around The Alhambra in Granada, Spain.

The Alhambra, which began as a 9th-century fortress and was renovated into a 14th-century Islamic palace, is sometimes called the eighth wonder of the world. Of course, there are officially only seven. (A goal of one of *Ring of Lions*'s characters is to have the Alhambra actually designated the eighth.) One date that recurs is 1492, when it was taken over by the Spanish Christian Royal Court of Ferdinand and Isabella, also named in the novel's pages.

The story, however, is set "not long ago." The wise narrator revels in time's bending, because "New stories are constantly being told, old stories forgotten, some deliberately suppressed, some hidden in the mosaics that form when a thing like the Inquisition rests edge-to-edge against an age of tolerance." With this promise of stories—new, old, suppressed, hidden, forgotten, and perhaps unearthed—we're off.

Allusions to the medieval Jewish philosopher Moses Maimonides (c. 1135-1204) and famed Arab Andalusian poet of the Alhambra, Ibn Zamrak (1333-1393), pop in across the novel, set up almost as honorary characters themselves. A recurring print of Pablo Picasso's Don Quixote, based on Miguel de Cervantes's celebrated seventeenth-century comic hero, also symbolizes the interconnections of culture and daily life, past and present. Knowing these authors and images must deepen your reading experience of *Ring of Lions*, but it's not required. Perhaps you'll finish the novel and seek them out next.

Most of the allusions in *Ring of Lions* are Spanish and Moorish. Its unstated inspirations, however, hail from the tradition of the English novel. Gothic fiction by 1790s British bestseller Ann Radcliffe informs the surprise workings of the title's intriguing lions. Historical fiction of the early 1800s by the sisters Jane and Anna Maria Porter stand behind this work, too, as it includes fictional and real historical characters and nudges readers toward greater insights about the thorny present and past.

I was delighted to feel the influence here, too, of A. S. Byatt's *Possession* (1990). Both it and Dalglish's *Ring of Lions* draw on the tools of detective fiction, although setting their stories among learned scholars and collectors. Both novels demonstrate that a thirst for knowledge and a penchant for solving puzzles aren't the only burning passions propelling such work. Late in *Ring of Lions*, one character jokes about the "exhausting practice of intellectual life." That's certainly a truth. A greater truth, however, as readers will no doubt experience across the propulsive pages of *Ring of Lions*, is it must be a joyful, compelling practice, too.

Devoney Looser, Regents Professor of English at Arizona State University, is the author, most recently, of *Sister Novelists: The Trailblazing Porter Sisters Who Paved the Way for Austen and the Brontës*.

ALSO BY CASS DALGLISH

Sweetgrass

Nin

Humming the Blues

NARRATOR'S PROLOGUE

There is a story I want to tell you about events that happened in Spain not long ago. I can't say exactly when because I don't relate well to time. It's always bending, and when it bends, I remember things differently. Perhaps I actually see them differently from the start. Like so many stories, this one depends on others, and it's possible you don't know the fine points on which my story depends—and why would you? New stories are constantly being told, old stories forgotten, some deliberately suppressed, some hidden in the mosaics that form when a thing like the Inquisición rests edge-to-edge against an age of tolerance. Others are kept secret, in the mad hope that someday they will be able to be told freely, in the open, at last.

I won't tell you all of them, but I will acquaint you with one of those old stories. It's a legend about a King who heard about a book full of animal fables, tales that would make him wise and powerful. The King was deeply curious, so he sent a philosopher to a distant land to retrieve the book. It wasn't an easy journey for the philosopher, and when he returned with the tales, the King was disappointed. He didn't like them. He said they were all about envious creatures who were deceitful and corrupt. He demanded that the philosopher go back and find a different kind of story—one that told of strangers who trusted and protected one another.

Since the philosopher believed nothing was equal to friendship, he was pleased to resume his search, to set out again to fulfill the King's demand. And finally, he found another story, this one about a tortoise, a crow, a rat, and a gazelle, and how they rescued one another from the hidden snares of the hunter.

Of course, my account of what happened in Spain isn't the same as the philosopher's story. Mine includes a great number of humans, and—in a large crowd—I often find it hard to detect the identity of a hunter. Even so, you might want to check this list of people who show up in my story, and don't forget, all of them come with stories of their own.

Graciela Corzal de Moreno, Director of the Alhambra, the Moorish castle-city of the last Emir of Granada. Her goal is to have the Alhambra named a Wonder of the World, and its centerpiece—the Courtyard of the Lions—cherished everywhere.

Rubén Torres, assistant to Graciela Corzal de Moreno. A Cuban, he is in Spain on a fellowship awarded by a synagogue named after a man he has always believed to be his ancestor—Luis de Torres.

Walter Drummond, an American. He is a retired FBI agent working in Europe as an authenticist—an investigator specializing in the study of documents, art, and artifacts. He is known for exhibiting discretion in distinguishing an original from a copy.

Ana Madrizon, a young New Yorker who has just completed undergraduate studies in folklore. Centuries ago, her family of mathematicians, philosophers, and story tellers fled to the mountains of the Alpujarra, when the Moors were forced out of Granada.

Ander Mendarte, a Basque artesano. He is working on renovations at the Alhambra.

Rafael Montoya, a wealthy scholar and writer. He is the Director of

Digital Resources for the City of Córdoba's Municipal Library, located in the garden of the Alcázar de los Reyes, alongside the Tower of the Inquisición.

Professor Yann-Hubert Lenhard, an Alsatian museologist and longtime patron of the Alhambra. He is in Granada as the leader of a group of French docents who are on a study tour of the Alhambra.

Marie Trouchon, dutiful assistant to Professor Lenhard. She is in charge of logistics, setting up and carrying out the French docents' study tour.

Marco Gutierrez, supervisor of craftsmen working on the Alhambra. Elena Goya de Gutierrez is Don Marco's wife.

Alberto Castañeda is a police captain, Province of Granada.

Julio Villanueva is Investigative Magistrate of the Autonomous Community of Andalucía.

Luis de Torres, the Jewish translator who managed to remain in Spain one day after the final date of the Jewish Expulsion Order. That one day was enough for him to make it to the coast and travel with Columbus to the Americas.

Maslama al-Majriti, a mathematician and astronomer, who is credited for giving Spain an Arabic version of the letters of the Ikhwān al-Ṣafā', a secret group of thinkers and Muslim Neoplatonists. Some call them the predecessors of the Masons. Al-Majriti was known as the man from Madrid.

Boabdil, Muḥammad XII, formally Abū 'abd Allāh Muḥammad XII, the last Naṣrid Emir of Granada. He reigned until the fall of

Granada in 1492, when the Roman Catholic Monarchs Isabela and Fernando seized control of the Alhambra.

Isabela y Fernando were also known as the Catholic Kings, (Los Reyes Católicos). During their reign, the Moors and Jews were driven from Spain, Columbus sailed to the Americas, and the Spanish Inquisición was set firmly in place.

Tomás de Torquemada, the Grand Inquisitor. He was advisor to La Reina Isabela.

CHAPTER ONE

G raciela Corzal de Moreno came down a wide stone staircase with a small overnight bag in her left hand. She had slipped an ivory-colored envelope into the outer pocket of the briefcase that hung across her shoulders, so no attention was required as she reached the bottom of the staircase. With her free hand, she opened the heavy door and stepped out onto the plaza. She was in her fifties, close to the age of La Reina Isabela when she had died. But it was not the sixteenth century, and Graciela Corzal de Moreno did not appear to be aging. Her gait was quick and strong, and her scholarly mind was the same. When you met her, if you didn't know you were supposed to call her doctora, you would have found another title to address her, maybe doña. She was the kind of person who entered your thoughts and remained there.

Her office was in the structure attached like an afterthought to the constellation of palaces in the Alhambra. The edifice was named after Carlos—grandson of Isabela and Fernando, as they were known in Spain, or Ferdinand and Isabella, as they were called in English-speaking territories. Carlos himself had two royal identities. He was Carlos V, Holy Roman Emperor, and also Carlos I, King of Spain. The palace he built was a huge, pillowy edifice, square on the outside and round like the Roman Colosseum at the center. It was called the Carlos Quinto, perhaps because it was a Renaissance structure well-suited to his Holy Roman identity. It was abutted to the old Moorish castles of the Alhambra, not just to show that he was King of Spain as well as Holy Roman Emperor, but also to maintain his romance with the last castle of the Empire of the Moors.

Doctora Corzal took the narrow path around the edifice toward the old castles and opened a small door to the Court of the Myrtles. A few steps away was a staircase on the side of a wall, and at the top was a wooden door with a large iron handle. She turned a key in the lock, entered the last Emir's castle through the room of the Abencerrajes, then walked past the small, rust-colored basin said to have been filled at one time with the blood of rivals.

The Alhambra was really a medieval city, with sunlight and water melting into grand rooms, towers, arches, and gardens. The walls were lined with tiled patterns of triangles and squares and covered with stuccoed writing—poetry ascending from the human word to the sacred, from lace and stars to the stalactites of the heavens, and, for those who could hear, to the music of the spheres.

Finally, she reached the Courtyard of the Lions, an open square surrounded by walls of slender pillars that appeared to be made of fine-boned china stretching from marble floors to their own lacy concrete shoulders. Channels ran from the four sides of the courtyard to meet in a circle at the feet of twelve lions where the water was invisibly sent up to a basin resting on the lions' backs.

Doctora Corzal's visit was in honor of the beasts, who were assembled in a circle to protect the Alhambra's magic, sunlight reflected in water surrounded by poetry written in flowing Arabic script. She approached the ring of lions and said nothing that anyone could hear, but she appeared to be promising the animals that she would be successful. Her work had become her personal life, the Alhambra her second home, the lions her family.

Inside the ivory envelope was a proposal that the Alhambra be added to the list of the Wonders of the World. This was her second attempt. The Alhambra had come so close in the past, and now that the competition was open again, she was determined that the Alhambra would achieve the status it deserved.

This was not a light responsibility for Doctora Corzal. For her, it was the duty of the director of the Alhambra to carry this Moorish city in all its magnificence on her shoulders. But she was not a woman who could disavow even distasteful episodes from the past. Her memory also supported images of Córdoba's tolerance being extinguished, Spain's monarchs expelling the Jewish and Moorish populations, blood splattering onto the sand of the Inquisición, and the land being thinned by Civil War and tyranny.

The vision Doctora Corzal held closest at that moment, however, was of the time in Spain when knowledge had been protected, when one language touched the boundaries of another without leaving a gap, when mathematics, science, architecture, dance, astronomy, and poetry linked scholars as if they were triangles joined to squares on the walls of the Alhambra.

Could Doctora Corzal be overstating the grandeur of that time? Certainly. She was aware that positioning Córdoba, Sevilla, and Granada as fountains of intellectual tolerance was an act viewed by critics as mythology. The power of Fernando and Isabela was overwhelming. Córdoba, then Seville, and then the last—Granada—had fallen beneath the hooves of powerful armies. She knew that even golden eras had moments of torment. She carried all this in her memory. But for Doctora Corzal, the real wonder of the world was that there had once been a time in Spain when people from different worlds had built a universe in which they could all thrive. She hadn't been willing to consider that the Alhambra might not be named a Wonder of the World.

When she had first read reports that some kind of biological deterioration had been detected in portions of the Alhambra, she refused to admit that it worried her, but the news caused her the kind of doubt that victimized only the fastidious. Just in case there might be a need to protect the centuries-old tubing in the lions' bellies from harmful micro-organisms, she sent one of the twelve lions—the one she called el noveno—to an atelier in Paris to be cleaned. If the process proved worthwhile, she would send the others as well. But when lion number nine came back, it hadn't seemed to be itself. It was suddenly performing its water magic again for the first time in five and a half centuries, and that was troubling. Was the decontamination process enough to explain the mechanical rehabilitation of the lion?

Before Isabel and Fernando had taken over the Alhambra in 1492, the lions had been fed from a network of waterways discarded by the Romans and redesigned by Muslim hydraulic engineers. The system channeled water clean enough to drink to the mouths of the lions, and the supply alternated, surging water more abundantly to the mouth of a different lion each hour. Lion one spouted water at one o'clock, lion two at two o'clock, lion three at three. No one had been able to make the lions produce water with such clocklike precision since the Christians had conquered Granada in 1492, when the workmen of the Catholic Kings disassembled the mechanism and the lions had never spouted water properly again.

Some Spaniards wondered if the workmen simply wanted to discover how the lions had functioned so flawlessly. Others believed Isabela had ordered the workmen to take the fountain apart. Had she been frightened by the control the Emirs seemed to have over the water flow? Did she imagine they were exercising magical powers to conjure the regulation of time, transmuting matter, practicing alchemy?

After the fountain had been tampered with, the lions had never functioned properly again. Until now. Until el noveno returned from the atelier and began spouting water every evening at precisely nine o'clock, performing in the exact fashion it had worked for the Emirs. And that was the change that was causing Doctora Corzal disquiet. True, the adjustment in the lion's behavior could have resulted from having its plumbing cleared, but Doctora Corzal couldn't help worrying. If a repair was that simple, why had no one been able to fix the fountain before? What if her centuries-old lion had been stolen and a forgery outfitted with a cutting-edge timepiece had been returned to the Alhambra in its place?

That was a concern she couldn't voice in curatorial circles, of course. The mere suggestion that she was anxious about the authenticity of el noveno would lead to troublesome rumors about one of the most highly regarded and controversial of the Alhambra's treasures.

Doctora Corzal's Peugeot was parked in the small space reserved for her behind the Carlos Quinto. Once inside her automobile, she headed down the red hill to Granada's post office where the ivory envelope was officially sealed and stamped and sent on its way. Then she turned onto the highway that meandered toward Córdoba. There, a small group of experts were gathered to talk about authentication and replication. For Doctora Corzal, that meant art and forgery.

Only her good friend, Magistrate Julio Villanueva, and Corzal's assistant, Rubén Torres, knew forgery was on her mind. Villanueva suggested that Doctora Corzal attend the conference, meet some of these authenticists. Doctora Corzal decided to send her assistant to Córdoba ahead of her. Rubén had begun working for her only six months before, and there was still so much he hadn't seen. He had asked for a few hours of personal time to breathe in medieval Córdoba's history, and he assured her he would join her at the conference as soon as she arrived. They were searching for an expert who could be trusted to take a look at the Alhambra's lions—a very discreet look.

In Córdoba, Rubén Torres walked through the bus station toward a busy avenue. He was carrying a black motorcycle helmet and wearing a backpack—no need for a suitcase, he'd be traveling back to Granada the next afternoon. He headed toward a moto rental down the avenue where a half dozen cycles were arranged outside.

Rubén was used to traveling poor and was hoping for a good deal. He'd come to Spain from Cuba for postdoctoral study at the Alhambra on a fellowship from the Luis Torres Synagogue in the Bahamas, a scholarly honor enhanced by little money. But for Rubén, it was enough to be in Spain in the name of the translator who had accompanied Cristóbal Colón on his first voyage five hundred years before. Getting out of Granada ahead of the director was his chance to visit the ruins of the old Umayyad city of Madinat al-Zahra just outside of Córdoba.

The rental manager seemed curious about Rubén's passport. "We get very few tourists from Cuba," the man said. "What led you to Córdoba ?"

Rubén Torres wasn't anxious to share with strangers the details that had drawn him back to the land of his ancestors. He saw no reason to describe the conference or what he and his mentor hoped to learn. But the manager was insistent. "Why have you decided to visit us?" he asked.

Rubén could see he was going to have to reduce the manager's concern about renting a bike to someone from across the Atlantic, make him feel it was natural to travel from the Americas to rent a motorbike for an afternoon in Spain.

"Adventure drew me," he said, then nodded to demonstrate respect for the manager's curiosity. "Splendor. Córdoba's splendor for a thousand years."

The manager smiled. He was going to accept the story. He took Rubén to the garage to see the merchandise and pointed toward the Kawasakis—a silver Z 125 for €65 a day, a fine looking, green Vulcan S 650 for €94, and a Z 900 for €108. An even better deal was offered if Rubén would take a three-day special, but Rubén was frugal. At the back of the garage, over in the corner, he spotted something dusty, maybe a black bike leaning against the wall. Rubén twisted his way between rows of polished bikes toward the old dirty machine.

"And this?" he asked, pulling the old bike up and checking the tires.

"Too old," the manager said.

"How old?"

The manager shrugged. "Maybe 1985."

"That's not so old," Rubén said.

"I don't rent that one anymore. Clutch goes out."

"If it's a good price, I'll take it."

"Young men like you, they don't know how to use a clutch."

Ruben asked for a rag and began to wipe down the old Norton. "How much?" he asked.

"You can have it for thirty-five euros," the manager said. "But watch it. I can't fetch you if you're stranded out there."

The tires were the only thing Rubén was worried about. He could see they were worn but still serviceable. "I've been fixing bikes all my life. That's what we do in Cuba."

Rubén walked the bike out to the pump, filled the gas tank, put on his helmet and took the Norton for a spin. It felt good enough to him, so he offered the manager his Alhambra identification, his credit card, his hotel information for security, 15 percent of the rental fee, and cash for the gas. Finally, he signed the necessary papers to assure that he would pay the remainder when he returned the next morning.

Soon he was riding away on a black bike toward Córdoba's Calahorra Towers at the end of the Roman Bridge to pick up materials for the conference that was taking place there. A woman at the registration desk suggested he wander around the Museum of the Three Cultures, a small, comfortable space inside the Calahorra Towers, to learn about the Moors, Jews, and Christians in Córdoba. "Then go to the roof for a presentation by your colleagues, nothing official," she said, "just a social event, but go up there. The view is amazing."

Rubén went straight to the roof. They were serving coffee, and he asked for a cortado, then moved to the far side of the seating area. He was comfortable at the edge of things. The rooftop had been a battlement—low walls alternating with gaps for weapons. Rubén leaned through one of the gaps to enjoy a perfect view of the Mezquita-Catedral.

He turned his head and was sure he could see the old Synagogue as well. This was a landscape he'd been hoping to view, one that invited him to gaze into his past. He had learned early in life to summon a panoramic view of history, a skill he believed came naturally to a Cuban who always had to glance over his shoulder to see if something new was approaching—a new religion, a new culture dressed over the old, a new government seated on top of the last one. And here he was now, conjuring up the history of Spain and imagining it as his family's story—the story of the Jewish translator who traveled with Columbus.

Rubén had begun to think about the translator as a grandfather in a long line of grandfathers, an ancestor with whom he was now sharing a transatlantic journey with but one exception. While the ancestor's displacement had offered him an escape from the history of Spain, Rubén's adventure was a quest for the recovery of an identity the ancestor had left behind.

As the group was called to order, Rubén crouched next to the enclosed wall to make sure he wasn't blocking anyone's view. The speaker was an expert who had brought three documents he referred to as letters written by Reina Isabela to her advisor, Tomás de Torquemada. He said one was an original and the other two were handcrafted replications of the original. The documents were set out for viewing on tables and the audience was invited to select the authentic one.

"Label the others as replications," said the expert. "I ask that you refrain from calling them frauds—just to be civil." The audience members were invited to take a close look.

There was a man standing next to the spot where Rubén was crouching. Slowly, he moved to examine the objects closeup. He used a strange eyepiece and then took a notebook from his shirt pocket and made notes. To Rubén, the man didn't fit the profile of a museologist, despite the eyepiece. He was dressed like a European, one with money—Italian boots, slacks with a sharp crease despite the heat of the day, a white linen shirt, and gold cuff links. Perhaps he was a collector, a serious one—not a dabbler. But for Rubén, there was an element of stealth in his demeanor. Too nicely dressed for plain clothes police, but maybe a gambler in rare goods. Or was he an informer? He'd known a few of those.

The man came back to his spot next to Rubén, who stood up and shook himself off when he realized it was odd for him to be crouching like a crow.

The demonstration was over, and the expert announced that a fellow who'd been working for a gallery in Florence was the only one to choose the authentic letter. The other two were replications. The original belonged to a private collector in Madrid and while it was not on the market, interested parties could let the expert know and he would pass their interest along to the owner.

The man next to Rubén glanced quickly across the roof and touched his fingers to his upper lip. As he closed his notebook and put it back into his pocket, he shook his head modestly. Rubén noticed that a fellow in a yellow sport shirt on the other side of the audience nodded back, then turned and left.

Rubén couldn't resist engaging. "You don't agree with the expert?" he asked.

"I don't have thoughts to share."

That was all the man would say, but he'd said enough for Rubén to catch his accent—the kind of universal diction newscasters use on American TV. Was it a journalist's voice? Was he a professor? Or was he another of the experts—one who disagreed with the presenter's declaration of authenticity?

"Are you saying it's a fake?" Rubén persisted.

"I don't believe I made any comment whatsoever," the man said.

Rubén asked if he'd be speaking at the conference.

"Just before dinner," the man said.

Rubén handed the man his card, which read, "Rubén Torres, Asistente de la Directora, Alhambra de Granada."

The man returned the courtesy by offering his own card. "Walter Drummond," he said. "Authenticist and Investigator, New York." The man disappeared into the crowd.

Rubén's phone buzzed with a text from Doctora Corzal saying she had just left Granada and would arrive in time for the late afternoon talks. They could go together and easily catch two presentations before tapas. No time to waste.

Rubén had about three hours left for a visit to the Madinat al-Zahra, the palace built by the first Caliph of Al-Andalus a thousand years earlier. Hundreds of marble columns, walls covered in gold, green spaces and gardens with fountains and statues created by architects from Baghdad. But even the Caliph couldn't sustain the glory of this creation. Madinat al-Zahra was destroyed in a civil war. Sacked by Berbers. Burned. Left in ruins. The Caliph's Versailles taken away in pieces. Stones. Statues. Fountains. Hauled off to other sites, other cities.

Hundreds of years later, much of it was still rubble, but that didn't matter to Rubén Torres. Madinat al-Zahra continued to fascinate him. He wasn't attracted to what used to be there but was devoted instead to what was missing. In his mind, Madinat al-Zahra was the original home of the twelve lions of the Alhambra, and he felt called to stand where they had once stood.

Rubén hopped onto his motorbike and sped toward the Palma del Rio. Once he reached the highway, he swooped down the entrance ramp and increased his speed until, from a distance, his figure on a black motorbike became a fleck of ink crossing the horizon toward Madinat al-Zahra.

Walter Drummond walked across the Roman Bridge toward the Mezquita-Catedral and tucked into a small café for lunch. Drummond's palate could be quite demanding, but all he wanted at this time was a glass of red wine. He was disturbed by the display he'd just watched on the roof, which had used a serious conference in a way that could open it to fraud. If they had needed a circus act to warm up the crowd, they should have hired jesters. Galleries, museums, collectors—they could all be so easily caught in a counterfeiter's net, as some already had been.

He had no doubt that the letters displayed were sophisticated, but there wasn't an authentic one among them. He'd signaled his opinion that they were all forgeries to his colleague from the Library of Congress, who had signaled back that he understood and quickly left the rooftop. They would talk later about specifics, then approach the presenter with information about how they knew his "original" was a fraud–the edges of the pages. A missing hook at the end of the "s" in the signatures, a telltale stroke Drummond had detected in all other authentic Isabela signatures he'd seen in his career. Drummond hoped that would be the end of the foolishness. The distasteful demonstration had destroyed his appetite.

And who was the curious young fellow with the motorcycle helmet? Drummond took another look at the young man's card. Rubén Torres, Asistente de la Directora, Alhambra de Granada. Was Doctora Graciela Corzal de Moreno still in charge? He hadn't heard otherwise. Someone would have told him if she had left. He'd read a number of her academic papers and remembered the internecine squabble when she won the coveted post as Director of the Alhambra, despite a well-orchestrated effort by rivals to paint her as an unworthy recipient of some sort of post-mortem nepotism that flowed from memories of her dead husband's lengthy term as the director.

It had all been silly gossip in Drummond's opinion. Graciela Corzal had been young and less than qualified when her husband had died, but in the decade after his death, she had studied deeply, honed her perceptions, and polished her curatorial skills to become the associate director of the British Museum.

When they had hired her, the Patronato had no doubt about Doctora Graciela Corzal's readiness. She was very clever, very steady. Responsible. She'd be happy to have missed the nonsense on the roof. It was odd they'd never met face-to-face. He'd been at the Louvre recently and had just come from the Prado. He was known in Europe. His clients trusted him to know what was original, what was a copy—even masterful copies like the ones he'd just seen. So, the motorcyclist was Doctora Corzal's assistant. Curiosity lifted his mood.

Later that afternoon, when Drummond scanned the audience before beginning his presentation, he saw Doctora Corzal next to her assistant about five rows back from the podium. Neither one of them asked a question during Drummond's presentation, but Doctora Corzal approached him after he'd finished and invited him for tapas across the Roman Bridge, at the taberna near the Mezquita-Catedral.

"In about thirty minutes?" she suggested, looking at her watch.

"Of course," he answered.

When they met, she told Drummond her assistant wouldn't be able to join them because he had other business to take care of.

A picture of the motorcyclist came into Drummond's mind. "An interesting young man," he said.

"He's Cuban, with a doctorate from the University of Buenos Aires. He's here on a post doc from the Luis de Torres Synagogue. It's in the Bahamas, named after Cristóbal Colón's translator."

"He shares a name with a man who sailed with Columbus?" That wasn't the story Drummond had been imagining for Rubén.

"He is quite excited about it. In fact, he believes he has found his Spanish ancestor."

Everyone was finding ancestors these days, Drummond thought. But he wouldn't be matching his DNA with someone from 1492. "Do you know if it's true?

"I hadn't thought of doubting him."

"I mean, has he found a family connection?"

"Apparently, his family has always talked about it, but I haven't quizzed him." Graciela Corzal was sipping a single glass of dark, sweet Pedro Ximenez, moving cautiously, making her way into her worries slowly. "We haven't had time to talk much today," she continued, "but he did mention that you were quite impressive this afternoon—the way you worked a fraud loose from that puzzling opening presentation."

Drummond smiled. He understood now. The quick conversation that afternoon with Torres had not been accidental. Rubén had been doing advance research.

Doctora Corzal finally switched the conversation to the Alhambra and her work on Wonders of the World project. As they spoke, it was obvious to Drummond that she was listening closely and parsing his responses.

A while later, she declined a second Pedro Ximenez and asked for Moorish tea—a crystal demitasse for each of them—and as she swallowed the sweet, apple-tinged liquid, she mentioned that she was acquainted with Drummond's friend, the magistrate, Julio Villanueva. She had known Villanueva for years. And she had, in fact, come to Córdoba at Villanueva's suggestion to meet experts and see who might take a look at the palace's popular centerpiece, the Courtyard of the Lions.

And then she told Drummond about el noveno, lion number nine, and how she'd sent the beast off for cleaning because of bacterial damage that had been detected in other parts of the Alhambra. She told Drummond how the lion had come back changed, acting as the Emirs had intended, marking the passage of time again by gushing at nine o'clock every evening.

Drummond could see that the lion had awakened a deep sense of curatorial responsibility in Doctora Corzal.

She leaned in toward Drummond, close enough to lower her voice, but discreetly enough to avoid arousing the attention of others in the taberna. "Will you come to Granada?" she asked. "Come and meet our spitting lion."

It was two days later that a pair of women were at JFK Airport at the check-in counter. The younger woman held her passport in one hand and rolled her bag as she moved along with the line of passengers. She appeared to be a college student. The other woman was older, with a few streaks of white through her thick, black hair. She was offering several twenty-dollar bills folded and neatly tied with a black ribbon to the younger one.

"No, Mom," the younger one said. "You'll need this. You've already given me more than enough." There were hugs, then the daughter said, "Thank you, love you, thank you," over and over again.

The mother said, "When you land, don't go to sleep right away. Stay awake until evening. See the city. Enjoy las tapas. Ajo blanco. Boquerones."

"Anchovies?"

"Con el pan sabroso de España." The mother was taking a deep breath as though she were smelling fresh bread, but she might have been holding back tears.

The airline agent called to the daughter and motioned toward the counter. "Come, it's your turn now," he said.

The mother backed up a few steps and made a slow turn to go her separate way. "Cuidate," she called to her daughter, then waved and walked to the escalator.

The daughter handed her passport to the agent who looked at her, then at her photo, then back at her, and finally said, "Ana Madrizon."

"Yes."

"What is your destination?"

"Madrid. Then Granada."

"Are you from Spain?" asked the agent. "¿Viene de España?

Ana answered quickly in Spanish. "No. Soy Americana."

"So you are American, and Spanish?"

"A long time ago," Ana said. "Not me, but my family. They came from Spain a long time ago. Is there a problem?"

The agent handed back her passport. "No problem. But you made me curious. Your mother spoke Spanish, and you have a good accent yourself." He shrugged. "I check passports, and you made me wonder, that's all. Have a good trip."

Ana couldn't really calculate the agent's intention. Was this some kind of security test? If it was a test, had she answered correctly? Did he administer this test to everyone, or only to Spanish speakers? Had she just been flirted with during a passport screening?

Her family had lived in New York for generations, but the agent's questioning was still causing her anxiety. Yes, she spoke Spanish, she'd been raised in the Madrizon tradition that required all the members of every generation to study Arabic and to learn Spanish. And not just the language, but everything that was important to the ancestor, the Moor, al-Majriti. That was the mathematician and philosopher who died in Córdoba before the Reconquista, long before the last Emir retreated into the Sierra Nevada.

Ana's family had what amounted to an archive of the Moor's writings, which had been handed down from generation to generation—mathematical treatises, an encyclopedia of philosophy, discourses on astronomy, and the folk stories that Ana loved.

"We have safeguarded everything, even the stories," her grandmother used to say.

"Keep them close," her father often reminded her, especially anything that would give away the family details about al-Majriti, the man from Madrid whose birthplace was part of their name, Madrizon. That was the way al-Majriti had lived—open to ideas, curious about science, dedicated to mathematics, attracted to the architectures of land and space, and fond of ancient fables—but always cautious with the details of his life. He and his company of sincere friends were free thinkers—free to investigate any idea, but careful to meet in secret. They hid their identities for fear that recognition would lead to persecution. They remained hidden so well that no one had ever uncovered all their names.

Now, the freethinkers were long gone, and Ana's father and grandmother had died. Her mother had become the curator of family mysteries, a guardian who believed in sharing wisdom rather than keeping it locked away. But secrecy is a strong habit, one that's hard to give up. So, while Ana's mother supported her daughter's dream of becoming a folklorist, she encouraged her to hold off on sharing the family's stories.

Ana made her way toward an enclosure that sheltered serpentine lines of passengers. As she tucked her shoes and backpack into a plastic bin, her mother's voice echoed in her mind.

"Cuidate," the voice was saying. "Take care. Take care of everything."

CHAPTER TWO

W ater, pure cold water. No wine could compete with the prospect of a glass of icy mountain water for Walter Drummond
at that moment. He'd just traveled in the heat of the day from the
flats of Córdoba, past mounds of olive trees, through hilltop towns
on curvy Andalusian highways, and the liter of mineral water coming toward him on a tray held by an amiable waiter was more inviting to him than any of the wines on the list.

Drummond unfolded the linen napkin and spread it on his lap.
He was looking forward to the kind of gracious afternoon meal that
seemed available only in Spain.

The waiter uncapped the mineral water, and it gave off a slight
whisper as it poured out of the green bottle into Drummond's glass.
Drummond nodded politely, lifted the glass to his lips, and let the
cold, wet fizz cool his throat and satisfy his thirst.

"Tenía sed," he told the waiter. Even though Granada was
cool in comparison to the 104 degrees he'd left in Córdoba, he had
worked up quite a thirst.

The waiter smiled, "When you drink the water of Granada,
the city becomes a part of you." It was Lorca's line, the waiter said,
and he seemed to bow ever so slightly as he poured effervescent liquid into Drummond's glass one more time. Again, Drummond lifted
the tumbler to his lips and enjoyed the mineral taste. When he had

finished his second glass, the waiter began to list the special dishes available for that afternoon's meal.

Drummond selected asparagus tips with olive vinaigrette along with a bowl of gazpacho—he'd never lost his taste for the cold tomato soup—and a plate of pescaíto frito, fried fish from the southern coast. The waiter told Drummond he was fortunate because today's gazpacho was even more savory than usual. Finally, Drummond opened the leather-bound wine menu and began to read. Now that he'd quenched his thirst, he could see that a glass—or two—of white wine would be a pleasant way to relax after his drive. It would be a simple meal, one that would go well with one of the Ebro River whites on the list.

When he'd visited Granada in the past, he'd stayed at the home of his friend, Julio Villanueva, the investigative magistrate for Andalucía. But this time, because he came to Granada at the invitation of the Alhambra's director, who was also chief historian for Granada's historic trust, he booked a room in the Reina Cristina just down from the Cathedral. It allowed him to keep a respectful distance from his friend, the magistrate, during the investigation. Drummond was about to embark on a business that might take him quite a while to finish and might end up sending him to a courtroom as a witness.

The good-natured waiter gave Drummond time to enjoy his gazpacho in leisure, and both his water goblet and his wine glass were kept full. The asparagus was tender, the fish was an excellent choice—breaded and fried in the lightest oil, not salty. Drummond ate slowly, allowing himself time to enjoy the satisfying meal. When it was time for coffee, the waiter brought two silver pots—a large one for coffee, a small one for heavy cream—and served up advice on how Drummond should approach the Alhambra: Don't drive up the mountain, the waiter advised, getting up and down the hill enmeshed a motorist in unbearable traffic. A stroll past the Cathedral would provide a chance for reacquaintance with Granada. Perhaps he'd like to stop at the graves of Fernando and Isabela? The daughter Juana? They were all there, in the crypts. The waiter thought it best to walk up the road to the Alhambra, listen to the people, enjoy the shops. Unless, perhaps, he had a reason to hurry.

No, Drummond said. He was not expected right away. But he'd visited the Cathedral many times, so he could forego the waiter's suggestions and delay the side trips. Perhaps he would have a nap instead before he walked up the hill.

When he'd met the Alhambra's director a few days before in Córdoba, Doctora Corzal had been worried about the lions in the famous fountain, "Come see them and then we'll talk," she had said. But she'd been careful to give him only enough information to wet his curiosity. She hadn't mentioned fraud, even though she told him she'd come to the conference on authentication to find an expert she could trust. Drummond was one of the speakers, there to talk about antiquities, precious documents, and forgery.

Forged documents had started him on the road to connoisseurship years before, when he was a young postal inspector. He loved the quiet precision that enveloped him when he was alone with papers. Why he'd left that job he was never sure. Why had he let himself be lured away by the FBI? Perhaps it was the enticing idea of doing good for society rather than spending his days alone at a desk. But in the end, he'd spent nearly a decade with a holster over his shoulder seeking perpetrators of distasteful crimes.

He was valuable to the bureau because he could recognize patterns in the actions of a guilty party, patterns that were intriguing and alluring—what he found himself defining as esthetically attractive. He was the detail fellow, relied upon for the fresh eye he brought to circumstances of wrongdoing, always expected to move closer and closer until facets of weakness were identified and tessellations of motivation were exposed. He believed he was leaning in close, focusing tightly on criminal skill yet keeping satisfactory observational distance.

Exactly what a good investigator should be able to do. Drummond wasn't showy. It wasn't about him. He saw solving a case as a proficiency, a dexterity that could be taught to young agents, until he learned that maintaining observational distance was difficult to teach. His young assistants seemed to be entangling themselves with suspects, and Drummond was having trouble extricating them. He could see that his belief in his own proficiency was causing the problem. His team was imitating his meticulous drive to move closer and closer to the crimes being investigated. They were copying his own rigorous study of the coarseness and harm that accompanied dishonesty. They were watching his fascination with the esthetics of violence—financial, psychological and physical. And it had become hard for Drummond himself to balance there on the thin edge of transgression. That's when he had decided it was time to distance himself, to go off on his own, back to the quiet life—to documents, to artifacts. Away from flesh and blood. Back to a desk where he could work alone.

After he left the FBI, collectors began to hire Drummond for his close eye, for his recognition of patterns, for his ability to magnify the inauthentic. Soon he had calls from the Getty and the National Gallery and the Louvre and the Prado, and once again he earned considerable respect, especially among those who feared fraud. Perhaps more importantly, he had established a reputation as someone who could be trusted to make his visits seem routine and keep his findings off the record until, and unless, a curator decided public disclosure was necessary. Working alone suited him well.

And so there he was, finishing a fine meal in Granada and thinking about his trip up the hill to the Alhambra. He had agreed to meet Doctora Corzal that evening to see what the lion might do at nine o'clock. Then he planned to stay for the evening tour of the palace at ten.

The waiter brought his bill and offered him a pamphlet boasting that Lorca had spent his last days at the hotel, at the start of the Civil War when the building was a private Andalucian home. Drummond thanked the waiter and slipped the pamphlet into his pocket. He climbed the wide marble steps to the third floor, circled around the open gallery, and unlocked the heavy door to a small but well-appointed space. He'd allotted two hours for a siesta and another for the walk up the hill, so he hung his sport jacket in the closet, slipped off his shoes, and stretched out on the bed. Soon, he'd have his stroll through the open-air shops, past the Cathedral, and up to the towers of the Alhambra.

G raciela Corzal's massive mahogany desk was covered with manila file folders and notes written on pages of yellow graph paper. The papers had been set out in a serpentine path across the desk by Rubén, and she was circling the material now, attempting to understand the organizational style Rubén had employed. Some of his notes were in Spanish, some in Hebrew, others in cursive Arabic. Odd that she could read most of his notes and still not be able to follow the narrative trail Rubén seemed to have been mapping, but she hadn't insisted on that kind of clarity. Not yet.

The real currency of Rubén's research fellowship from the only Synagogue in the Bahamas was honor, not money, and since she couldn't add much to his stipend, she was lenient. Still, she enjoyed the energy he brought to his work. Perhaps that was another reason she was too easy on him. But where was Rubén now? In return for a free day on Sunday that he could fill with travel to Corpus Christi fiestas scheduled across Andalucía, he had promised to spend that Thursday afternoon organizing material on the lions and interpreting his research for Inspector Drummond. Now the afternoon was fading into evening, and he still wasn't there in her office where she had expected to find him.

Graciela had been telling herself there was no cause for concern—there were always issues that ensnared young men as the weekend neared—but she was beginning to wonder if Rubén had come across something unexpected. Lately, his performance had been erratic as well as inspired. He'd been staying late into the evening when the Alhambra's Palacios Nazaríes were open for moonlight visits, disappearing in mid-afternoon, huddling with the craftsmen, chatting with that young Basque artesano, Ander, who was working on restoration projects throughout the site. Still, Graciela Corzal considered herself lucky to have Rubén around. His specialty was medieval architecture, and his interest in the Fountain of the Lions had given him the kind of obsessive edge that Graciela found essential in a scholar.

Like Graciela, Rubén had found it puzzling that el noveno had come back from the atelier functioning as it had not functioned since the fifteenth century.

"Some would be pleased," Graciela had told him, displaying a method her mentor had used on her students—continually testing the quality of their curatorial skepticism. Graciela had hoped the test would work on Rubén.

"I'm more interested than pleased when an artifact displays this sort of difference," Rubén had replied.

That had been the correct answer to Graciela's quiz.

CHAPTER THREE

Rubén crouched down to tie his boot and slipped sideways into the soft earth next to the Río Darro. The bank of the Darro was a mixture of loam and pine needles, a dark mud created by the short burst of rain a few hours earlier. His shoes were covered in it. More than his shoes—his stockings and left trouser leg. And his hands. He supposed his face was smeared with the stuff as he wiped away heavy drops of perspiration that gathered on his forehead in the heat.

The artesano should have been there long ago, but the fellow was either late or not going to show up at all. Ander had told Rubén there was an opening in the brush on the riverbank below the Torre de las Armas. He'd heard talk of it among his friends, the ones who pushed wheelbarrows of gravel for the renovation project in the Alcazaba up above.

Ander had noticed Rubén's sketches of possible underground exits and entries, and he'd promised to take Rubén to see a real opening in the hill—one Ander believed could be followed into the Alhambra if centuries worth of debris were cleared. "It is, perhaps, the cave where the princesses hid when they came back after riding horseback all night in the Sierra," Ander said. "Or maybe it's where Boabdil escaped from the palace when the Catholic Kings were going to kill him."

"But they didn't kill him, Ander," Rubén replied. "He rode out on horseback, through the Gate of Justice, in plain sight. He'd already surrendered. They let him go."

"Because they didn't think he had anything left to give them," Ander said. "The people say he slipped out earlier—before the Catholic Kings arrived—to hide his treasures."

Rubén was keenly aware of his status as a visitor in Spain, even though his family routinely recited a list of ancestors that traced their line back to August 3, 1492. So he was always careful when he spoke to the young workers who'd come from provinces across the north of Spain to labor in Granada on the Alhambra project. They may not all be Granadinos, but they were Spaniards, and Rubén was something entirely different. He was a Cuban. And he had the sense to know it was bad form to challenge Spaniards about Spanish history.

He hadn't told the artesanos that his family went all the way back to the embarkation by Cristóbal Colón from the port of Palos. He hadn't specifically mentioned the person he called "abuelito," Luis de Torres, Rubén's obscure "grandfather," the translator and astronomer, the Spanish Jew who knew Latin and Spanish and Arabic, and who had signed on with Colón to leave Spain the day after all Jews were forced out. Abuelito is what Rubén still called his grandfather when he imagined him riding out of the Sierra Nevada toward the sea, hurrying toward Cádiz just as Boabdil had rushed toward the Alpujarra.

The way Rubén's family told the story, Luis de Torres had understood for a while that his people were being scattered. Laws were being enacted. Documents were crossing his desk. Decrees were needing interpretation. Rubén's grandfather, Luis, could see a diaspora coming.

As the Christian armies of the reconquista rode toward Granada on Andalucían horses, the planned dispersal of the Jews rode alongside them—right there—in the packs of documents that messengers were delivering from city to city. Among them were new laws and orders. Don't let the Jews sleep outside the ghetto. Don't let them sell their wares at the market. Don't let the doctors be doctors. Move the young people away from their families when they marry. Let everyone convert or leave Spain. These were the messages conveyed in the documents Luis had been ordered to prepare—more of them every year. Move the Jews out.

And then there were the letters about Granada that contained troubling orders to collect more taxes to pay for the army that was marching on the last stronghold of the Moors. The Jews were being moved around like pieces on a game board and the sultans were down to one last mountain crag. Which would come first, the expulsion of Luis's people or the reconquista of Granada?

The story passed down to Rubén was that some of the ancestors believed there was safety in conversion. After all, wasn't Fernando's grandmother a Jew, and didn't everyone in Spain have such a grandmother? But Rubén imagined abuelito telling his wife it was time for them to leave rather than convert. They should set up a home in Greece, maybe Turkey. Even Portugal would be safe.

"Travel day and night to find a spot," Luis would have told his family.

Those were the words of Maimonides, the philosopher the people called RamBam. His advice was to choose exile as an alternative to giving up one's identity.

In the end, Luis's wife had gone into the Catedral one afternoon and had come out with water on her head and oil on her lips and hands and feet. The conversion was done. They'd be safe if Luis would only do the same, the story went. Rubén's grandmother had received a certificate in Latin identical to ones Luis would have first seen ten years before.

The certificate was stiff and made a dull rattle in her hands. It carried the scent of the Catedral. The ink was heavy, the strokes bold. The seals of both church and state were pressed into amber wax. No need to stop believing, she must have reminded Luis. Even RamBam understood necessity. Luis would have countered that RamBam also understood risk. They'd be taking a risk that neighbors might notice their lack of orthodoxy or catch them making a mistake. Something as simple as failing to genuflect could threaten their lives.

In Rubén's rendition of the family story, Luis had gone home, opened a deep drawer in his desk and rummaged to the bottom of a stack of discarded papers for a piece of parchment identical to the certificate given to his wife, who was now to be called Catalina. The parchment Luis pulled from the drawer contained everything his wife's parchment did except a name, two seals in amber wax, and an accidental drop of holy oil spilled during a ceremony.

Fortunately, Luis had what was needed to correct those missing elements—wax, a government seal, a church seal, and a small silver flask of consecrated oil that carried the aroma of the Church. He'd been gathering these things over the years as he translated decrees coming into the Governor's palace…in case conversion became expedient. Luis wouldn't have told his wife about the forgery. It was better for her not to know.

In Rubén's cherished version of the story, Luis rolled the certificate and put it into the leather pack he was filling for the ride up to Granada. He'd been asked to accompany the Catholic ambassador on a visit to the court of the Emir. Talks were beginning, and Luis was the most capable interpreter in southern Spain. It was December 1491, and the kings wanted to settle things by Christmas.

This family story had been handed down from generation to generation in Cuba. Luis Torres, the famous abuelito, had been inside the Alhambra while Boabdil was still in charge. He'd served as interpreter as Boabdil considered surrendering.

This was the story Rubén was hiding from Ander and the other workmen while he was asking about five-century-old rumors that they'd picked up on the streets of the Albaicín. Rubén didn't know if the workmen had any religious loyalties at all. He wasn't sure whose culture they were remembering or how old the secrets were that Ander insisted you could hear if you leaned into the hill and pressed your ear against the earth.

"Whose rumors are these?" Rubén asked.

"They belong to the people," Ander told him. "I hear them every day. At work, afterward when I have apple tea in the plaza. Everyone knows these stories. All of Granada knows. Boabdil hid all the gold and jewels somewhere—out of the reach of the Reyes Católicos—and only after the wealth of the Moors was safely hidden in a cave did he go back and surrender."

"The other workers here—they believe this?"

There was a good deal of talk about a lost route, Ander said, so much talk lately that his supervisor threatened that if the storytelling continued, he'd cut the pay they were getting for all the extra hours they'd been assigned.

"We think someone wants to keep us quiet," Ander told Rubén.

"One of the master masons?"

Ander shrugged. Rubén had the feeling the question made Ander even more nervous.

"I still hear the stories…" Ander said, "but I don't talk about them anymore."

About that time, Ander had begun hiking home alone after work every day, down the hillside, through the brush, across the Río Darro, back up the hill on the winding streets of the Albaicín. He told Rubén that one day he noticed a soft spot in the hill below the Alhambra. More than a soft spot. There was an opening in the hill.

"Can you show me?" Rubén asked, promising to pay Ander for the hour it would take to lead him to the cave. They agreed to meet Thursday afternoon at the edge of the Darro directly below the Torre de las Armas. From there, Ander promised, they could climb to the secret spot. But Ander phoned Rubén just before noon and told him he'd have to postpone their walk. Could Rubén meet later?

Rubén said he could arrange things. Yes, he could meet later. Spain was a complicated place and being Cuban, Rubén understood complication. He was secretly happy to have a few extra hours to sort through his notes in Doctora Corzal's office. At four, Rubén left the pages on the mahogany desk sorted into an order that only he understood, but which would serve him well when he spoke to Doctora Corzal's visitor. He locked the director's office and took the road behind the Carlos Quinto, down the hill toward the Darro. But Ander never appeared.

Rubén waited for another half an hour before giving up on his friend, and then spent another twenty minutes scaling his way back and forth below the tower in search of the secret entrance, pushing through brush and moving stones that could have been piled as gestures of secrecy. By 5:30, he was ready to give up on Ander and the path he claimed he'd been using every afternoon to get home from the Alhambra. Rubén had his own work to do for Doctora Corzal, and he wasn't going to get it done before her guest, the authenticist, showed up to see the lion.

Rubén walked a bit farther. It was steep and rocky. He had to hold onto a Poplar branch to pull himself to the small plateau about halfway up the hill, and when he moved a branch out of his way, he saw a shoe dangling about twenty meters away. He worked his way up the hill until he could see the shoe had a leg attached to it, and the leg was attached to a young man's body. Ander was lying in the brush at the edge of this strange plateau, his legs twisted in an alarming way.

Rubén crawled over to Ander, who seemed to be staring at him, and touched his cheek. Ander's face was cold despite the heat of the afternoon. His neck was twisted oddly, and the side of his head was covered in dried blood. Rubén leaned over, putting his ear on Ander's chest. There was no movement. No sound.

Rubén leaned back against the hill and pulled his cell phone from his pocket. His first instinct was to call Ander's family, but they were somewhere in Basque country. He didn't know them, didn't even know where Ander was living in Granada, so he phoned the policía and reported that he had found the body of a young man on the hill above the Darro just below the Torre de las Armas. Yes, of course, he would stay there and wait for the policía to arrive.

Rubén couldn't take his eye off the twist in Ander's neck. And his legs, the way they were bent around him. It didn't appear that he had a simple fall. Rubén used his cell phone again, this time to take a photograph, and that's when he noticed a scrap of paper sticking out of the boy's left shoe. Carefully, he gripped the scrap of paper between his thumb and forefinger and pulled the note away from his would-be guide's foot. It was written in large, childish letters and in words that were not Spanish.

One phrase at the top of the scrap, one at the bottom: "ibai-le-hoi," the note said, "lehoi-hezle." The boy had said his family came from the north, and Rubén recognized the words in Basque. "Lion tamer," the letters said. "River lion," or was it the sea rather than the river?

The policía arrived and slid down the soft path above Rubén, weapons drawn. Behind them came a pair of médicos carrying a stretcher, medical bags and an oxygen tank.

"I'm glad you're here," Rubén told them. He realized he was expecting them to revive Ander.

Within minutes, the policía turned away from Ander and were looking at Rubén. They insisted Rubén stand and give them his papers and the teléfono that he'd just tucked into his pocket. Rubén gave them his phone.

"Password, now," an oficial said, holding the phone so Rubén could tap in his code and frowning when the photo of Ander's body appeared on the screen. How could Rubén be so cold-blooded as to take a photograph of a dead body? And there was a note in the fellow's shoe. Where was it now? Was Rubén hiding it?

Rubén handed over the note. While one of the policía was trying to read the note, the other was reading Rubén's passport. "Why should we believe you? A Cuban? A student? Why are you visiting Granada?"

"I'm on a fellowship here at the Alhambra and working on a postdoctoral project," Rubén explained. "An architectural project."

"And what about languages and scribbles like these? Are you an expert? Can you translate these words you were hiding in your pocket?"

"Perhaps, but my specialty is really architecture."

"What do you think these scribbles mean?"

"Meaning is hard to fix," Rubén answered.

"Give it a try, por favor."

"It could be a phrase for a circus person, like a lion tamer," Rubén said. "There may be a mention of the sea."

"The note mentions the sea? So, you admit you have taken this evidence from this victim. Or have you brought this evidence with you to leave with the victim?"

"I found it, here," Rubén said.

"A sea lion?" The oficial twisted the paper around so he could see the blank side and then twisted it back again. He didn't seem to know what to do with it. He started to put it in his pocket and then thought better of it. "You come here from Cuba, and you find a body, and it has a note in Basque, and you are climbing here in the brush on this hill, and you read Basque. Please, tell me why this coincidence is happening."

"I've been here in Spain for six months."

"And Basque?

"Languages come easy…" Rubén said.

The oficial looked again at the photo of the dead young man. In the photo, the note was protruding from his left shoe.

Rubén reached for his phone, "I'd like to call the director of the Alhambra, Doctora Corzal. She's expecting me for a meeting on a topic of importance to the Patronato. I'm late."

The oficial took a deep breath before he told Rubén there would be no more climbing and no more translating and no call to Doctora Corzal. For now, all Rubén would be doing was sitting still and touching nothing. "You've tampered with things quite enough," he said.

CHAPTER FOUR

Ana Madrizon had been up all night on the flight from New York, then she had two hours in Madrid before her plane took off for Granada and finally taxied to its gate. When she checked in to the Hotel Guadalupe up on the Alhambra hill, the desk clerk asked where she'd learned Spanish.

"My family," Ana had responded.

"They are from Andalucía?"

"Yes, Córdoba, Granada, the Alpujarras…"

The clerk lifted a pamphlet from behind the desk. "We have excursions into the Sierra Nevada—right up to the point of The Moor's Last Sigh."

"Washington Irving's story? As the sad prince rushed to the mountains, he paused to look back at Granada and was overwhelmed with grief?"

"Precisamente," the clerk said while handing Ana a brochure. "We can also take you to the room in the Alhambra where Irving wrote about Boabdil. Your name—we would pronounce it differently. It does not seem entirely Spanish."

"The family changed it somewhere along the line."

"Americans change everything," the clerk said, handing her the key to her room. "You never really know who anyone is."

That's when Ana first noticed people speaking French in the lobby. They were gathered in small clusters and holding fliers that

advertised the afternoon sightseeing tour around the city of Granada. Ana's French was good when she was reading, passable when
she was listening, but not dependable on only two hours of sleep.
She couldn't say for sure who these people were, but they seemed to
be in Granada for a conference. Maybe they had a good idea, taking
a bus tour. Not a bad way to stay awake.

In one of the clusters, Ana noticed a tall, silver-haired man in a
caramel suit who seemed to be an authority of some sort. The others
were nodding at him with reverence. The man left the group, crossed
through the lobby, and stepped into an elevator. Ana entered just before the door closed and noticed a page of equations sticking out of
the man's jacket pocket. He'd been speaking French with the people
in the lobby, but his French had a lilt to it, a tone unlike the others.

The man got off on the second floor, and Ana went on to the
third. She settled into her room quickly, shook the wrinkles out of
the dress she wanted to wear to the Alhambra in the morning, and
hung it in the closet. She took her iPhone out of her carry-on and slid
it into the front pocket of her messenger bag so she'd have a camera
at her fingertips.

Then she went down to the lobby again, to the bar to munch
on a cheese sandwich. Her mother was right about the bread. Warm
and crispy.

When the French group started for the door, Ana wrapped the
last of the sandwich in her napkin and stuffed it into her bag. She
waved to the waiter, pointed at the ten-euro note she was slipping
under her plate, and followed the French people down to the parking lot and onto the big red tour bus. For most of the afternoon, she
sat on the top deck as the bus steamed down the Avenida Reyes
Católicos, around the Catedral, and past the bronze statue of the man
commissioned to find a new trade route to India.

The bus circled the park where the green veranda of Lorca's
house was now the entry to a museum. Ana breathed in air scented
with basil and mint and whispered, "Green the wind, and green the

branches…" She climbed down from the roof deck to ask the driver if she could hop off the bus and spend the afternoon there at the Lorca museum, but the driver discouraged her. "School children," he muttered. "Buses full of them." He was sure they wouldn't let her in.

The bus was hovering near the Plaza de Toros when Ana overheard dissonant sounds—an American man and woman, the only other English speakers on the tour. They were debating the fate of the toros, animals that had been pressed into service only to be maltreated and forced to die as victims of a ruthless spectacle.

"Odious. Indecent," the man said.

The woman admitted enjoying bull fights back in grad school in Mexico. Bulls had a better life than chickens on corporate farms, she argued.

The man's voice got louder. "And you continue to mistreat our animal brothers by cooking them up for dinner?

"It's an old argument," the woman said. "Who's to be the judge?"

Ana wondered if she should break in to tell them they were engaged in an ancient debate and offer them a short version of a third century story about a man who thought animals were created to serve him. It was a fable she was often told as a child whenever she neglected her duties to keep water in the birdbath or refill garden birdfeeder. Her father would take on the role of the knowledgeable and prudent Kalila, a character from the wisdom fables, a jackal who could think, speak and was always just.

But the pair then lapsed into silence as the bus moved away from the bull ring, and Ana, entirely comfortable with silence of any kind, was relieved that the debate had ended quietly.

The bus moved toward the Carthusian Monastery before it turned back to the center of town and on to the Mirador San Nicolás. "You can see for miles and miles here," the driver called over the microphone. Then he turned up the narrow, cobbled streets and the bus navigated around the white houses of the Albaicín, the medieval Moorish quarter.

Ana wished her mother were with her to talk about the precious gardens walled inside the whitewashed houses. Cármenes, her mother called them. The family had abandoned Spain, but they'd held onto their memories. "Go walk where your family has walked. Learn what they have known." Her mother had spoken about Granada so often Ana half-expected to recognize someone on the streets, to see a corner that was familiar, or to peek over a wall covered in bougainvillea into the faces of a family who would know her name.

But why should anyone know her? The last of her family had left Spain long ago, and the family name had been Americanized to sound like Madison.

After the Americans ended their boisterous debate about toros, Ana began to hear French voices talking about mathematics. She enjoyed being among so many French speakers. It was good for her. Her French was getting better.

She heard the word "Pythagoras," and then a man's voice talking about numbers, and another about the quality of life. It was the kind of banter her father and her grandfather often fell into—a little investigation, a bit of persuasion, a good deal of gesturing. Ana might have talked that way if she'd applied herself to the family's other tradition—mathematics—instead of folktales. She wondered if these people were astronomers or engineers, but then decided they seemed too philosophical to be engineers. Were they architects?

She leaned toward the woman in the seat next to her and asked in the best French she could muster, "Qu'est-ce que vous étudiez, les gens de votre groupe, étudiez-vous les mathématiques?"

"Oui… et non," the woman responded rather coldly.

"Oui?"

"Oui!" the woman said again.

"Mais, non aussi?"

"Exactament!" she said. This time she smiled at Ana. "You are American?"

"Yes. Oui."

"But of course," the woman said in English. "I will speak English. Here we will study the geometry of the Alhambra, among other things. We are museologists, what the Spanish call 'aficionados.' Docents from the south of France, just above Spain." She gestured skyward as though France were a heavenly body floating above them.

The tour bus crossed the Darro, headed for the Plaza Nueva and pushed up Cuesta de Gomerez toward the Alhambra. So many people on the streets, in and out of the tiny shops that opened into the hill. Finally, they were in the parking lot below the Alhambra, right down the street from the Hotel Guadalupe.

As the bus driver was saying his goodbyes, he reminded his passengers of the words of a poet, "What a tragedy to be a blind man in Granada!" He repeated the line over and over in French and English and Spanish.

Though Ana had ended her first afternoon in Granada, she had done little more than stay awake long enough to comply with the first day travel rules her mother had given her—"Stay awake and enjoy las tapas." Ana walked away from the French docents toward the pavilion where tourists were returning the headphones they'd used during walks through the Alhambra. She noticed a garden café across from the ticket pavilion. It was early evening, too early for a full Spanish meal, but the café was serving tapas. The fellow in the caramel suit was seated alone at a table near the bar. He waved to someone behind Ana, and the woman from the bus brushed past Ana and walked to his table. Just then, a waiter approached Ana and led her to a spot on the other side of the bar. She asked for a tall bottle of water and watched the bubbles dance as the waiter filled her glass.

"Ajo blanco," Ana said, "y boquerones."

Within minutes, the waiter was back with a basket of crispy bread. Ana leaned toward the basket and took a deep breath.

CHAPTER FIVE

The siren started as a low whine riding so deeply under Graciela Corzal's thoughts that she didn't notice it right away. Then the sound became clearer as a police car climbed the hill. Graciela went to the window as a squad car twisted around the corner past the librería and antiguedades shop. She watched it bump over the low brick steps beneath her window.

The ambulance customarily stationed at the top of the hill followed behind the squad car edging alongside the Carlos Quinto. The vehicles' tires squealed on the cobblestones as the car slowed for tourists then passed through the Wine Gate. The vehicles had to be headed for the Alcazaba. Perhaps a tourist had collapsed from the heat or taken a fall. Why did people sit on those walls in the sun? The Patronato would need to take action, make new safety rules.

Then Graciela began to wonder if something had happened to Rubén. He so rarely disappointed her with tardiness. Could he be the one who had fallen? No, of course not. Rubén knew the Alcazaba almost as well as she did. It couldn't be Rubén. It had to be a tourist. Some simple accident. Graciela comforted herself and went back to work sorting through the yellow graph pages Rubén had left on her desk.

She'd been working about twenty minutes when she noticed another low whine, then another siren. Just then, her telephone rang and Rubén's cell phone number appeared. Like a worried mother, Graciela lifted the phone to her ear and began talking before the caller had begun to speak.

"Where are you?" she demanded. "Are you all right?"

Then, without waiting for a response, she scolded him for being late. "We have Inspector Drummond coming here at any moment and it doesn't appear to me that you have arranged things properly, not at all."

The voice that responded was not Rubén's. It was the official de policía who had taken Rubén's phone. "A young gentleman is here on the side of the hill beneath the Torre de las Armas. A Cuban gentleman. He seems to be involved in a very suspicious death."

The news stunned Graciela. "He is alive?" she asked.

"He is very much alive," the voice said. "But his companion is very dead."

"What companion?" Graciela asked. Rubén didn't really have friends.

"It seems to be one of the young men who was working on the renovations."

Of course. One of the workers Rubén had been talking about, the ones with all the stories about Boabdil and his fortune. She'd told him not to get mixed up with that folly.

People were needy in Granada these days. It was too easy for them to get their hopes up about dreams of hidden treasure, and too easy to get involved in spats over false leads and fairy tales.

"We think he may have been involved," the policía's voice said.

"That's nonsense," Graciela said. "Is he all right? Let me talk to him."

"You can't speak to him. We want to question him at the station."

"Well, you can't take him right now. I need him this evening. We have an important visitor coming from America, and Rubén Torres is essential to the visit."

"The visitor is the Inspector Drummond you mentioned when you answered my call? Is it something of a criminal nature?"

Graciela was not about to discuss the lions with the police. "The investigative magistrate is fully aware of today's visit. If you like, I will ask him to contact you."

The official relented only slightly. "Come to the Alcazaba if you like."

"Por Dios," she said. "I will be there directly. I trust that you will not arrest my assistant in the meantime."

Perhaps she should have been more watchful of Rubén. It was inevitable that the young locals, whose heads were full of treasure tales, would latch on to the young scholar, whose head was already full of tales about an ancestor who was an interpreter for Columbus, a Jewish linguist who spoke Arabic. Rubén was a scholar who could read the walls of the Alhambra just as his ancestor had done. Why had she presumed he would resist the romances of the people of Granada?

Graciela remembered one of Rubén's favorite questions—"Why do you think Columbus was imagining sultans at the end of the voyage to the far East?"

Graciela took a card from the top drawer of her desk and dialed the Hotel Reina Cristina. The man at the front desk told her that Inspector Drummond had left the hotel on foot about thirty minutes earlier. She set down her phone and left her office.

CHAPTER SIX

The first cruiser squealing up the Cordera sent Walter Drummond diving into the doorway of a local shop to avoid being struck. The pilgrims ahead of him jumped quickly out of the way, a man bumped into a rack of silk scarves and a woman knocked over a set of chessmen carved in the costumes of Christians and Moors.

After the commotion stopped, Drummond stepped around the tourists and kept walking up the hill, but as a second police car became enmeshed in the pedestrian traffic, Drummond fell into an old habit. Instead of getting out of the way, he ran toward it, his ID in his hand. He was there at the invitation of the Patronato, as Magistrate Julio Villanueva was well aware, and he needed a ride to the top.

Drummond leaned into the driver's window of the squad car. If ever there was a time to use his Spanish, it was now. "Necesito que me lleve arriba," he said, reaching for the back door as the officer clicked it open.

He pulled out his phone and thumbed through his contact list. Doctora Corzal and Magistrate Julio Villanueva were on the list, but Doctora Corzal's number went to messaging and Julio's home number wasn't answering either.

The squad car roared up the road and took a hairpin turn around a restaurant across the street from a ticket pavilion, pausing just long enough at the guard hut for the watchman to raise the arm, and then taking off toward the Alhambra.

Ana looked up and saw the silver-haired gentleman spring to his feet. He pulled bills from his pocket, pressed them into them into the waiter's hand, left his companion seated there, and quickly headed up the hill behind the police. And now, the woman was sliding out of her chair and was approaching Ana's table. Ana found the practice of assigning motives to strangers intriguing, and these people had aroused her curiosity. Who were they?

"May I join you?" the woman said to Ana as she gestured up the hill with her chin. "The professor has been called away."

Ana had just torn off a piece of crusty bread. The woman moved her hand across her skirt as though she were brushing Ana's breadcrumbs away, then waived at the waiter and ordered a café for each of them before Ana could respond.

CHAPTER SEVEN

The promenade from the museum to the Alcazaba was full of tourists, some sitting on benches that circled the oak trees near the Wine Gate, others walking from the royal palaces to the military towers. Graciela cut through a group that was moving too slowly. When she turned, she saw a police car rolling across the stones and shimmering in the heat. It was approaching rapidly from behind her. A beeping horn pulsed above the wail of the siren, and tourists scattered to make room as the car bumped its way up the stony incline to the gate of the Alcazaba, finally stopping abruptly in one of the spaces reserved for dignitaries.

An official opened Drummond's door and tapped his boot impatiently, a sign to the person in the rear that he was taking too much time exiting the vehicle. "Señor," he said gravely, "Adelante, por favor."

"Oh yes. Que pena," Drummond said, letting English slip back into his Spanish as he tucked his cellphone away. "Gracias, muchas gracias." He asked the officer for his name so he could tell the investigative magistrate how grateful he was.

"I am Alberto Castañeda, Capitán Castañeda, and I know the investigative magistrate quite well. Now I would like you to leave me to my work."

It was obvious that Capitán Castañeda also spoke fluent English. "Of course," Drummond said, tilting his chin in a slightly apologetic nod. "If perhaps you could also help me locate the director? Doctora Corzal?"

Doctora Corzal was right behind him. "Aquí estoy," she said. "I am here." She moved between the two men and stretched her hand toward Walter Drummond. "Señor Drummond," she said.

Drummond nodded as he had when they'd parted in Córdoba. Graciela would have found it charming if she weren't on her way to see what kind of trouble her assistant had gotten himself into.

Drummond straightened his shoulders. He had obviously come upon the Doctora at a difficult moment.

"I'm afraid there's been a dreadful accident, One of the artesanos working on the renovation. He may have fallen. I'm afraid the fall was fatal."

Drummond's gaze followed the officer who was running toward the Alcazaba.

Graciela was walking briskly toward the admission kiosk as she spoke. "My assistant, Rubén, seems to have been with him. We must see what's going on." She handed her identification to the woman at the entrance and explained that she and her visitor needed to follow the officer inside. She told the gatekeeper there was no need at this point to close the entrance. And yes, she would send word if that became necessary.

Graciela shielded her eyes in the late afternoon sun and asked Drummond to come with her. She looked at her watch. "They've been at this for some time. They're quizzing Rubén somewhere just over the precipice."

Walter Drummond noticed a man in a khaki suit rushing toward them as though he were an old friend, but his action seemed intrusive. He pretended to ignore the man for a while to see if he intended to clarify his presence.

Graciela climbed the five steps up to the Torre and paused briefly at the top, facing the intruder. "Professor Lenhard, you've come back to us again." There was a friendly tone to her voice.

"I've brought you a group of French docents," Lenhard said.

"You're back in France now?" Graciela asked as she began walking again, moving quickly across the flat roof of the tower toward keystones at the far edge. Drummond was just behind her.

"In Paris, for a while…" Lenhard said as he tried to catch up. "There seems to be some police business here." He was at Drummond's side now. "I trust there's no problem."

Drummond explained that a young man had fallen. He turned to look over the wall. Heads in uniform caps were visible in the dense bushes below.

Graciela waved a pleasant goodbye to Professor Lenhard and led Drummond toward a circle of bricks jutting out of the roof of the Torre de las Armas. In its gaping throat was a rough stone staircase that spiraled down into the dark. At the top, the brick circle was covered with a heavy mesh screen and a large, rusty padlock. Graciela reached into the small leather purse she'd been carrying over her shoulder, removed a large key, twisted it in the lock and lifted the circular screen. She stepped onto the stairs that coiled downward and motioned for Drummond to follow.

"Hadn't you better lock that behind us?" Drummond asked. "Unless you want a parade of sightseers like that Lenhard fellow straggling after us?"

"It's spring-loaded," she said. "The padlock is a visual warning more than a security device. Just an extra precaution."

Drummond nodded and cleared his throat. "We'll be able to get out?"

"I suspect we'll choose a more comfortable exit," Graciela said, leading Drummond down the narrow staircase that spiraled into the yellow clay earth. Halfway around the first full turn was a sign in both Spanish and English that stated: Mazmorras. Dungeons.

They made their way down four or five more spirals before they touched the hard-packed earth at the bottom of the pit. "We'll use the walkway to cross over to the Torre de la Vela. It will lead us to the old barrio of the castrense. My guess is the policía have taken Rubén there. He wasn't on the hill when I looked down. You didn't see him did you?"

Drummond said he saw no one who appeared to be Rubén Torres. "All of the men were dressed in police uniforms," he explained

The twisted staircase ended abruptly at the edge of a road that Drummond believed came from somewhere in the direction of the palaces or the Generalife, the royal garden home of the Emir. The path was dark and cool, high enough that a man mounted on a horse could ride comfortably without touching his head to the ceiling and wide enough that two could move side by side.

"The barrio of the slaves and the castrense—you know this word, yes?"

Drummond nodded. Castrense—castrated servants. Men who were regarded safe in the presence of the royal women. Doctora Corzal interrupted his thoughts. "We'll soon be near the hill where the investigators are working on the unfortunate young craftsman."

The walkway opened into a large room, and Rubén was sitting on the hard-packed earth with his hands restrained behind his back. Two battery-powered lanterns cast light toward the young motorcyclist.

An oficial was quizzing him in a voice much louder than it needed to be considering that he was leaning into Rubén's face as he spoke. "You are friends, this craftsman and you?" The timbre of intimidation was recognizable. "Were you in the habit of meeting in such inaccessible places?"

Graciela recognized the voice, and she was not keen on the rude demeanor. This was the man who had telephoned her. She had no patience for his professional style.

She approached the officer, interrupting his interrogation and speaking first to Rubén, a signal that the this was her territory in a national preserve, not a space in a city park. Was Rubén all right? Yes, he was fine. Would he like to stand? No, he was comfortable sitting.

Graciela was still facing Rubén when she began speaking to the policía. "I am Doctora Graciela Corzal de Moreno, Directora of the Alhambra. There is no need for you to treat my assistant in this manner. Please unbind his hands." Graciela's voice was assertive. The officer said nothing as he stepped back from Rubén and went to the door.

The Capitán, who had given Drummond a lift, had been leaning against the wall. Now he moved toward Graciela and nodded.

Drummond was only a visitor here, one with no authority in Granada. In fact, his mere presence could antagonize the police and place the young scholar in greater jeopardy. He thought he should get out of the way. Doctora Corzal was the only one who could demonstrate strength in this situation.

Drummond walked quietly toward a narrow set of stones that ran like a staircase directly up the exterior wall near the doorway. He waited there in the light that was coming from an opening above.

The Capitán glanced at him and quickly looked back at Rubén and Doctora Corzal.

"At the very least," the Doctora was saying, "I must insist that you respect the autonomy of the Council of the Alhambra. Authority is shared here. We are not a simple city monument. Dr. Torres, the gentleman you have shackled here on the ground must be afforded a private interview with the Director of the Alhambra. As an employee of the Patronato, he is entitled. I am sure you are aware that it is my responsibility to exert that privilege."

The Capitán was taking in the scene—glancing from the Director of the Alhambra to the policía who were a good five meters away but close enough to assure that the Cubano was securely detained. "I most certainly respect your responsibility," he told Doctora Corzal, and then nodded to the policía before he stepped back toward Drummond.

Walter Drummond had rested his boot—a sturdy but well-polished black ankle boot—on one of the stone steps. It was part of a uniform that offered kinship to police and military wherever he met them. As Drummond had become independent, his taste in boots had gravitated toward a narrower more European style. To the unini-tiated, he would appear to be clad in Italian dress shoes. It was only when he lifted his foot, as he did at this moment to place it on the narrow step, that the influence of police styles on his fashion choice was apparent.

The Capitán was watching him, just as Drummond had hoped.

Drummond's attention was on the stone staircase he was about to climb. "These stepping stones—are they originals?"

"They are very old."

"Would this have been a way to the top of the Torre back in the time of the sultans?"

"A medieval fire escape, you might say," the Capitán answered. "One that goes up rather than down."

"Would you mind if I scaled it quickly?" Drummond was half-way up the stones by the time he finished his request. "Por supuesto, it's up to you, of course …"

"Cuidado, señor." The Capitán seemed concerned about Drum-mond's climb. Was it the staircase or the view from above that wor-ried him?

Once Drummond had reached the top, the Capitán scaled up behind him. They emerged onto an open platform on the tower that extended over the edge of hill.

Below, Drummond saw the young man's body still on the prec-ipice. He slipped a small case from his jacket pocket and snapped it open. Drummond always carried this set of high-strength binoc-ulars with him. He turned the nob between the lenses and focused on the young man's face. Blood had streamed from his forehead, blood that did not appear to have originated from his black hair. Little chance the lad had simply fallen to his unfortunate end. The forehead wound looked like it had come earlier, before the boy had hit the ground.

Drummond turned to the Capitán and asked, "So, this convinced you this was a red death, as the Moors called it, rather than a simple accident? Death looking through a face as red as Lorca's moon?"

"Sin duda. The body is sprawled like a rag doll. He was dead or unconscious before he was thrown from the tower."

From below, Drummond's boots became visible to Graciela first, then the sharp crease in his gray flannel trousers as he made his way back down the narrow stone steps. The Capitán came right after him, making his way down to the hard-packed dirt floor where Rubén was sitting. Both men turned to Doctora Corzal, who had stepped in front of Rubén now, casting a barrier between her assistant and the policía.

Graciela took a deep breath and scolded the Capitán. "What possessed you to think it would be necessary to shackle this young gentleman?" she asked again.

"His papers, they are not exactly what we expected," the Capitán answered. "What exactly is his home? Havana? With a degree from Argentina and a fellowship from the Bahamas?"

"At this moment, his home is Granada." Graciela selected her words and her tone carefully. There was no reason to believe that the presence of an academic researcher from Havana should pose political complications to Spain, but the word "Cuban" had syncretic power, and she did not want to impose any additional meaning onto this delicate situation. "He is here on postdoctoral work. He is invaluable to the Alhambra."

Rubén looked directly at the Capitán and said nothing.

"And the Cuban intellectual, can he speak for himself?" the Capitán asked sarcastically.

Rubén nodded and said, "My parents live in Havana. It is the place of my birth and home to my ancestors since 1492. I have recently finished my studies at the university."

Graciela intervened. "His country of origin is hardly the question. It is deeply disturbing that the young worker fell to his death, but that has nothing to do with Doctor Torres or his work as my assistant here."

"Perdón, Doctora Corzal, but your other visitor seems to agree we could have a homicide here. The question is whether the Cuban visitor to our country might have been involved."

"The question is whether he will now be allowed to go with us back into the Alhambra." Gabriela looked at her watch, it was a quarter past eight. "We have work that we must accomplish this evening. Work that is related to the history of Spain, and for which this visitor, as you call him, has much to offer the Alhambra."

She looked at Drummond, who was standing shoulder to shoulder with the Capitán. Somehow, Drummond had established a connection with the officer, and perhaps the link could be of use to her at that moment. "Inspector Drummond has come from America specifically to meet with me and Doctor Torres," Graciela told the Capitán.

"Indeed," said Drummond. "If possible, we would like to get back to work."

The Capitán lifted the note that had been found in the victim's shoe. "And this note about the lions?"

Graciela glanced at Drummond and then leaned in to see the note. "This is Basque?"

"Your linguist says it is."

Graciela thought for a moment and then said, "That a young craftsman like our unfortunate victim would write a note about lions … It doesn't surprise me. This is a football fantasy. A bet on the Bilbao Athletic Club."

"And why did your assistant try to remove this note from the scene?"

Drummond stepped to Rubén's side. He hoped that ignoring the Capitán's comment, and the note as well, would make it seem less important to Rubén's interrogator. "I am sure you realize now that this young scholar, Doctor Torres, is an innocent witness who has had the shocking experience of coming upon the death of an acquaintance."

"He could leave the country," the Capitán protested.

"He is going nowhere," Graciela insisted.

"You will be responsible for him?"

"Absolutely," Graciela said.

"You will keep him here, on the hill?"

The Capitán's tone was softening. Graciela calmed hers as well. "I'll find a room for him nearby."

A voice echoed just outside the door. "I have an extra room in the Guadalupe." It was Professor Lenhard, standing in the doorway. "One of my group was unable to join us. The young gentleman is welcome to have his room."

"Very kind of you," Graciela said to Lenhard. "Thank you. We will bring Doctor Torres to the hotel after we have finished our work."

In Drummond's opinion, this Lenhard fellow was a bit of a specter, always emerging when they were not expecting him. Maybe that's what he disliked most of all—the fact that this man was not someone he had come prepared for. Of course, he understood the notion of chance. He could grant himself a single surprise. But he was uncomfortable with the reality that he had been surprised by Lenhard twice that day. He probably should have known the man would ignore Doctora Corzal's dismissal when they first met as they crossed the plaza. When they hurried down into the dungeon, the man had seemed to step back. But Lenhard had been close behind them all the while, close enough to hold the automatic lock on the gate. How long had he been listening from the shadows?

Nevertheless, Drummond knew his discomfort should not be indulged. Any interference in Graciela's negotiations might give the police an excuse to keep Rubén longer. He smiled at Lenhard, and the two of them helped Rubén to his feet so that the Capitán could sever the nylon cord around his wrists. Graciela signed a page that placed Rubén under her care, and the four left through a door to yet another staircase that took them directly upward into the rose gold light of dusk.

Graciela thanked Lenhard for his help and told him they would find him after dinner. Lenhard went on his way toward the tourist gate, and Graciela took her companions through the Alcazaba to a garden path that skirted the crowd. She noticed that Drummond had been looking over his shoulder, watching Lenhard during his departure.

"He's harmless," she explained, smiling. "He's a brilliant man, a gentleman from Alsace who was never able to establish an enduring link with a university. You have these eruditos independientes? He visits us with great regularity. Sometimes we forget he isn't one of our own."

"Not unusual for him to follow you into the torre then?"

"Not at all. When he's here in Spain, he's a regular at my museum lectures, and he's been here a great deal this year."

Drummond thought he had picked up on something more than intellectual curiosity.

"I've been told he has a bit of a crush," Graciela said.

"He's an aficionado," Rubén said. "He's drawn to the palace. It's taken control of his imagination. This happens to people here."

"You know one another, then?" Drummond asked.

"I don't really know him," Rubén replied. "I've seen him a few times. We've traded congenialities. Actually, I first met him in Paris in the fall before I began my work here."

Rubén rubbed the red marks made by the cords on his wrists, "I'm sorry to have caused such a delay."

"You'll tell me all about it in the morning," Graciela said. She wanted the whole story, but she also wanted Drummond to see her lion, and the precise moment—nine o'clock—was all but upon them.

This unfortunate accident, and Rubén's proximity to it, had been an intrusion that she found disconcerting. It had kept Rubén from focusing on the issue at hand and had consumed several hours that might have been spent in discussion with Inspector Drummond. She preferred to gather evidence methodically, bit by bit until her doubt was drowned in certainty. What a relief the police had released Rubén to her custody. With Professor Lenhard's generous offer, Rubén would not be out of her reach for the next twenty-four hours.

The three walked briskly past the public entrance to the Mexuar and through the small gate between the Court of the Myrtles and the Palacio Carlos Quinto. There was a staircase appended to a squared-off wall on the Alhambra side of the path. Rubén stepped back as Doctora Corzal led the way up the steps to the wooden door and turned a key in the lock. Drummond checked his watch—8:43. The nine o'clock stream would flow from the mouth of the ninth lion in seventeen minutes.

CHAPTER EIGHT

Rubén took deep breaths as he walked, hoping evening air would clear the heaviness in his lungs and ease the dull headache he'd been harboring since he'd found Ander. He wasn't frightened by the police. It wasn't fear he was feeling at all. It was the sight of Ander, his friend. The twisted ankle. The listless body.

Rubén took another breath. And then one more. Doctora Corzal would be expecting a full explanation for his abandonment of work he'd been assigned to complete before the American arrived, and he would have to be ready. She had behaved as his caretaker for the last hour, but she would shed her nursemaid persona just as soon as she was sure Inspector Drummond agreed with her first principles. Doctora Corzal was using this walk to the palace to set straight the historical record by detailing the ninth lion's behavior over the previous five centuries. Soon she would know how the American reacted and if he shared her apprehensions.

Until then, Rubén knew Doctora Corzal's thoughts would be focused entirely on the business at hand, and not on the advice she'd given him to stop meeting with the masonry apprentices. In her opinion, they were living in a fantasy world, visiting Sacromonte at night to dance in the caves with gypsy entertainers and pass secrets and conspiracy stories to tourists.

Doctora Corzal led the way, past the small rust-colored basin of the Abencerrajes, then through the narrow hallway and into the

Courtyard of the Lions. The space was still. The last tourists had straggled out and the guards had gone off for supper before their night shifts would begin. The walls were washed in rosy light from the electric candles that became visible as the sun moved behind the hills. The lions were straight ahead, circling around the fountain.

"Tomorrow, we'll come back to enjoy the Alhambra as a whole," Graciela said. "Tonight, we see it as it was imagined—red against the sky."

Rubén caught the eye of the lion that had recently returned from Paris. It was only a statue, of course, but Rubén had been studying this creature for weeks, trying to see if this ninth lion had even the slightest variation from the other lions that stood with him in this pious circle.

Drummond walked to a point under an archway that appeared to be made of sturdy, stony lace. He breathed deeply, inhaling the cool night air and reveling in the view of the fountain at the center of four water channels, each impeccably flowing in mathematical precision toward a point somewhere below the hind quarters of the twelve lions. Were these creatures smiling or snarling as they bared their teeth at him? His first task, he knew, was to take this all in. To let the courtyard, its water channels, its textured walls and ribbons of script, tame his response to the creatures he'd come to observe.

Authenticity was not a state that was easily defined. In his years of work with artifacts and museum pieces, Drummond had learned that a work that looked reliable was often a fake created by an artist who was more accomplished than the creator of the original. He stood motionless. He could hear streams of water, although he was not sure he could see everything that he was hearing. His job was to validate the gush of water from the mouth of a single lion at a specific moment, something the lion may have been created to do but had not done, according to his hosts at the Alhambra, since the Moors had surged out of the Red Palace and rushed toward the Sierra Nevada.

Drummond watched the water flow freely from four channels into the base of the fountain and he saw the generous gush into the basin above the backs of the lions. But the water spilling out from the mouths of the lions was modest. How was that small spill from each lion keeping things from overflowing? Was some of the water leaking away underground? If so, where was it going? Was it being purposely diverted?

Rubén was on one knee, leaning toward the ninth lion as if he were having a face-to-face conversation with the beast. As Drummond moved toward him and was nearing the fountain, the lion made a low, gurgling sound before the light stream coming from its mouth thickened and began to bubble and spurt, squirting up and then falling down into the channel at the animal's feet. The spray curved as if it were echoing the geometric proportions of the archways that surrounded the courtyard on four sides. This enthusiastic water show lasted precisely sixty seconds—fifteen seconds of bubbling at the start, thirty seconds during which the stream achieved the full status of a water arch, and another fifteen during which the flow slowed until the angle diminished to a trickle that wet the lips of the lion as he sounded a low, throaty gargle. Then once again lion number nine relaxed like his comrades, water filtering from all their mouths in a miserly flow.

"Impressive," Drummond said.

"Magnificently, mathematically precise," Rubén said.

"And disconcerting," Doctora Corzal added.

"The officer called you a linguist," Drummond said, turning to Rubén. "Perhaps you can tell us what we should think of the script on the basin?"

"Not a linguist," Rubén said. "I'm an engineer and an architect. In my work with language, I am simply another enthusiast."

"But you can read these lines?"

"I can recall what I know. It's the work of ibn Zamrak. It begins here—" he touched the stucco script. "They say it is a verse in homage to the prince, the ruler at the time this courtyard was assembled."

Drummond noticed the cautious way Rubén had spoken, "They say..." he repeated. "You're not sure?"

Graciela answered. "No one should be sure. The palace was redecorated from time to time and the writing is in stucco. Lines could have been added or subtracted. But we believe this passage belonged to ibn Zamrak, the palace poet in the fourteenth century."

"What about the subtext?" Drummond asked. "The grace I feel flowing here?"

"In the water?"

"In the writing."

Rubén moved around the basin about forty-five degrees and touched the point where another ribbon of language began. "What is it but a mist... drenching toward the lions..." Rubén seemed to be reciting the poem from memory. "...behold the lions while they are crouching... timidity prevents them from becoming hostile..."

Rubén continued to touch the Arabic script, and Drummond imagined the young man was reading with his fingertips, "Silver melting... a running stream... what is solid, what is fluid, what is the truth?"

Drummond was now studying the Cuban as attentively as he'd been studying the lions, and Graciela noticed.

"And what do you make of lion number nine?" Drummond asked Rubén. "You and he had a bit of a tête-a-tête."

Rubén stepped back from the fountain. "I visited the atelier in Paris, just as they were loading this guy into the crate. Doctora Corzal asked me to travel with el noveno since I'd made plans to fly through Paris on my way from Havana."

"That's how you met our friend Lenhard?"

"That's when I met him," Rubén replied. "Lenhard was not connected with the atelier, but he frequents the café nearby. He spoke to me when he saw I was carrying a book about the Alhambra."

Drummond was touching the lion's forehead. "When you looked into this fellow's eyes just now, what did you hope to see?"

Rubén summoned a professional reply. "I asked myself the question I have been asking since I arrived. How were these lions made? Are they identical, or was each fashioned individually?"

Drummond smiled as if pleased by this response. He began to move slowly around the fountain. "We would expect small differences in the authentic," Drummond said. He removed a notebook from his jacket pocket and jotted a few lines.

"Shall we return tomorrow in the daylight?" Graciela asked. "Or are you finding this a good time for more investigation?"

"Actually, I enjoy the lack of tourists," Drummond said.

They could hear footsteps coming across the marble courtyard—Capitán Castañeda. Graciela left Drummond and Rubén and went to meet Castañeda at the far end of the courtyard. He clicked his boots to greet her and spoke in a hushed tone. The gentleman who offered the convenient hotel accommodation was waiting outside. It was time for her assistant to leave the palace. Castañeda gestured a sort of sideways nod toward Rubén.

Graciela turned to follow the Capitán's glance and saw Drummond nod an ever-so-slight acknowledgment of the Capitán's authority. Drummond seemed to be working on the Capitán, continuing to build trust. Graciela hoped so. She wasn't about to supply this fellow with rumors he could take back to his unit. She didn't want the policía attempting to take jurisdiction of the Court of the Lions.

"Ah!" Graciela made the sounds of assent. "Sí, sí, sí." She turned and led Castañeda away from the fountain, assuring him that she was keeping a close watch over Rubén. She thanked Castañeda for his attention and bid him a good evening, managing to coax him out of the patio and into the hands of the Alhambra's night guard who was back from his dinner break.

Graciela's shoes made a sandpaper sound as they slipped over the stones on her way back to the fountain, but neither Drummond nor Rubén noticed her approach. The two were moving quietly from lion to lion, as if their stealth might keep the creatures from waking. What a shame to pull Rubén away, Graciela thought, but there would always be tomorrow, as long as she could keep the policía at bay.

"I'm afraid we must leave soon," Graciela said. "I've promised there'll be no additional difficulties this evening."

CHAPTER NINE

Sacromonte was a bulky pointed shadow dotted with lanterns. It loomed behind the ginger-gold Alhambra tower as tourists lined up for a nighttime view of the palace. Ana sat in the plaza, watching fragments of sunlit cloud scatter across the sky that was shifting from flat blue to deep aqua to indigo. She had no more travel guidelines to fulfill. She had avoided sleeping too early after the flight, she had eaten her mother's prescribed meal, and she had walked up the hill from her hotel to the Alhambra for the requisite bedtime exercise. Now, she intended to watch the palace flush in the sunset and glow against the night sky, a vision she'd be happy to carry with her into sleep. If only she were tired.

An ambulance moved quietly across the plaza and headed down the hill with no flashing lights, no siren. There were still two police cars in front of the Alcazaba and one of the officers had been crossing back and forth between the fortress and the palace for the last hour. The Frenchman—the one who seemed to be a professor—had gone back and forth as well. She decided that if the professor came by again, she'd ask him what had happened. But when he did show up, he was part of a small parade of people who were walking quickly away from the palace toward the road that led down to the pavilion, the garden restaurant, and her hotel.

A young man was leading the parade, if you could call it leading. His head was turned over his right shoulder and he walked almost sideways, glancing back at the woman behind him and occasionally speaking or whispering to her. She moved with the casual authority of someone in charge—nodding occasionally but not speaking. The young man seemed about Ana's age, maybe a few years older. He had a full head of hair—black and shiny.

Behind them was the professor. How many times had Ana seen him that day? He walked side-by-side with a tall fellow Ana believed to be an American. He was mixing a bit of French into his Spanish, and she could hear the problem he and most Americans have with the "r" sound in both languages.

Last came the policeman, following the other four. Was he part of this band of disparate associates? His connection with the group seemed tenuous. Was he holding the rear as some sort of guardian, or was he there in quiet pursuit?

Ana slipped her iPhone into her bag. She'd been using it as her camera and was pleased with some photos she'd made of the tower. She'd take more pictures tomorrow. She stood, stretched, and headed back down the hill on a stone path alongside the myrtle hedges, through patches of darkness, behind the odd assortment of companions. When the group turned at the gardens and went up onto the sidewalk that led to her hotel, she slowed her pace. She didn't want to interfere. This was beginning to look like a coherent group.

Once inside the lobby, the professor took over, inquiring at the desk about a room that had been booked for one his party, a room that was still unclaimed. It was to be booked now for Doctor Rubén Torres. When the young man stepped to the counter, the policeman followed. So that's what the officer was doing—keeping an eye on Doctor Rubén Torres.

The American noticed Ana standing between the desk and the elevators, observing. He smiled at her. She smiled back, walked to the elevators and pushed a button. It was time for Ana to stop her casual surveillance and go to her room.

An hour later, Ana gave up her attempt to rest. How long had it been since she'd slept? Had she really been on her feet for thirty-six hours? Why wasn't she tired? A glass of wine was called for, and whatever kind of snack she could find in the little bistro in the lobby. She pulled on her white cotton sweater and a pair of jeans, slipped into her sandals, and took the small, brown guide to the Alhambra off the dresser.

The lobby was surprisingly quiet. Two people sat at the bar, and the black-haired young man sat at a table off to the side. No policeman. No professor, no American, no woman of authority. The young man was alone, eating a sandwich. When she sat at the octagonal table next to his, he looked up at her and grinned.

"Are you following me too?" he asked in the English of a Latin American.

Ana smiled and said, "Perhaps."

"Every time I look around, you're there."

"How did you know I speak English?"

"Your jeans. Your sandals. They shout Yanqui."

"New Yorker," Ana said, smiling. "And I'll guess you're Latino, not Puertorriqueño, not Venezolano. If I follow you long enough to hear you speak Spanish, I'll tell you where you're from."

"Soy de la Habana," Rubén answered.

"What happened to your escorts?" Ana asked.

"They left."

"So, they decided to trust you?" Ana was a great deal more relaxed with the young man than she expected herself to be.

"Unless you are one of their spies," he said.

They had begun a sparring match, as though they actually knew each other, as though they had something in common. Was Ana surprised that she was behaving in such a forward manner? She was certainly wondering about it. She was curious about their camaraderie. Was it surfacing because they were both itinerants, two wanderers on their way back to Europe from the Americas? From two very different Americas, Ana had no doubt about that, but they seemed to be forging a connection, and she was curious about its origins. Perhaps it was simply generational.

The bartender approached with a menu and Ana asked for a glass of red wine—the house would be fine—and a sandwich like the one the young man was eating. Was it Manchego?

"I've been awake forever," she told the young man. "I left New York last night and I may never sleep again. It's been a long day."

"Sin duda," he said, noticing how easily she had talked with the waiter. "You're from Andalucía… long ago? Or perhaps your family?"

Ana answered his question with a question. "It would be the same, wouldn't it?"

The young man moved his chair so that he was closer to her.

Ana said, "Something happened in the Alhambra today. Lots of police."

"Difícil y triste," he said. As he spoke, Ana could hear the clipped delivery of his Cuban accent.

"The ambulance left late and without a siren," she said. "I couldn't help but notice."

He nodded.

"And you, with your band of colleagues…" All so different. The Spanish woman. The American man. The French professor. The policeman. Very protective. Were they strangers? Helping one another? She wondered. "You looked like you were in the company of friends," Ana said.

People in Ana's family were always looking for the company of friends. No matter how difficult the circumstance, no matter what size the misfortune, somebody in the family would suggest the whole thing could be resolved if strangers would help one another, if they could develop a strong bond. If only they'd become a company of friends.

"Friends, perhaps—with one exception…" the Cuban said.

Who would she exclude from his curious society? The policeman?

She decided not to intrude further. The silence was filled by the waiter clinking the cutlery and landing her plate on the wooden table. Her sandwich and glass of wine had arrived.

The young man finally spoke. "My friend died there on the hill today. I found him, and I called the policía. And now they think I may have killed him."

Ana took a sip of wine, saying nothing. She remembered feeling sincerity in the Cuban when she had first noticed him up on the hill. It came across in the way he'd been talking to the Spanish woman.

He shrugged. "Por supuesto, I didn't kill him."

Of course. He wouldn't kill his friend. He was obviously a thoughtful person. He was like the kindly crow in the story about the friends and the hunter. That was a story she sometimes shared with people. "It makes me think of a folk tale," she said.

"Is your story American or Spanish?" he asked.

"It's a story my family brought with them when they moved to New York, an animal story. A fable of kinship."

"And...?"

"And there's a crow, and he's kind to his friends..."

Rubén broke in. "I know a story like yours... in the letters of philosophers and mathematicians who influenced the architects of the Alhambra. A society of freethinkers so secret that no one knows exactly who they were. I thought maybe you'd heard about them."

Ana took another sip of wine.

"The group of friends," he continued. "Their work came to Spain from Basra in the tenth or eleventh century, complete with animal stories and meditations on numbers. Numbers invite the mind on a pilgrimage toward the sublime."

Ana smiled but said nothing. She'd been taught to speak of the philosophers in hushed tones. She'd been raised to be respectful, to hold their secrecy tight.

"Do your stories have numbers in them?" he asked.

"Not this one," she said.

He stood and walked to her table. "Perdóname for having been so forward. I should have introduced myself. I am Rubén Torres, assistant to Doctora Graciela Corzal, Directora of the Alhambra."

Ana took his extended hand. "Mucho gusto," she said. "I am a traveler, from New York. My name is Ana Madrizon."

Rubén returned to his table and took his seat. "Not from Madrid?"

"From New York City," she said.

"Madrizon is one of those American names?"

"The desk clerk had the same question."

"You know your Spanish family?"

"It was long ago," Ana said.

"Maybe your American Madrizon is really Madrit?"

Rubén took a small notebook out of his shirt pocket and opened it. That's when Ana felt she'd revealed enough, in a bar, in the middle of the night, talking to a murder suspect, kind and sincere though he seemed. He intended to write things down, and Ana didn't want a stranger tacking her story to a cork board like a euthanized butterfly.

Rubén continued. "There was a scholar, the man from Madrid, an editor of the "Rasā'il"—a kind of encyclopedia full of ideas that show up here in the Alhambra. Hay cuentos, fables like yours. They called him al-Majriti."

Ana wrapped what was left of her sandwich in a red paper napkin and called the bartender with a slight wave.

"You come from a Morisco family. That much is clear," Rubén said. "Maybe your family's related to the man from Madrid."

Her father's hesitation to claim connections to the philosophers had begun to encircle her again. She was embarrassed. She'd let the conversation flow too far. No further analysis would come from her. No casual chat about secret philosophers, or what their writings had to do with the story of the animals, or with the mathematical design of the Alhambra. "In my family, they were just tales," she said, "and you know how folk tales are, they have lives of their own."

Rubén stood again as Ana moved away from her table.

"I really must get some sleep," she said. "I have morning tickets for the Alhambra."

"Perhaps I will see you," Rubén said. "The Directora has a guest and I'll be showing him around."

"The Frenchman and his docents?" Ana asked.

"Not at all," Rubén answered. "Professor Lenhard is perfectly comfortable on his own."

The American then, Ana was sure the American must be the guest. She could feel Rubén's gaze as she left the bar and crossed the lobby. When the elevator came and the doors opened, she stepped inside and turned casually, expecting to wave at the dark-haired young man, who would then nod at her from the bar across the lobby. But when she glanced at the table where he'd been sitting, he was no longer there.

CHAPTER TEN

If restoring el noveno's pipe lines to a fifteenth century standard had been Graciela Corzal's goal, near perfection had been achieved. That fact alone told Walter Drummond it might be easy to diagnose the truth about the ninth lion's behavior. Tomorrow he'd check each of the other eleven animals, comparing them to el noveno to see how they were different and if they displayed what the inexperienced might perceive as flaws.

In Drummond's mind, a flaw was often a mark of variation, and a keen eye would expect to see variation in an authentic work created eight centuries ago. His visit that evening had given him a sense of the unique, rather than the uniform. And that was good, as far as authenticity was concerned. But before Drummond could assert that lion number nine had retained its eccentricities, he needed more time and a much closer look at the beasts—all of them.

Young Torres had seemed to understand the cardinal rule of authentication—that perfection was most often a sign of replication rather than originality. Where had the motorcyclist learned that? He said he'd accompanied the lion back from Paris. Had he gleaned other information from the atelier that he had not shared?

Drummond hoped that with some sleep he would regain his focus and be capable of separating his investigative task from the unfortunate homicide that had been dropped into their hands that afternoon. Perhaps "drop" was not the best way to characterize the boy's fall. Drummond made a mental note that from that point on he would need to describe the young artisan's death in the most precise terms. A simple fall from the top of the citadel would have been a tragedy. What had happened that afternoon could well have been something more.

After they had left Rubén Torres with the Frenchman in the Hotel Guadalupe, Drummond walked Doctora Corzal back up the hill to the Carlos Quinto. Light from the Alhambra was tinting the black asphalt a ruddy gold. She asked if he would like to wait for her while she tidied up a few things, then she'd be happy to give him a ride back to his hotel in the center of Granada.

He declined her offer. He needed the walk, he said. It would help him clear his mind—at least help him file the events of the evening into their proper mental compartments.

She told Drummond he should set aside her academic title for the moment and call by her given name, Graciela. She didn't like so much formality between colleagues. Situations like this one required close work, and formality set up barriers and stunted collaborative thinking.

Drummond realized no one ever called him by his given name, just "Drummond." He hadn't gone far down the hill when Graciela drove by, tooted a short beep on her Peugeot, and rolled down her window. She had forgotten her bag in the Guadalupe, she said. Nothing much in it, she was sure. No worry, really, but would he tend her car while she ran inside?

When they got to the hotel, Drummond offered to retrieve her bag, and he went inside where he saw Rubén alone in the bar. He waved and the Cuban returned his greeting. There was no sign of Lenhard. Drummond walked beyond the bar to the main desk where the brown leather pouch was lying on the counter.

"This belongs to the Directora," he told the night clerk. "She's right outside."

The clerk walked far enough toward the door to see for himself that the Directora was waving from the Peugeot, and then handed the bag to Drummond, who brought it out to the car.

Graciela offered once more to drive Drummond to the Reina Cristina, but he declined and told her he'd come to her office after breakfast to pick up his pass for the Alhambra. He promised to keep his profile low by mingling with the tourists, as if his presence hadn't already been detected by some of the people Graciela wanted to keep in the dark about her suspicions. Surely, someone had done a quick search on Drummond and found that he'd given up his work as a federal agent and turned his talents toward the authentication of art and artifacts. It wouldn't be a stretch to notice that the authorities at the Alhambra needed something authenticated.

As Drummond walked through the Puerta de las Granadas, the street took a steep decline, and Drummond could feel himself being propelled down the Cuesta de Gomérez in semi-darkness. He passed shuttered shops where doorways had been draped in fuchsia and azure shawls in the afternoon, where windows had been full of wooden carvings and flamenco dresses. Now the tourists who had been pushed into the shops by the police cars were gone to their hotels or to late night suppers with the rest of Granada.

At the bottom of the hill, Drummond crossed through the plaza and walked past the Cathedral where Ferdinand and Isabella, the Catholic kings, were buried in the Royal Chapel. He wondered if Isabella had been more comfortable resting in her first grave on the top of the hill in the Convento de San Francisco, the old Nasrid Palace that Isabella had taken over after evicting the Emir.

In the plaza cafés, people were enjoying a late Spanish dinner. Drummond took a seat at a table beneath a canvas awning and asked for a bottle of agua con gas and a glass of the house red wine. There was gazpacho on the menu, and Drummond thought a cold soup would calm his hunger. He pulled the medium-pointed black fountain pen he was fond of from his jacket pocket and opened a narrow Moleskin pad.

He thumbed through the notes he'd made earlier until he came to the fist blank page and printed "RING OF LIONS" in thick black letters. Beneath that heading, he filled the page with his first reactions to the lions, especially the ninth lion. On the next page, he made a list of the day's events and drew a sketch of the Courtyard of the Lions, the hill where Ander's body had been sprawled, and the dungeon where the police had held Rubén. His plan was to describe the day and the people he'd encountered. He assigned a page to each one—Graciela Corzal, her Cuban apprentice, the French professor, the police capitán, and the dead boy.

The waitress wondered if she could bring him something more, and Drummond asked for another pour of the red. He'd rearranged his life to avoid what he now thought of as a grisly fascination with crime, but he still found murder an intriguing affair, a moment when someone exercised an enormous degree of power over another. So had he already decided that this was murder? Or had the boy's death been caused by some other person's accidental grasp at life? The answer would be easier for Drummond to evaluate once he had another glass of wine in his hand.

He could see the Capitán coming toward him from the far end of the plaza. The Capitán raised his hand when he noticed Drummond and walked toward his table. He asked if it would be all right to sit.

"I don't mind," Drummond said. "How can I help?"

The Capitán offered a cigarette. When Drummond declined, the Capitán asked if Drummond would allow him to smoke. Again Drummond said he didn't mind. The two were being extremely polite to each other, just as they had been earlier that day in the Alcazaba.

"You do not stay up on the hill?" the Capitán inquired.

"No. I'm located here a few blocks away." He closed the small notepad and slipped it into his jacket pocket.

"You are enjoying the traditional Spanish dinner hour?"

Whatever Capitán Castañeda wanted, he was taking a circuitous route to get there.

Drummond smiled. "Would you care to join me?"

The Capitán shook his head. "No. Gracias." He glanced at Drummond's pen, still there on the table next to his wine glass. "You are writing notes about the murder?"

"A traveler's chronicles, nothing more."

"You write a great deal in your chronicles?" the Capitán asked.

"A habit," Drummond said.

"You have some idea who killed this young boy?"

"I am not a homicide investigator, as you know."

"A quarrel, perhaps, a fist fight that went too far?" the Capitán asked.

For Drummond, the questions meant the Capitán had done his research. He knew art forgery hadn't always been Drummond's field. "Your investigative team must have some idea by now," he answered.

"We have not given up interest in the Cuban."

Drummond finished his wine and stood. He asked the officer to pardon him, he hoped the officer would understand—he'd been traveling most of the day, and it was time for him to rest.

The Capitán stood with him. Drummond shook his hand firmly, turned, and gestured to the waitress. The Capitán wandered back across the plaza.

Back at the Reina Cristina, Drummond paused in the bar long enough to sip an espresso and then went to his room. He arranged his pen and notebook on the table by the window so he could continue writing about the day. He hung his jacket in the closet, removed the onyx links from the cuffs of his shirt, and rolled his sleeves to just below the elbow. He was ready now to make a list of details, including the story Rubén had offered, doubts the Capitán had expressed, and Graciela's reactions to both.

He started with the policeman who had hijacked him as he was enjoying a much-deserved glass of wine. "THE CAPITÁN," he wrote at the top of a page. The officer had intruded on Drummond's analysis of the young artisan's death. He'd taken the liberty of sitting down at Drummond's table, and when he had offered a cigarette, there was an aura of pretext about it. Drummond recognized the tactic. The policeman obviously had hoped to engage Drummond in talk about the murder, get him into an offhand chat about Rubén Torres, maybe bring the Doctora into the mix. One thing was certain, the Capitán would be back.

The Capitán wasn't the only one with an air of manipulation about him. At the top of a second page he printed "DEAD BOY." There was something less than genuine about the victim. Why had he postponed his meeting with Rubén and what was he doing in the Alcazaba?

Also, Rubén's explanation of the whole affair was not what Drummond considered forthright. Drummond flipped to the next page and wrote "MOTORCYCLIST." He searched his vocabulary to find a better word for what he was feeling about Rubén. Duplicity? No, no, if that were the quality he was sensing, it would be easy to discern the counterfeit and the counterfeiters. What was present on the Alhambra hill was not so recognizable. It was a mix of the authentic and the incomplete, an ether of partial truth that seemed to have attached itself to the entire afternoon and evening. Perhaps the undefined ether Drummond sensed had come into the Alhambra long before—a haze of doubt that had been on the hill even before the lion had been sent away.

Was the Directora aware of the partial truth that hung in the air? Drummond started to write "DOCTORA…" then crossed it out and wrote "GRACIELA." She had asked him to call her by her given name.

She seemed both trusting and suspicious. Trusting that Drummond would be able to dust away any gray areas, authenticate the lion as the Alhambra's own artifact, or expose it as a counterfeit. And she was also suspicious of the change she had witnessed in her lion's behavior.

Was it Rubén Torres, her apprentice, that Graciela distrusted? Certainly not. She demonstrated no doubts about him, not even in the trying circumstance in which he was currently enmeshed. And her reaction to the French professor was trusting as well. His occasional fawning didn't bother her in the slightest. She had been told the professor had a crush, and she seemed to think his behavior was routine for a middle-aged man in that condition.

So, what condition was she attributing to Drummond? Her request that he stop calling her Doctora, that he use her given name, Graciela—what was that all about? Had Drummond been behaving too formally?

Drummond also questioned Graciela's reaction to the police. She wasn't happy they had surfaced in her world, but she was neither impressed nor frightened by the officer's imperious demands. The question of trust had nothing to do with her reaction to the officers. For her, the issue was one of expectation. Graciela expected certain behaviors from the officers, and the officers expected certain behavior from her. Each understood the boundaries of the other's authority, and neither was disappointed.

On the surface, Graciela's role in the day's events was simple, clear, and administrative. But Drummond could see that something had disturbed her well-disciplined world. He had filled Graciela's first page and begun a second.

He noted that Graciela was moving carefully yet forgetting things like her bag. She seemed slowed by a weariness that came from carrying a layer of doubt beneath a softly confident shell. Drummond was sure her malaise—he liked that term, it seemed to fit Graciela—had nothing to do with her Cuban apprentice. The Alhambra was Graciela's life, and Rubén's family story tied him to the castle's early days.

Clearly, Graciela was as devoted to Rubén as a mother might be to her only son. Any disappointment she exhibited over his failure to complete his assigned tasks was quickly erased by appreciation for his brilliant interpretations of the architecture and beautiful translations of the writings on the walls. She had enjoyed the way the young man appeared to communicate directly with the lion, staring deeply into the creature's eyes. Her devotion was strong enough that Rubén could be deceiving her. But Drummond doubted that deceit was Rubén's intent.

Drummond went back to the page labeled "MOTORCY-CLIST." There was more he needed to add. Rubén was hard working and enthusiastic, and he was possessed by a desire to follow his quest, to solve a mystery that few others seemed to care about. Or, perhaps, this mystery was one that many cared about but few were willing to pursue. After all, it was clear that one person who did pursue the mystery—Rubén's friend, the young craftsman—had not survived the quest.

Rubén did have a surname that carried its own secrets. Was he really a descendant of the Torres who'd been Columbus's translator on his first trip across the sea? That Torres had been part of a small landing party that remained in the Americas when Columbus returned to Spain. There was a story that everyone in that landing party was dead when Columbus returned on his second voyage. But there were also claims that Torres had survived. Was this enough to explain Rubén's passion and his fidelity to his ancestor, or was Rubén hoping to excavate something more?

Drummond paged through his notes to the next blank page. He wanted a new space for the fawning French academic. He titled this page "THE FRENCHMAN." It was good fortune for Rubén that Lenhard had a spare room reserved at the Guadalupe. He had certainly made himself useful—and omnipresent. The professor knew the Alhambra almost as well as the Graciela, and he seemed capable of popping up everywhere. Drummond didn't have more to write about him yet, but he wanted to find out more, so he left the rest of the page empty.

Drummond hesitated before capping his pen. There was one more person who had captured Drummond's attention that night—a young woman who'd walked behind them down the hill from the Alhambra and hovered while Rubén had checked into the hotel. How had she come to insert herself into the day? He didn't know what to call her, so he left the first line blank.

The young woman looked as Spanish as the waitress who'd brought him his wine, but the tendency of the young to dress alike no matter where they lived had made defining nationality more challenging. But he could see clearly that this woman moved with a certain urban invisibility, a style often exhibited in cities much larger than Granada. She exhibited the fashionable habit of hanging at the back of a crowd in the belief that if the hanger-on kept silent, no one would notice her presence. Yet Drummond had noticed her, and he thought Rubén had too, perhaps because she and Rubén were close in age. Tomorrow he would see if there was another link between them.

Drummond pulled off his boots and placed them at the side of the bed. He phoned the night clerk, asked for a wake-up call at six o'clock and explained that he'd be checking out first thing in the morning if he could obtain a room on the hill. He wanted to spend the next few days and nights closer to the Alhambra.

The clerk suggested a vine-covered hotel at the top of the hill, a family-run place wedged between the Palace of Carlos Quinto and the Convent of San Francisco. The clerk knew from personal experience that the breakfasts were delicious because his cousin was the cook.

A few moments later the clerk was at Drummond's door with a handbill promoting the location of the little hotel. The flyer said—in Spanish, French, English, and German—that the hotel was "…within the walls of the Alhambra…" and the phone number was listed on the back. Drummond called the number and a young woman told him in Spanish that he was fortunate. Then she repeated in English that she had one room open overlooking the inner patio. He could check in tomorrow morning since there was no one in the room for the night.

CHAPTER ELEVEN

The humidity of the Guadalquivir River hung hot and damp in Cordoba's evening air as Rafael Montoya finished another day at a job he found foolish. He locked the door of his office and stepped across the reception area through another door, which he locked as well. Once outside the offices of the Municipality of Córdoba, he made his way along the hallway that ran under stone arches, across a polished concrete floor, and out into the gardens of the Alcázar de los Reyes.

Montoya knew the work he did for the city of Córdoba was beneath him. His brother had said it to his face more than once. He used to joke that Rafael spent his time at internet cafes pretending to be a highbrow. Now his brother would tease that the good thing about Rafael's municipal job was that it provided him with a desk and a phone number. But why, he'd ask, didn't Rafael find a position that suited the Montoya family station?

If only Montoya could have disagreed. He was Doctor Rafael Montoya, a scholar and a writer. He deserved better. The family was right. He'd taken a post that could be handled by anyone, but with Rafael's experience, he should have become director of the entire municipal library and all its historic material. That's the position he'd applied for.

But he hadn't been selected. His rivals in Granada had made sure of that. The director's position was left vacant while the municipality continued its search, and he was offered an appointment he would never have considered if he weren't exhausted by all the criticism. Even worse, it was only luck and his fascination with computers that landed him a job at all. He was called the Director of Digitization, but Montoya knew the title "Director" had little to do with administrative responsibility and a great deal to do with the city's inability to pay decent salaries. Instead of the remuneration employees deserved, they were given inflated titles.

Even so, Montoya invested great energy in his work, as he had always done. In the few months that he had been employed, he'd embarked on the creation of a digital catalogue that would open the Reconquista to scholars worldwide, and he'd connected Córdoba's Alcázar to a network with links to precious collections in Granada and Seville, as well as in Madrid, Rome, and Paris. The ambitious scope of his project surprised his colleagues and left Montoya both drained and exhilarated by the genius he mustered every day. Soon, all his projects would come to fruition, and he would have the acclaim he deserved.

But that night, instead of working into the evening in Córdoba, he should have been in Granada meeting with thinkers who had come from France to learn about his work on the Alhambra. Montoya was respected in that circle. In fact, when it came to the riches of the Alhambra and the history of the Nazrid Princes—especially the last prince—he was considered a top scholar. He espoused the idea that the romantic longing for a castle in Spain had a basis in reality. He was close to demonstrating that the Moors had abandoned treasure when they were forced to abandon Spain—treasure that remained to this day in every castle in Spain.

Montoya was meeting with French colleagues who understood the importance of his theory. They often gathered in Granada, and those trips to Granada had been profoundly satisfying. He had planned a presentation for this weekend that would have confirmed his brilliance, but at the last minute he'd been forced to reschedule, to postpone his dramatic revelation.

With only a few days' notice, the library board had announced it was his responsibility as the newest director to stay in the municipal library during the feast of Corpus Christi. Of course, he protested, but it was clear he'd have to dance with that ugly tradition to keep the respect of his colleagues. He attempted to trade favors with several fellow directors, but none would take his place. To Montoya, it seemed that someone was laughing at him again.

Certainly, there was no reason for a faction of Spain's prestigious academics to pounce on him as they had years before when they had laughed him off the podium at a conference and knocked him out of contention for every position of academic and curatorial stature. There was nothing wrong with his theory about the castles of Spain, but the intellectuals were still after him, he was sure. He'd been denied the library post he had wanted in Córdoba, had been forced by circumstances to accept the lesser position, and now his academic work was becoming just a hobby.

There were other scholars who were still interested in his ideas, however, like his French colleague Professor Lenhard and the aficionados he brought with him. They would have arrived in Granada already. They'd be settled in their hotel, and he should have been with them. A room at the hotel had been reserved for him. Instead, he'd left a message for Professor Lenhard and Mademoiselle Trouchon stating that his position of great responsibility in Córdoba had forced him into a role he could not talk about, one so significant he could not arrive in Granada until Sunday evening at the earliest.

What he planned to reveal demanded an element of surprise, and his colleagues promised to maintain the confidentiality of Montoya's presentation until he arrived. And, of course, his friends were attentive to the tension between Montoya and Doctora Graciela Corzal. She had joined in the ridicule he had suffered after his presentation at the British Museum conference, and the very mention of his name to Doctora Corzal might have caused her to question the motivations of Lenhard and the French museologists.

Montoya continued his stroll through the Córdoba gardens, planning how to make the best of things. He would travel to Granada on Sunday night. He'd take a sick day on Monday, perhaps Tuesday as well. When he gave his demonstration, there would be no doubt that he had been right all along, and he would be recognized for his important work. Shortly after he learned he would be on duty for Corpus Christ, he had moved the materials he needed for his presentation to a secure location in Granada. One of his French colleagues had agreed to set up things properly so the demonstration could occur as soon as he arrived.

As Montoya neared the far side of the grounds, the scent of the dirty river began to blow away. Once he exited the castle gate, it would be only a short walk to his apartment. He would stop at a café for a small plate and a glass of wine. Perhaps he would pick up some bread to have with his coffee in the morning before returning to the Alcázar for another day in the municipal offices.

CHAPTER TWELVE

Rubén woke up as the sun entered a bank of windows in Docto-ra Corzal's office. He'd fallen asleep in her chair. A browned and brittle file folder lay open on her mahogany desk, a few pages were scattered on his lap, another page on the tile floor. Two papers were still pinched between his thumb and forefinger. He began re-reading the letters in his hand, then stood, stretched, and walked to the copy machine a few steps away. When he turned, he noticed he was not alone.

"Good morning, Rubén," Graciela said in her firmest voice. "Am I to assume that your room in the Hotel Guadalupe was not up to your liking?"

The American investigator was at her side. Both were staring at him like teachers who had discovered their star student's excuses were counterfeit.

"Have you found something I missed? Something I forgot to put away when I left yesterday?" Graciela walked to the round table at the center of the room. "Bring the papers here. Let's have a look at what you found, shall we?"

She was locked in a fixed stare with Rubén, a connection that seemed physical, one that Drummond was not about to obstruct. Drummond moved to the other end of the counter without crossing Graciela's gaze. There he found a tray holding a tea pot, cups and saucers, and a box of tea bags. On a shelf above were an electric kettle, a tin of McVities Biscuits, and several liters of spring water.

He opened the water and poured it into the kettle. "I think we'll want a cup of tea, won't we?" he asked.

He slipped seven tea bags into the china teapot, then meticulously draped each string and adjusted its orange paper tag precisely over the edge. When the water began to bubble in the kettle, he poured it over the bags and moved the covered pot to the center of the round table. He popped the lid off the biscuit tin and arranged three cups and saucers at compass points equidistant from the tea pot. That done, he picked up the file folder marked "Conditions of Surrender" that Rubén had left on the desk and slipped in a brittle page that must have fallen to the floor when Rubén dozed off. He took the file to the table where he was the first to settle in.

Graciela followed. Rubén stood, thumb and forefinger still pinching the browned parchment pages he had intended to copy.

"Rubén," Graciela's voice had lost its sharp edge. "How did you open that cupboard?" She pointed her chin toward a mahogany credenza and cabinet across the room.

"You gave me a key to the office," Rubén replied.

"I wasn't asking about the office, I was asking about the cabinet." Graciela recalled locking the doors to the cabinet the day before. At the end of each day, the keys always went into a zippered coin pocket in her briefcase, and the briefcase was routinely slipped inside a drawer in her desk. She was sure she had spun the tumbler on the drawer's combination lock before she had left her office.

Rubén came to the table and placed the pages on the polished wood. His explanation came slowly. "I came up the hill to the office," he said, "because after you had left, I realized that Ander's death was related to your concern about the lion. I'm sure you realized that too. Ander was about to lead me to a crevasse that opened to the Alhambra's underground—a shaft, or cave, or whatever—a route that would show someone had altered the flow of water to the lions."

Rubén looked at Doctora Corzal and took her silence as a signal to continue. "So it was obvious," he said. "Last night, I knew my appointment with Ander led to his death. And I knew I had to see the Alhambra's subterranean plans."

He was sure there would be drawings of pipes and passages in Doctora Corzal's office that would make things clear. If passages had been built close to the exterior surface of the hill above the Darro, Rubén figured he'd be able to predict where Ander was going to lead him. And that would explain everything.

"So, this is different from the work you've been doing already on the waterways—the information you were going to show Inspector Drummond?" Graciela asked as she poured tea into each cup.

"No… and yes… Of course…"

"And the documents you took from the secure cabinet…?"

"All connected," Rubén said. "Todo. But I didn't understand how clearly they were connected until last night."

Graciela settled into her chair. How did Rubén plan to convince her the folder he'd taken from her locked cupboard was connected to engineering studies drafted in the late nineteenth century? Chronologically, hundreds of years separated the engineering files from the fifteenth century parchments. And thematically, there was no connection at all.

"You'll need to clarify," Graciela said. "And tell me about the cabinet. How did you open it?" She glanced at the leather pouch that she'd had with her at the hotel. But no. It was not her practice to put the keys in anything but the zippered coin pocket of her briefcase, which always went into the locked drawer.

Rubén stirred a spoonful of sugar into his tea. He took a sip, glanced at the credenza, whispered, "Sí, sí, sí, sí, sí," and then he began to lay out his theories. There were drawings of the subterranean waterways made in the nineteenth century, when attention was first given to the Alhambra's restoration. Rubén had located the diagrams showing the flow of water to and from the Palace of the Lions.

To prepare for the visit of Inspector Drummond, he had traced the water path all the way to the fountain. He was convinced that lion number nine had come back from the atelier decontaminated, but otherwise untouched.

"I saw no reason to believe the lion had been tampered with or replaced. On the other hand, my research suggested there had been tampering on the waterways leading to the fountain. Unauthorized work. And that's what was giving lion number nine his heroic flow."

Graciela shook her head. "The work being done on the waterways was authorized. It was all part of the current renovation. Your young friend was on the crew."

"Yes, Ander was on the crew," Rubén said. "That's exactly how I knew someone had instructed the crew to look for more than biodeterioration. They were doing extra work—looking for riches hidden by the last Emir, Boabdil, before he handed over the Alhambra to Fernando and Isabela."

Drummond interrupted. "You found something more in Doctora Corzal's files, something you were just about to copy?"

Rubén tapped the corner of one of the parchment pages. "Sí," he whispered.

"A rare document of some kind?" Drummond asked. "One that contains evidence?"

"Evidence," Rubén repeated. "Ander was killed to hide evidence that would reveal that Boabdil actually did leave some kind of treasure here in the Alhambra."

Graciela sighed. "This is a very old tale here in Granada," she said. "A fantasy."

Rubén walked to the window that overlooked the Emir's palaces. He pointed dramatically toward the Patio of the Lions and then crossed his arms and stood there confidently, as if there were no question that his late-night visit to Graciela's office was justified. "Sin duda," he said. "There is evidence."

For Drummond, Rubén's story was one that merited applause, rather than belief. Perhaps the Cuban protégé had finally been caught in the process of deceiving his mentor. But if deceit was Rubén's goal, Graciela would not be easily misled. Drummond noticed that Graciela had put a white glove on her right hand and then gently placed the browned pages Rubén had been holding into the file.

"Normally, we wear gloves when we look at these, Rubén. I believe you know the protocol." Graciela poured more tea into Drummond's cup before turning again to Rubén. "You had a difficult day yesterday. It may have caused you to place too much trust in your young friend's mythology. The tales the local people tell about the Alhambra are even more elaborate than Washington Irving's stories. Everyone believes treasure is lurking behind the walls, or under the floors, or in the hills."

Graciela sipped her tea quietly. When she finally spoke to Rubén again, her voice carried a sad tinge of mockery. "And how does all of this relate to your breaking into my documents case?"

"You left the keys on your desk," Rubén said. "Right there, for anyone to use. I did not break into the cabinet. But I did search it."

Drummond was looking at the leather bag he'd retrieved from the hotel. It was there on the table where Graciela had set it down that morning, after they'd entered the office. He wondered if the chaos surrounding the murder and the police had caused Graciela to break her pattern. Had she tucked the keys into her leather pouch instead of the briefcase? Had someone removed the keys before the bag was turned over to the hotel clerk? Had Rubén done that?

Drummond took a pair of white gloves from a box next to the cabinet of precious papers. After he slipped them on, Graciela handed him the file. The two pages Rubén had been about to copy were composed in the Castilian dialect of the Golden Age and appeared to be handwritten transcriptions of identical material. The handwriting of the documents was similar but not identical. The lettering was accomplished with characters of roughly the same height and width, but one document appeared to be a line longer than the other. It was dated "25 noviembre 1491." The other was dated "2 enero 1492," the day of the Moors' surrender. Drummond could see that Torres had identified the discrepancies. Perhaps the young man had wanted copies so he could look for more anomalies.

Drummond gave Rubén a pair of white gloves. "Please, show us what you found here."

Rubén placed the papers side by side in front of Doctora Corzal.

She had known about the variants for a long time, ever since she'd been asked to take them into her custody to protect them from whatever zealotry might cause harm to the historical record, conflicted though it now appeared. She had also known there would come a day when the existence of the two agreements would be revealed. She just wasn't expecting it to be this particular day.

Graciela studied the telltale phrase that had caught Rubén's attention. In the middle of the page of the document dated "25 noviembre 1491" was a line that did not appear in the document dated later. She took a deep breath that sounded like a sigh as Rubén gave his interpretation.

"In the first document," Rubén explained, "it says that there must never be a repetition of Córdoba, the animals—the lions, this phrase has to mean the lions—they must never be removed from the garden. In the later document, there is no mention of the lions."

"And Córdoba?" Drummond asked. "Perhaps the Emir was scolding the Church for turning the Mosque into a Cathedral?"

"So much was lost," Rubén said.

Drummond could hear the fervor in Rubén's voice, and the tone made Rubén's interpretation less than objective. "Do you believe the first draft is the actual statement of the Emir's conditions for surrender and retreat?"

Rubén pointed to the signature lines on each of the documents. Both carried the name Abu 'Abdallah Muhammed XII. "This is Abu

'Abd Allah, successor to both his father Abul Hassan Ali and his uncle Abū `Abdallāh az Zagal," Rubén said. "He served two reigns and eventually became the last Emir. The Christians called him Boabdil."

Drummond wanted a more specific answer. "Do you believe this shows that not only the Emir, but also the Catholic Kings, knew that something had been hidden in the fountain—or in the conduits that supply the fountain?"

Rubén stared at Drummond and said, "What I believe is that these two documents show the rumors Ander gave his life to prove may be based on more than fairy tales."

"You were not so sure of this yesterday?" Drummond asked.

"No, not as sure as I am now."

Drummond removed the white glove from his right hand and slipped a small black gadget out of a case hooked to his belt. "Do you mind my looking through this?" He offered the gadget to Graciela, who took it and turned it over. The device had a dial, a small screen, and directional buttons like a television remote.

"Push the red button," Drummond said. "It will turn on the magnification screen."

Graciela pressed the button and stared at the screen before handing the device back to Drummond, who gestured for Rubén to place the two documents on the table again. "This is a microscope, a modern replacement for the jeweler's loupe, which I also carry out of respect for times past."

Drummond focused the digital microscope on the dates and invited the others to look closely. In the earlier document, the year "1491" was clear. In the document with the official surrender date, the numerals in 1492 were written with just enough hesitancy that the ink had beaded halfway around the top slope of the "2." In the November document, the X of Muhammed XII was the product of two bold single lines that crossed exactly at the center. In the official surrender signature, there was a hair-line repetition, as though the X in XII had been written over.

"Do you detect concern or fear in the hand of the person who served as notary on the second document?" Drummond asked.

"I detect variance," Rubén said. "These were not written by the same scribe or signed by the same Emir."

"Do you believe the first document was written in the hand of an experienced—perhaps a specific—scribe and interpreter?"

"It is certainly well done," Rubén said with an air of satisfaction. "The bold strokes of the 'X' lead to that conclusion. The entire document is written in a confident hand. The Emir would have signed the November document with certainty that an agreement about the lions had been reached and embedded in the contract."

Drummond believed there was more to the discovery than Torres was letting on. "If we conclude that the second scribe was counterfeit, what can we ascertain about the first?"

Rubén and Drummond were gazing at each other, saying nothing.

Graciela finally broke the silence. "There is an established way we can examine the question," Graciela said. "It was the habit of the scholars of the time to leave a mark, something that would allow the writers, scholars, and interpreters to prove their connection to the work they had done. This was necessary in the event the royal court should try to withhold payment, something that happened with regrettable frequency in those hard times."

Graciela ran her forefinger under a line that mentioned animals, the line Rubén believed referred to the lions. "You see, here we find a reference to the lions in one document... but there is no such reference in the other. And look at what happened in the scribal parsing of the lines. The Spanish words do not fall in exactly the same places on the page on the second document."

Drummond offered the magnifying device, but Graciela declined. "The mark I'll show you is not so difficult to find as to require your device," she said. "Read the beginning letter of each of the last six lines of this paragraph—the one that includes the reference to the lions."

Drummond called out the letters. "Hache, a, ele, e, v-chica, i,"

Rubén drummed his fingers on the table and said, "H-a- L-e-v-i. This is an important name, HaLevi or ha levi."

Graciela nodded. "There were many infants named for Levi, the child whose mother Leah hoped would be her connection to Jacob," Graciela said. "The name is repeated many times in the list of Spanish scholars and poets."

Drummond recognized the trick. "HaLevi wrote the famous Purim letter from London," he said. "A poetic treatise on the difficulty of spending a holiday alone, among strangers, with no wine."

Graciela smiled, pleased her hired authenticist had been able to place her reference so easily. "HaLevi employed this style of encrypted authorship claim," she said.

Rubén added, "The Purim Letter writer—he turned on his people with unfettered violence. Penalties. Expulsions. Forced conversions. Autos de fé."

"But he gave us this model of encrypted claim that we can employ here, in the Alhambra, at our scribe's suggestion." Graciela said. "The notary has embedded a reference right here in this text."

Rubén's response was almost a whisper, "In finding the reference, we have also found a surname. And there is more! Look, above these lines we see a first name as well—Yosef. It is the Hebrew name of Luis de Torres, Yosef Ben HaLevi."

Drummond studied the young man. Except for the drumming of Rubén's fingers on the table, Torres exhibited no emotional change. Did his nonchalance demonstrate that he had already deciphered the meaning of this encryption? "Luis de Torres," Drummond repeated. "The interpreter who traveled with Columbus. Of course."

"Yes," Rubén replied.

Graciela leaned in as though she needed a closer look at the newer document, although she knew the importance of this name. Turning to Rubén, she said, "Your ancestor, the one you so admire."

Rubén continued with his theory. "The second document, if you notice, makes use of small increments of space to create the illusion that there has been no change."

Drummond had already noticed the rearrangement and agreed. "On the second document, only the 'I' and the 'L' remain at the beginning of a line. And so, the encryption of authorship disappears."

Graciela sat back in her chair. "And for this reason you wanted to make a copy of these papers?" she asked Rubén.

"Yes. But I didn't break into your locked case. As I said, you left the keys on your desk. At least, I presume it was you."

Graciela couldn't believe she would leave the keys behind. But the day had been significantly troubling. She carried the folder across the office to a console, below a reproduction of Picasso's Don Quixote. She lifted the painting off its hook, placed it against the console, tapped her code on the keypad on the thick iron door set in the wall, and slipped the precious papers into a more secure space. Could Rubén be telling the truth? It was possible. Still, she decided her young apprentice would benefit from closer supervision.

"Inspector," she said to Drummond, "you should take Rubén with you to the fountain. No need to disguise yourself as a tourist. Perhaps the two of you could also take a tour of the work that was done in the waterways."

"I've already included Doctor Torres in my plans for the day," Drummond said.

Graciela filled her arms with several additional files she wanted to switch from the cabinet to the wall safe.

She motioned toward her desk and said, "The passes I ordered are there in the wire basket. I will expect you both for tapas."

CHAPTER THIRTEEN

Drummond and Rubén were standing in the patio of the Cuar-to Dorado, the Golden Room, looking at a tall, filigreed façade of flowers, leaves and Arabic inscriptions encased in geometric forms on the south wall. There were cutouts in the façade for five arched windows and two doors. The door on the right led back through the room where they had entered. The door on the left opened to a hallway that exited on the Court of the Myrtles.

Rubén had seemed hesitant to talk the night before, but he wasn't hiding his thoughts now. He told Drummond they were positioned at a crossroad about to choose between magnificence and separation. He pointed to a verse carved on an ornate wooden band above the honeycombed plasterwork and said the verse was a sign they were at that crossing.

"The very magnificence of the Alhambra teaches me to read this verse. It is the castle speaking to us," Rubén said. "This wooden band is the castle's crown—a sign of the power of the throne—and of the Emir, the man responsible for the radiance of the Alhambra."

Drummond was confused. "Orient me," he said.

Rubén translated the verse, "'In me, the West is the envy of the East.'"

Drummond fumbled in his jacket pocket for his compass, and finally held it shoulder high. "Exactly what are you calling the West?"

"The West is the Alhambra," Rubén explained. "It is so spectacular that even the rising sun—the East—has become jealous of it."

"Ah," Drummond responded with a whisper. "So simple. A doorway to the exquisite."

Through the door on the left, Rubén led Drummond into the Alhambra, leaving behind the door to the mundane on the right. "We should walk through the Court of the Myrtles. We didn't see much of it last night."

The hallway to the courtyard was dim, a honeycombed ceiling hung above their heads like young stalactites. Drummond stepped carefully—up one step and then another, finally onto a zig-zag of black and white tiles that gave the floor a dizzying effect. As he moved into the open patio, he understood Rubén's passion for this building, and he could feel a stirring inside himself too.

He stood motionless for a moment and took in the brilliance of the sun splashing off the marble floor and the water channeling through it. The light was shocking, almost overwhelming. At last, he followed Rubén down the marble path alongside a well-groomed hedge of myrtle that stretched from one end of the courtyard to the other on both sides of the water channel. At the north end, the Comares Tower rose above seven arches covered with plasterwork diamonds of fine geometric lace. The air was light and fresh and calm.

They took a turn through another door and passed through another chamber that felt like a vestibule. Drummond slipped his digital microscope from its holster to survey the ceiling. "Do I see evidence that the Alhambra's beauty has undergone significant repair?" he asked.

Rubén nodded and said, "Work was done in the seventeenth century to restore the ceiling after a nasty explosion in the gunpowder shop a hundred years earlier."

"And before that?" Drummond was examining a corner where the rooms and patios seemed glued together against their will. From what he knew of Arab comfort in open spaces, the buildings were meant to stand on their own, close but not connected to one another.

"I wonder if a collection of individual palaces might have been merged when the Catholic Kings imposed mortared connections between the walls," Drummond said.

"Yes, I'm sure of it. The Palace of the Lions was built as a separate rustic villa, with no connection at all to the Comares Palace that rose above the Courtyard of the Myrtles. They should have remained detached," Rubén said.

"The lions belonged to a rural respite, set in the center of this urban fortress."

"You know the theory then. The Palace of the Lions may have been a school, a madrasa, a center for reading and learned discussion."

"Maybe a center for poets," Drummond added. "Or a place of respite for mathematicians and mystics."

Drummond and Rubén moved along the perimeter of the Courtyard of the Lions through rooms known as the Mocárabes, the Sisters, the Kings. The last room they entered was the chamber of the Abencerrajes, a room with a marble basin stained with streaks of dark red and a dome filled by an eight-pointed stalactite star. The chamber had compellingly bloody legends attached to its history.

"You must have heard the stories of what happened in this room," Rubén said. "The murder of the Banu Sarraj? I believe Washington Irving took great pleasure in that story."

Drummond bent over the basin to capture digital images of the dark red stains. He knew of texts from the sixteenth century that told about that slaughter, but he also knew that Graciela enjoyed laying the blame for the tale's popularity on Washington Irving's fiction. Apparently, Rubén agreed with his mentor.

As Drummond turned away from the basin, he had a perfect view of the lions framed in the double-arched doors to the Abencerrajes. He was positioned exactly at the far end of one of the four marble channels, the east-west axis, with the lions and their fountain at the center. He paused a moment, taking it all in.

That's when he saw the young woman who had followed them down the hill the previous evening. She was directly across the courtyard. He moved toward the lions and began to circle the fountain, getting microscopic digital images of each of the twelve beasts. Oddly, the young woman seemed to be working her way around the circumference of the lions as well. Rubén was standing still, looking her way, watching her.

So Drummond had been right in assigning significance to her presence the night before. He bent down to focus on the basin that seemed to rest on the hindquarters of the lions, but from this point of view it was clear the basin was positioned on a central pedestal so that it would hover just above the standing beasts. Water flowed through their right rear legs, spilling delicately from their mouths into a low channel that was open on four sides to the canals that crisscrossed the courtyard. Was it an illusion, or was the water flowing into and away from the fountain at the same time?

Drummond's interest in these lions had begun years earlier when he had first visited them and noticed they were unlike other lions of their time. All other lions were hostile, crouching on their haunches and ready to leap onto intruders. These animals, however, were standing at ease and gazing straight ahead.

The Near Eastern style of the beasts was obvious and rarely disputed. They reminded Drummond of creatures he'd seen in the museum in Baghdad and in collections of Mesopotamian art. He had read the arguments about where these lions had been created. Was it in Córdoba, when that city was the most significant intellectual center in Europe, during the time of the Umayyads? That would certainly account for their style since the Umayyad sultans had relished the art of Baghdad and Samarra. Or perhaps they were manufactured later by artists emulating Mesopotamian ways.

Drummond liked the first theory, that the lions came from Córdoba, procured—as so much of Granada's art had been—in the aftermath of the fall of the great Umayyad metropolis after the destruction of the medieval palace Madinat al-Zahra. It seemed obvious to Drummond that they certainly had not been created in the Byzantine studios of Christian artists as Washington Irving had suggested.

Drummond moved slowly now, capturing the digital information from each lion that would yield proof of material and aging, scratches and repairs, humidity shifts, and biological change. On the surface, the lions all appeared to be of the same age and material and carved with roughly the same craftsmanship—give or take the requisite sculptural whimsy that Drummond used as a marker of authenticity. He saw nothing that suggested questionable provenance.

When all the digital imagery was available on his laptop, he would be able to look closer to compare the information from the lion that had traveled to Paris with each of the non-migratory statues. For the moment, he chose to look like an enthusiastic American, perhaps a slightly greedy traveler who wanted to fill his camera with as many photos as possible. His small instrument was not all that different from the android device the young woman was using as she and Drummond circled, always at 180 degrees from one another.

Drummond paused at the ninth lion to capture digital data and noticed that Rubén and the girl had ended up exactly across the way, at lion number three. Drummond wanted them to think he was ignoring them, but it was impossible for him to be in that position without hearing their conversation. They were both speaking in Spanish, but Drummond had no trouble understanding.

"So, you're alive and well after all," the young woman said.

"¿Y por qué no?" Rubén said. "Why wouldn't I be?"

"You sort of disappeared last night."

"I thought you were tired. Didn't you say you needed sleep?"

"Your friend is taking a lot of photos."

"He's American," Rubén said.

"¿Y nosotros?"

"Of course. We are too."

"He's listening to our conversation."

"I would not be surprised. Let me introduce you," Rubén said.

Drummond nodded to Ana and continued walking around the circle of lions while maintaining his studied pace—number ten, eleven, twelve, one, two. As Drummond finally reached lion number three, Rubén introduced him to Ana Madrizon from New York City, USA.

"Señor Drummond is your fellow countryman," Rubén explained.

Drummond laughed, acknowledging Rubén's subtle reference to his status as a Yank, and then he turned to the young woman. "Forgive me," he said. "I don't mean to be impolite, but I noticed the geometric nature of your meanderings just now. You've been paying close attention to the division of the quadrants here in the courtyard."

She smiled at Drummond. There was no hesitation in her answer. "It's something I do—something my father taught me to do."

Drummond pointed at the notes Ana had penciled into her journal. "Justice is number 4" was at the top of the page in letters three times the size of her ordinary notes. She had drawn a set of six angles next to six sets of ten dots arranged into triangles, some of them inverted.

Ana closed her journal but kept her eyes on Drummond. "Family philosophy," she said.

"Her family is full of ideas like that," Rubén added.

It was clear to Drummond that Rubén had spoken to this young woman before, that he found her extremely charming, and that he would have enjoyed parting company with the American authenticist he'd been saddled with so that he could have a civilized lunch with her. But Rubén was a very useful guide for Drummond, and Drummond wasn't going to excuse him yet. He still needed to go down to the work areas below the courtyard. "Perhaps you'll join us later?" he said to Ana.

"Tapas, perhaps?" Rubén added.

"Perhaps," Ana said to Drummond. Then she smiled again, this time at Rubén, and wandered off through the Hall of the Two Sisters.

There was a small door just inside the arches of the Abencerrajes, and Rubén inserted an oversized skeleton key into the lock that creaked as the key turned. Rubén held the door for Drummond, and they walked into a space between the stone walls. The narrow passage widened into a workspace at the bottom of three worn steps. A balding man in a white shirt was talking to several workers there. His shirt was marked with the yellowed sepia of damp Alhambra clay. It had been soiled recently, as had his hands and knees. The soles of his shoes were dry.

"Don Marco," Rubén said, "I am here with our visitor, Professor Drummond. I want to show him how we are doing in our renovation work. I hope you don't mind."

The man waved the workers away and wiped his forehead with his handkerchief. "My men are still very upset. Yesterday. The death. Their companion. You'll forgive us. We will not be of much service to you. Another time will be better."

Rubén and Drummond exchanged quick glances. The man seemed to notice and turned to walk away.

Rubén called after him, "We'd like to do a simple walkthrough. Si es posible."

"Today is very difficult," the man said.

"Tendremos cuidado," Drummond said in Spanish that was good in small bursts. "We won't disturb anyone. I am a guest of the Patronato and want to fulfill Doña Graciela's request."

"Then go ahead," the man said, wiping his forehead again.

"One question," Rubén said. "If you would remind me. The hatch that we opened when el noveno came back and we secured its connection to the water source. It is this one, isn't it?" Ruben touched a wooden door, about a meter wide.

"You are as good as any of us down here," the man said. He wiped the clay from his hands and shook the dust from his handkerchief.

"Has the crew been working in the tunnel that circles the fountain?"

"Not today."

Drummond wanted to speak, but he was hesitant to assume any more authority than he had already. This was not the place for a visitor to take on the task of interrogation. Instead, he asked Rubén, "Is this something that is checked routinely?"

Rubén repeated the question to the foreman, who was growing irritated.

"Isn't that my work?" the man said. Then he looked quickly at his watch and said he had to leave, he had an appointment, there was someone he needed to see. Rubén and his friend would have to continue on their own.

CHAPTER FOURTEEN

O nce Graciela had cleared away the teacups from the large round table, she went back to the safe behind the Picasso print and retrieved the archival box. She needed to look at the surrender documents one more time. Wearing the white gloves of her trade, she opened the box and touched the red velvet lining inside. Archivist. Museologist. Guardian of the past. She was among the few who had access to the lives of the long dead—kings, scholars and peasants alike. Her mentor, one of the university's first academic women, had reminded her often of the privilege afforded archeologists. But close as she had been to the remnants of ancient lives, the rules of her profession had always kept her from the sensual appreciation Rubén had enjoyed the night before when he had fallen asleep with history open on his lap while touching a page he believed his ancestor had touched, feeling the texture of the parchments.

She carried the box toward the two armchairs near the windows and set it down on the coffee table between the chairs. The windows were tall and there was good morning sun. She wanted to see the documents in that light.

She opened the box and removed the document that Rubén believed his ancestor had translated. The coded signature was impossible to ignore. She replaced that page and lifted the second one. She had noticed the discrepancies, the lack of conformity, but had allowed herself to be lulled into acceptance of both because she knew they had been verified.

The documents were among a very select number that anyone could claim to be from the fifteenth and sixteenth centuries. Graciela knew the Catholic Monarchs had interests in the writing of the time—official, literary, personal and architectural. They were curious about the poetry carved on the walls of the Red Palace. They had set up a guild of translators and town criers—the Romanceadores del Cabildo—to translate the verses of the lived-in book. But none of those translations survived.

There was another well-known set of texts that came from the work of Morisco Alonso del Castillo—a Moor turned Christian turned translator for the Crown and the Inquisición. His work, imperfect as it was, had become the foundational material of scholars. But much of that work had also disappeared. No one was certain whether any of his original documents had survived. The exception was one highly prized copy registered in the library in Madrid, but Graciela wasn't sure that translation was truly his work.

Castillo had been part of a counterfeit scheme creating records to smooth over differences between the Catholic Kings and their Morisco citizens. Falsified documents and relics were found in the ruins of the Mosque, and a trove of counterfeit missives engraved on lead disks had been unearthed on the Sacromonte Hill.

Forgery in all its romantic splendor. Romance with all its imitation of truth. All of it had been woven into the cultural fabric of Granada. And now it seemed to Graciela that few people were capable of separating reality from fantasy. Fictions arose from the red fortress on the hill and seeped into literary chronicles. These chronicles assumed a value equal to the history that had been burned—either by Archbishop Cisneros in Granada's central square or by nature in the library fires.

But the two documents in this archival box were real. Both had been created during the last days before the Reconquista. What Graciela had not done is focus as tightly as Rubén had in comparing the two documents of surrender. She had not considered the possibility that one of them could be a forgery committed in the first days of 1492 before the Emir had left Granada.

It was almost miraculous that both of the manuscripts had survived. The scholar who unearthed them had gone unnamed. It had been dangerous to take too much credit. But somehow, Graciela's mentor had acquired the documents and kept them in her office at the university under her sole care because she felt they were safer under her stewardship than they would have been if dispersed into the hands of any churchman or politician.

Those were the times in Spain. Nothing was safe. It was when Graciela's mentor had become ill that she told Graciela about the documents, which were hidden in plain sight among the books in her office. Later, when Graciela had become director of the Alhambra, her mentor had instructed her to find a space for them. Graciela had repeated her mentor's pattern and hid them in plain sight behind the doors of her personal book cabinet above the credenza alongside the most ordinary documents—payroll records and annual budget files. Yes, she had preserved them, but she had never given them enough attention.

Now, she wondered why she had never guessed the documents would be among the treasures Rubén was seeking. And that he would find them. The documents had emotional weight for him beyond being two of the few extant writings from the fifteenth century. They signaled the intersection of Rubén's family and the Fountain of the Lions, stone beasts that had survived great peril. The lions had most likely been produced long before Mohammed V had built the palace, long before they had been set up like Solomon's oxen with a basin on their backs. They were creatures out of time.

The beasts were figurative, and like the representational paintings of monarchs in the Parlor of the Kings, the lions would have conflicted with the orthodox iconoclasm that dictated palace friezes full of vines and fruits and flowers and words rather than living beings.

Even more puzzling, the lions depicted in the fountain were not muscular animals with hair flaring out like sunbursts. They were small creatures, although one would never call them stunted. Their ears were rounded and cupped. They resembled the ninth century Hittite Lions at Tell Halaf in Syria. For Graciela, they brought to mind the Queen of the Night, her birdlike feet curled over the backs of crouching lions in the Burney Relief. Graciela loved those lions and visited them regularly when she'd worked in the British museum. But it seemed unlikely that Boabdil meant to save the Fountain of the Lions simply for the sake of art. There was no record of his being an art enthusiast. Graciela wondered if Rubén really believed the Emir had hidden treasure in the lions—or in the tubes that supplied them.

"Castles in Spain." That expression was at the core of the treasure dreams, and now it annoyed Graciela. All because of that Montoya fanatic. She wouldn't want him to get his hands on these documents.

Graciela closed the archival box and went to her desk. She keyed her password into her computer and began a search for the email Professor Lenhard had sent the previous day listing the names of the museologists he was bringing with him. Was Rafael Montoya among them?

Lenhard had befriended Montoya during his fall from grace at the antiquities conference in London. Graciela had been on the other side. In fact, she had led the other side. That was when she had landed the job at the Alhambra and Montoya had suffered a bitter loss. He had been convinced he would be named director of the Alhambra. Of course, he lost his bid after all his foolishness about treasures in the castles in Spain. He had nothing but conjecture to back up his theories, and scholars in general agreed with Graciela including those who sat on the board of the Patronato. The only person who was at all tolerant of Montoya was Lenhard, and that was only out of kindness.

It would have been difficult for Lenhard to see a man experience such total defeat. Still, if Montoya was holding onto his dream of turning the Alhambra into headquarters for his semi-intellectual rants, Graciela could not let the lions become his pawns. Was Montoya still blaming her for his loss?

Graciela scrolled through the names on Lenhard's email. Montoya was not among them. She breathed deeply, closed her email, and returned to the coffee table where she'd left the archival box.

What was it that these documents were saying about the Courtyard of the Lions? Ibn Zamrak had written on the basin that the lions and their fountain had been crafted for the Nasrid palace, for Muhammad V's Garden of Joy. The palace poet called them noble ideas to grace the Imam's mansion. But there was another story that the lions had been moved to the garden from the palace of the Jewish governor Yusuf Ben Nagrella, whose palace had once dominated the space now taken by the Alcazaba.

Rubén had not mentioned that second story to Drummond. Rubén was behaving cautiously, hiding both his linguistic skills and his ancestral politics. He'd read from Zamrak's poem a lyrical passage describing the hydraulic system, but he had not offered Drummond lines from the Jewish philosopher and poet Ibn Gabirol, lines that were nowhere to be found inside the Alhambra.

Rubén had often used the poem as proof that the lions had come from the home of the Jewish governor. His favorite passage connected the Alhambra lions poetically to the palace of King Solomon, where a basin rested on a phalanx of oxen.

"...not on oxen ..." Rubén would quote Gabirol, "but there are lions, in phalanx by its rim..."

The phalanx of lions still encircled a basin in the Alhambra, but there had been many alterations to the fountain with each generation of politicians, artists and craftsmen believing their modifications were improvements. The original cylinder from the center of the basin had been moved into the Patronato museum on the level just below Graciela's office. She was certain anything left in the base of the fountain would have been found and removed centuries earlier. Especially treasure. Nonetheless, she decided to have a look at the original cylinder, the one that would have regulated the flow of water long ago.

Graciela carefully locked the archival box in which she had sequestered the documents of surrender and slipped the key into a small pocket on the inside of her vest. She walked over to the safe and placed the box inside. She shut the heavy door and tugged the handle to be sure it was locked, then replaced the Picasso print for the second time that morning. That done, she removed her gloves.

As she left her office, she double-locked the door to make sure that no one, no matter how trusted, would enter in her absence.

CHAPTER FIFTEEN

The American had been right about the way Ana was approaching the Lion Fountain. She had been meandering in a distinctly geometric fashion. That's how she used to wander the whole of a Sunday afternoon with her father, paying attention to the shapes of squares and rectangles. "It is important for you to understand this motion," her father would say. "If al Majriti were here, he would teach you."

They would roam through parks and plazas and university campuses—the school where he taught and any other campus that caught his attention on a particular day. As they moved through spaces both planned and unplanned, he would draw her attention to elements that consisted of four lines—equal in length, opposing in position. "Most things are made in fours," he would say, and Ana would run her foot over the length of one line, then another, another, and another.

What about the diamonds, she'd once asked. Her father said she was looking at a masquerade. "Look carefully," he'd said. "You will see the diamonds also have four external sides."

She wasn't certain, but she imagined all this work must have been done by the great source of wisdom her father was always deferring to in discussions with her grandfather. At the time, she gave the geometric walks very little thought. It was simply one of her father's practices, his "mystical practices" as her mother called them now.

Ana left the Hall of the Two Sisters and walked back through the Garden of the Lions to the room on the other side, the one with the red-stained basin at the center. Above her head was a ceiling that reached down and pulled her up into a honeycombed star with eight points. It held sixteen windows in a firmament of stalactites with a tiny eight-petaled rose at its center.

"Numbers lead the mind on its journey toward beauty." Was that how Rubén had put it when they had met the night before in the bar? Fairly well phrased—not far from the experience she was having as she looked up at this ceiling. She had a stash of sayings like that one stored in her memory. They'd been repeated so often by her father that she could call them up and slip them into conversations at will. There were similar lines in the material she'd been reading about the Alhambra, descriptions of rooms in the fortress castle based entirely on the ideas of people Rubén had called architects and mathematicians.

Ana didn't believe the workers who had built the Alhambra were mathematicians. Many of the books she'd read called them architects, but just as many scholars called them carpenters and craftsmen, practitioners, laborers following a routine—more craftsmen than philosophers, with esthetic principles based on practice rather than theology, repeating their training each day in rote performance. Why should they meditate on immaterial concepts like the passage of life through seven spheres of heaven when they were busy honeycombing eight-pointed stars into a plaster firmament that would become the ceiling of this castle?

Ana thought these workers may have been doing her father's thing, "mystical practice," work that appeared mundane to others but came to a celestial conclusion, such as a cupola of stalactites that formed a star that appeared to rotate on the square space below. Hadn't they created a universe? Surely, they must have shuddered at the energy that dripped from mocárabes as they worked them into the plaster ceiling, considered every leaf and flower, paused in the

beauty of each cursive line of poetry. And how was it that they copied the lines of verse so perfectly that they coincided with the length
and width of the rooms?

The craftsmen who had built the Hall of the Ambassadors
would have traced the sides of squares as they laid the stone floors
and counted the four panels that made the sides of the ceiling. And
wouldn't they have been aware that they were assembling seven ascending sets of stars in the ceiling, seven being the perfect number
and the number of spheres through which the soul would want to
pass on its way from this life to a meeting with the great source of
wisdom? To study numbers, her father had told Ana, was to study
the source of all knowledge.

If Ana had chosen to major in mathematics, she probably
would have advanced further through the seven heavenly spheres.
Perhaps that's why her mother had sent her to Granada—to give her
a mathematical education to go with her degree in folklore.

She had decided Rubén and the American must have been deep
in the science of numbers when she had run into them at the Lion
Fountain. The American had an instrument that was capturing photographs as it measured. A great gizmo. Ana thought she'd like to
have one, if she could figure out what it did or why it would be
valuable, but she could see the American had little time for chatter,
so she'd excused herself. When she looked back, they were going
through a small door that seemed more theatrical than real. They
disappeared so quickly that Ana imagined they'd vanished, that the
wall had swallowed them whole.

Ana's plan had been to spend the afternoon walking back
through the Alhambra, retracing her steps, gathering as much
memory as possible. One of her professors claimed he could recreate myth by standing in the shadowy footprints of the hero,
allowing the legend to unfold once again. That's what she wanted
to do—re-live the Alhambra stories—and she would take photographs while she was at it. She would meander geometrically,

as Rubén's friend had noticed, to gaze at spaces that had been inspired by very complicated notions.

She pulled her phone from the messenger pack slung over her shoulder and left the Court of the Myrtles to take another look at the mocárabes. Then she continued backward, against the flow of tourists, until she came to the Hall of the Ambassadors where she counted four panels. She made long gestures with her right hand, pointing her forefinger as though she were running it along the lines on each side of the rectangular space. She glanced upward at the ceiling to measure the seven balconies of stars. She was stepping into that place that would have forced the craftsmen into the physical performance of mystical practice, whether or not they were aware of the nature of their routine at the time.

Ana was overstaying her ticket and the welcome that went with it, but since she hadn't left the palaces, no one seemed to care that she had entered with the earliest morning group and was still there. She had only one more place she wanted to see, the Whisper Room, the space that had become famous for the way it carried sound from one point to another.

Whisper rooms were Ana's favorites. They were usually constructed in a circular hollow where sound as soft as a whisper could be reflected directly from a focal point on one side to another point across the circumference of a dome. Ana and her roommates used to play a whisper game in the gallery at Grand Central Station, but the Alhambra Whisper Room was not a play space when the castle was a working fortress. If the wrong person was listening across the way, whisperers could be killed for a simple murmur.

As Ana entered the room, she saw a man in a madras shirt whispering into a sand-colored corner. He was mouthing his comments oh-so-quietly in hopes he would still be overheard. Ana located his intended audience, a woman in a turquoise dress standing across the room from him. Ana switched the phone to video and made several attempts to capture the scene and its science, panning and dollying to mimic the path of the sound wave, hoping the video captured by the phone's lens could demonstrate the elliptical path that she knew the sound waves would be taking.

That's when her travels began to catch up on her. She was tired and warm. She saw an unoccupied chair and sat down to re-arrange things. She'd been holding her pocket-sized notebook and ballpoint pen in her left hand as she used her right to capture the scene. Now, she put everything but the phone into the bag. She wasn't ready to make the decision to stop shooting photos, so she tucked the cell phone into a small pocket in her travel vest. She took a deep breath, closed her eyes and listened.

CHAPTER SIXTEEN

Graciela took the convex staircase that circled down to the main floor of the Carlos Quinto where the lion fountain's original cylinder was kept in a secure, glassed-in cabinet. She studied the seamless, hollow tubes on display. Five hundred years before, it was simplicity that encouraged water through these pipes in the same way air coaxed music from a flute. There did not appear to be a hiding place for gold or silver to melt into a running stream as Zamrak's poem may have led the young workers to believe. Boabdil would have chosen a better place to hide a treasure. He would have sheltered valuables deep in the walls, embedded them in fissures running through clay. If Rubén's interpretation of the artesano's discovery was right, there would have been a crevice, a gap under the fountain that appeared as an accidental indentation but eventually led to the hills above the Darro.

Graciela stood straight. Look how quickly she'd been drawn into that speculation, into a mythology of hidden treasure, one she had rejected long ago. Yes, a young man had died, and yes, she was deeply saddened. But if wild rumors about treasure had led to his death, Graciela had no intention of scattering that gossip any further.

It wasn't until Drummond was standing directly beside her that she noticed he'd entered the museum. A film of amber dust covered the sleeves of his white shirt and his khaki trousers. There was a spray of the powder on his forehead, and it was lightly streaked across his nose and cheeks. His appearance made Graciela realize she'd never seen him so connected to the physical nature of his work.

Drummond leaned over the glass-enclosed cylinder. "The conduits rise like the arms of an upended squid," he said, taking a step backward and wiping the dust off his forehead with a handkerchief. "Perdón," he said. "My passion overwhelms my good manners. I should have cleaned up."

Graciela was pleased, not with his apology but with his enthusiasm. "You have engaged directly with the environment, I see. And you found something?"

"Several things."

First on Drummond's list was that the traveling lion appeared to be the genetic brother of the other eleven. He'd know more once he completed his analysis, but there were no outstanding features that signaled forgery. Second, the cleaning of the tubes had been done very well. There was no evidence of residual biological material in the waterways that connected the Alhambra's plumbing to lion number nine.

"Clean as a whistle," he said. "Cleaner than a whistle. Perhaps getting cleaner every day. Short of someone having actively scrubbed the plumbing, I would guess it's a result of the theatrical rush of water that we've witnessed emanating from our lion at nine o'clock every evening."

"So, the water pressure is continuing to cleanse the pipes."

"Exactly. Under normal circumstances, there would be some small residue building up each day. But there is no evidence of any bacterial growth at all. Which leads me to question the source of the ebullient flow of water."

"Are suggesting that the water is coming from somewhere other than the Alhambra's natural springs and ponds?"

"Precisely," Drummond said.

"City water."

"Chemically treated."

Graciela glanced at Drummond's clay-dusted clothing. "You climbed into the tunnels?"

"We did—Rubén and I. He was in search of the passageway that his young friend had promised to reveal, but we didn't find it. The space narrowed abruptly. Pipes went off through the earth toward the Darro. Excavation would be required before continuing."

"The passageway is one that's been used to check the flow in and out of the gardens since the fourteenth century."

"And it's been renovated much more recently, it would seem. We did not find a connection to a new water source, but there are signs that motorized implements have been used in digging around the pipes and widening the space for human intervention. This is not work from the fourteenth century. And it was not done by hand."

"What does this mean?"

"Our lion may be entirely authentic, but his dramatic spitting seems to have been managed."

"To what end?" Graciela asked.

Drummond moved his chin, ever so slightly toward the direction of the staircase to signal that he'd like to answer Graciela's question in her office. He suspected the artesano, Ander, was part of a scheme, and Ander's willingness to share the information with Rubén may have been the cause of his death. The public museum was no place for that kind of talk.

French museologists were gathering across the way and Graciela's friend Lenhard was there circling them. Flighty guy, Drummond thought, always pacing, checking his watch, glancing at the door, and, of course, noticing Drummond and Graciela wherever they were. Graciela walked Drummond toward the stairs, and within seconds Lenhard was with them. He apologized effusively and asked if they'd seen Mademoiselle Trouchon. She was supposed to meet the group but had not appeared. After a polite exchange of trivialities, he turned and left.

Drummond thought he was doing a good job masking his annoyance at Lenhard's constant appearances, but Graciela's smile told him that he'd failed.

"He's actually harmless," she said.

CHAPTER SEVENTEEN

The rush of things exhausted Marie Trouchon. Vite. Vite. Hurry. Hurry. The rush and the dust, dirt, clay, sand. She'd been hurrying all morning, and she was still hurrying. Vite, vite, she thought. She should have reached the group by now. They'd be wondering where she was.

She squinted at a haze of fog gathering around her colleagues as they exited the museum. Was it humidity or perspiration starting just below her eyes? She raised her right hand and waved at the group to let them know she would be with them soon, bientôt. She pointed one finger, un moment, then moved quickly toward the services pavilion next to the Wine Gate.

By the time she made it into the women's restroom, dampness had begun to diffuse over her cheeks, and in the mirror, she saw a drop of sweat mixed with the fine dust of Alhambra clay slipping down the vertical groove in the middle of her upper lip. She turned the cold-water faucet. It squealed, but no water streamed. If there had been a paper towel dispenser, she could have blotted the moisture from her skin, but there were no paper towels. The Alhambra had installed air dryers—more sanitary she supposed, and quicker if all you needed to do was dry your hands. But her hands were not in need of drying. She needed to wipe away the clammy dust that was rising from her shoulders up the back of her neck and staining the white starched collar of her linen shirt. Inside her bag, behind her notebook, she found a single tissue, and she used it to dab the skin under her eyes. Within a few seconds, the tissue was drenched. Instead of getting clean, her face was taking on the taupe shade of the mascara running from her eyelashes.

In the mirror, she saw four women standing at the four sinks along the wall gazing at her. Not a single one offered a handkerchief, a towelette, or a few drips of hand sanitizer.

She turned on the cold-water faucet one more time and waited.

"No funciona," one of the women said. It doesn't work.

Was she all right? Necesita ayuda? Should they call the matron?

The women were talking about her.

Marie Trouchon turned the handle on the warm faucet one more time. There was a squeak and a hiss, but no water came out.

She went into a stall and sat down. She needed to get away from those staring women. She removed her jacket, held the silk lining over her face, and breathed in deeply. Once, twice, three times. She untucked her shirt, turned the hemline, and smoothed the end of the linen under her eyes. She slipped her arms back into her jacket and left the stall.

The women were gone, so she stopped in front of the air dryer and let it blow on her neck until she felt dry. Her perspiration was stopping. She stood, feeling cooler.

She remembered the tourist kiosk where there would be bottled water. She would be fine. But as she exited, Professor Lenhard was just outside the door. He slipped his arm around her waist. Was he being attentive, or had her tardiness disappointed him?

"Marie, what has happened? Where have you been? Are you well?"

"Pas mal," she said.

But he stayed close. "We've been waiting for you," he said. He steered her toward the entrance to the plaza, toward the taxis, and held the door as he slipped her into the back seat of a checkered cab. He had always been considerate.

"To the hotel. Back to the Guadalupe," Lenhard said. "Take some time."

What was he telling her?

"Rest. Put on something fresh."

The fog had lifted from her vision, and she noticed her shirt tails hanging below her jacket. She hadn't meant to wrinkle her shirt like this. But Lenhard was smiling at her. That was good. No worries. She would get a cup of tea and freshen up. She would meet the group at the hotel.

CHAPTER EIGHTEEN

How long was it before Ana felt a touch on her shoulder and heard a man's voice? English, Cuban lilt, standing at her side, a bit of clay-colored dust on his upper lip, and on the cuffs of his white shirt, just above his wrists.

"I could have stolen a phone from a sleeping woman," Rubén said, pointing to the phone standing upright in the pocket of Ana's travel vest. "You have been in very deep contemplation."

"I must have dozed off for a minute." Ana took the phone from her pocket and noticed it had been running while she dozed. "Longer than a minute, I guess." She shook her head, stretched, and tucked the phone into her messenger bag. "I was going to walk through the gardens, but it seems I'm too late."

Rubén knew a quick way to traverse the path to the gardens of the Generalife, he said, his pass would work for both of them, so no need to worry about the entry time. He took Ana's hand and led her out under the mocárabes of the squared pavilion. They moved quickly, along the exterior walls of the Palace of the Lions and then down the hill on a cinder path the sultans had reserved for horseback travel when they needed to move with speed between the Alhambra and the summer getaway.

The royal path turned up over a private bridge that would have taken the sultans' horses directly through the stables into the palace of the Generalife, the sultans' safe house—a garden estate that had been there on the hill before the palaces were built. The Generalife was a retreat to leisure, entirely separate from political conspiracy and artful excess. It was simple and calm with useful buildings that offered solace rather than power.

Instead of following the cinder path into the stables, Rubén led Ana into the orchards. They crossed the greenway and continued behind the amphitheater to the top of the water staircase. Laurel branches created an awning that shaded the clear water flowing down the stairway.

"I think it's best that we stay on the perimeter," Rubén said.

"Are we trespassing?" Ana asked.

"No," he said. "Y sí. Posiblemente."

"Las dos a la vez?"

"At the same time, yes. I have a pass, but it would have been better to use it in the early hours."

Ana was happy to stay right where she was. It was late afternoon, and she was finally feeling the effects of her flight across the ocean. The prospect of exchanging a hike through the gardens for a chance to sit in the sun, listening to water flowing down the staircase, was inviting. She sat down on the soft grass, leaned against a bench under laurel trees, and slipped off her sandals.

"Let me show you the photos I've been taking," she told Rubén. She pulled out her phone and tapped in her code, then handed the device to Rubén. He sat down beside her and touched the photo icon. As he scrolled through Ana's images, she rested her head against the bench, enjoying the scent of fragrant leaves, and she fell asleep again.

CHAPTER NINETEEN

Back in her office, Graciela went to the credenza beneath the book cabinets and pulled out the shallow top drawer—nearly a meter wide. This was where she kept her maps, each lying flat in a brown paper folio, a dark brown ribbon tied gently around the entire set. She lifted the corners of three folios until she found what she wanted, the fourth folio in the bundle. Gently, she tugged it out, placed the folio's contents on top of the credenza, and smoothed the map with both hands.

She leaned over to adjust her focus and called to Drummond. "Here," she said, pointing to a spot that she wanted Drummond to consider. The spot seemed to be a knot in a tangle of kinks and coils. "This is the point you are describing—where you said the path stopped, where you thought it would have to be excavated to continue on. This would be the clay corridor housing the waterway that refreshes our lions and keeps their fountain flowing."

Drummond traced his finger from that point, round and round on the map, along circuitous lines that had a cursive character similar to the poetry written on the walls of the Nasrid palaces. "Where do these go?"

"The city is a nest of passages, with a web of legends—and rumors to match," Graciela said. "Tunnels run under the Alhambra, down the slopes and under the plazas of the city. There's another tunnel where people still hunt for gold dust drained from the mountains by the Romans."

Drummond was aware of the tunnels. Years before, he'd been invited to accompany his friend, the chief justice, to a gathering of artists and law enforcement officials. The judicial branch was looking for a way to guide young people away from nuisance crimes like the graffiti tagging that was occurring all over the historic district. The plan was to create an arts program, perhaps an exhibition with sculpture, painting, and large format photography—art to be encouraged in public spaces and displayed on the streets. They hoped it would result in cultural enrichment for the city's teenagers and less desire to deface public property.

After the exhibition opened, Drummond and the chief justice were invited to tour the secret spaces under the home of the host, a sculptor who taught at the University of Granada and had a reputation for work that was unbounded by either the traditional or the surreal. They entered through a small opening just inside the cármen and walked through labyrinthine passageways that had been braced and illuminated.

"There are many points in the mesh of tunnels where it appears the end has been reached," Graciela told Drummond, "but nothing could be further from the truth. Rubén believes his unfortunate young friend was about to demonstrate a mastery of these burrows."

Drummond had not seen any clever architectural trickery beneath the lions, no hint of a ruse, no trompe. "To me it appeared that the path had been rather bluntly machined shut," he said.

"In which case, it might easily be reopened."

"The sand was substantial and well packed," Drummond said.

Graciela walked toward a coat rack at the back of her office. She stepped out of her pumps and into a pair of utility shoes, a cross between garden boots and sneakers. She removed her suit jacket and slipped on a pale, rose-colored duster. "Will you accompany me?" she asked Drummond. "I think I need to have a closer look."

They left her office and went to the point where the Court of the Lions connected to the Hall of the Abencerrajes. Using the same entrance Drummond and Rubén had accessed just hours before, they descended three stone steps.

It was quiet in the empty workspace under the Lions' Fountain. No sign of Don Marco, the foreman. Tools had been wiped clean and hung back in place on the pegboard wall above the work bench. The floor had been swept with a straw broom, which was leaning now against the tool bench.

Graciela turned on the fluorescent lights that hung from the ceiling and looked around the room. She touched the workbench and looked at her fingertips. They were clean.

"This space is quite tidy, isn't it?" Drummond commented.

"I see they've taken my advice to avoid tracking dirt and dust up to the public level," Graciela said. "I've been after the workers about the mess they've been spreading into the palace. Our visitors come here to experience history, with a bit of magic thrown in. We don't want them to notice workaday rubbish."

Drummond had been listening carefully for any trace of irony in her voice as Graciela spoke. Perhaps there was none. After all, she hadn't seen the room that morning. The clutter. The tools scattered about. He was unsettled by the orderliness he encountered now. "Siesta time?" he asked.

"That as well," Graciela answered quietly. She went to the wooden door that Drummond and Rubén had entered in the morning, turned the brass doorknob, and unlocked the top half of the door. She reached inside to grasp another handle then gave it a tug. The lower half of the door glided open.

"We didn't use the whole door this morning," Drummond said.

"No, it's apparent from the clay on your clothing that you did some crawling," Graciela said. "This way is a bit less taxing."

It was dark and the lamps on the walls were not functioning. Graciela pulled her light torch from the pocket of her duster. "We mustn't stare into this light. It has some sort of laser in it." She moved ahead of Drummond, down the track, alongside the water pipes and the wooden benches built into the base of the walls. The track did appear wider than she had remembered, the pipes more accessible.

"We were able to continue beyond the bend," Drummond said. "But not much further."

"There's always been a deception here," Graciela confessed. "A clay barrier that moves like a screen turning on a spindle. You can move it forty-five degrees, turn it on its axis and enter at either side."

Her lamp gave out the bright light of mid-day and Drummond could see the point at which he'd thought the pipes ran straight into the walls.

"Here, let me show you how the screen opens," Graciela said. She shut off her torch and set it on the bench, then pushed on the wall until it became a door that creaked and turned.

Drummond shook his head. He was surprised by the barricade wedged into the wall and by the tamped earth that completed the seal. Rubén had said nothing to him about this deception. Maybe the young man had never gone past this point.

With his jeweler's loupe, Drummond examined the edges of the screen, the surface of the wall, and the floor. He stooped low as he continued beyond the point that had been blocked a few hours earlier. He was beginning to pick up a change in the texture of material on the floor. The sand had a scattered quality to it, but there was also a ridge no more than a millimeter or two on the right side. He followed the ridge as it grew in size—three millimeters, four. Something had been dragging a trail of sandy clay.

Graciela switched on the torch again, letting the beam of light do the walking. Wooden benches continued along the wall. Further in, at the point where the edges of the beam began to dim, there was a mound—light shades turning to dark, thick shapes tapering to narrow.

Graciela and Drummond rushed toward the mound. What bit of contour startled them? The outline of a boot at the end of a ridge of clay? A glimmer of light in the pearl button of a shirt cuff? A sepia stain on the worn leg of a pair of trousers? A man on his side, knees drawn up, one hand in a fist, the other arm invisible under his torso.

"Don Marco?" Graciela's voice was a whisper. "Don Marco." She stood at the figure's feet. It was dark, but when she held the torch high, she could clearly see that it was Don Marco and that his chest was utterly still. She moved closer and crouched down, touching the spot on his neck where she hoped to feel a pulse. She leaned in, her ear close to his mouth. He was not breathing. Drummond was kneeling beside her, repeating the litany of urgencies that Graciela had performed.

Twenty years before, Graciela had knelt this close to her husband as he died. His was a simple death in the presence of his young wife and the physicians who had gone to great effort to keep him alive. Her husband had directed the Alhambra for years and fell in love with Graciela when she was a young scholar drawn to the poetry, light, and water of the castle that he kept. He had left her the means to study abroad and encouraged her to leave Spain and devote herself to the level of scholarship demanded for her to find her way back to the red castle. His quiet death had signaled that his work was completed and hers had begun.

How different Don Marco's death. When Graciela had closed her husband's eyes, she had brushed the wrinkles from his pajamas, folded his hands just below his ribs and pulled a white cotton blanket up to his chest. She wanted to do the same for Don Marco. He had worked at the Alhambra since the days when Graciela had first arrived. She had visited his home and noticed small things—a photo of him with Graciela's husband, an award from the province of Andalucía—signs of the family's pride that Don Marco's work at the Alhambra made him a part of Spanish history. Now she knew she would need to visit one more time.

Graciela raised her hand to close Don Marco's eyes. This small act would put things in proper order, but Drummond interfered, gently blocking her hand with his arm.

"Perhaps we should not change anything," he said, pointing to the twist in Don Marco's left ankle and a buildup of fine clay dust on the heel of his work boot.

"Is it possible he's been dragged from the revolving stone door?" Graciela asked.

"From just this side of the door."

"You suspect someone has done this to him?"

To Drummond, nothing was clear. "I don't know. He could have pulled himself. Look at his hand. He has been clawing the clay."

"Do you believe he fell behind the door? Maybe that's why you were unable to open it this morning?"

Drummond knew the two incidents could be connected, but he doubted that the timing had been so neat. Besides, someone had done cleanup work in the area below the Lion Fountain and in the tunnel as well. Drummond was not a forensic scientist, at least not so far as human bodies were concerned, but Don Marco's body was still warm when they arrived. To Drummond, this clouded the timing of the cleanup.

And what had caused the man's death? There was no sign of bludgeoning, no knife wound or blood. Had he accidentally fallen by the stone door and then been dragged away? Was it a thoughtless attempt to hide a simple accident? Drummond tried to trace the path that could be taken out if one continued deeper into the dark. It didn't appear that anyone had walked over the dusty floor.

Without his asking, Graciela handed him the torch. "The tunnels run from the top of the red hill down to the Plaza then across to the Albaicín. They continue under the Catedral into the cármenes."

"Could we follow?"

"With care, and with effort. And perhaps with a dog that has a good nose."

"Will your cell phone work down here?" Drummond asked. "I think it's time we call the Capitán who spent so much time with us yesterday."

Graciela didn't respond. Something was bothering her, making her feel distracted. Was it a scent? Mildly sweet? Her eyes had become damp. Was it pepper? She felt a bit dizzy. She extinguished her torch. "I don't think we want to use a phone right now," she said. "There's something in the air."

Drummond pulled his handkerchief from the pocket of his shirt. He gave it to Graciela and told her to cover her nose and mouth. He put his arm around her shoulders and gently turned her away from Don Marco.

"Let's go back," he said, giving her a push toward the secret door.

"Yes, now," she said, holding the white cloth over her nose and mouth. The space was small and the ceiling low. Graciela moved quickly with her knees slightly bent. Drummond followed. Running through his mind was a catalogue of cave gasses and news stories about spelunkers who had died after walking into pockets of bad air. What had they sensed back there by Don Marco's body? Hydrogen sulfide? That gas was heavy and could easily collect in a space like this. If it could sneak into sewers, it could meander into passages alongside the plumbing of the Alhambra's waterway.

Hydrogen sulfide had a nasty, rotten egg smell in small quantities, but neither he nor Graciela had detected anything until they'd spent some time checking the body. Of course, people don't smell gas when it's at a lethal level, so maybe that's why they hadn't smelled anything right away. To Drummond, though, the sweet smell he noticed was more like pineapple than eggs. The scent reminded him of a wicker basket full of freshly washed linens. A childhood smell. Like when his mother would take the linens down from the line, fold and stack them in a basket, and ask him to carry them inside. He enjoyed the clean scent of bleach that emanated from the sheets and towels as he carried them. It was a scent that never seemed to leave the fabric. A scent that had been abundant in his bath water that morning, and one of the clues that led him to check the bacterial level in the water at the lions' fountain a few hours before.

City water was bereft of bacteria because it carried many chemical purifiers, and the lions' water had the same characteristic purity. If the gas they had just inhaled was chlorine, it could have come from the supply that had taken over for the old natural springs. Depending on the dose, it could have knocked out Don Marco, or it could have killed him. Had he become disoriented and crawled in deeper rather than toward the door? Or was someone with him—a good Samaritan, perhaps, who tried to drag Don Marco to safety rather than a killer attempting to hide the corpse? If another person had been with Don Marco when he collapsed, who was it, and where had he gone?

Drummond's nose was dry and so was his throat, but they were approaching the small door of the workshop below the Lion's Fountain. Graciela turned the knob and pushed it open. They had made it back to fresh air.

CHAPTER TWENTY

Both of them—Ana and Rubén—had been sitting upright against a garden wall, enjoying the afternoon sun when they had fallen deeply asleep, so deeply that Ana didn't notice Rubén's head leaning on her shoulder. Unusual. They weren't friends yet, were they? Ana didn't want to disrupt Rubén's rest, so she tried to move his head gently off her shoulder before she slipped sideways and stood up. Success.

She sat down across from him in a spot where she could watch him draw air in and then puff it out, pull air in again, sniff, and then exhale—still not waking. His shirt seemed to have caught a clay-colored shadow, but on further inspection she could tell it wasn't a shadow. It was dust. A trace of it had settled on her shoulder where he had rested his head.

The dark green grass had an earthy, country scent to it and Ana began to amuse herself by pulling the strongest blades of grass and stacking them into formations like mason's bricks, repeating unity. One blade of grass, and one, and one, and one, until finally the wall of grass revealed a number to be the principle of its own structure. Did she remember her father's concept correctly? She was missing her father now. She'd been missing him for quite a while—since high school, since his heart attack. She made another wall of grass. And another. And another. A four-sided shape again, four for justice.

Finally, Rubén unfolded himself, stood, stretched, and crouched next to the grass walls. "I've heard it said that the Moors were better at geometry than algebra," he said.

"And the meaning of this?"

"I've finally concluded that you are the lost daughter of one of the sultans. That's why you spent your time in the Alhambra tracing geometric patterns—attempting to call Pythagoras back into the mix."

This was amusing to her, this game they were inventing, trying to unlock each other's family histories. "Perhaps I am more likely the reincarnation of one of the palace servants who cleaned up after the artesanos who built this magnificent castle," she said. "And you? What shall I guess about you?"

"Think of me as one of the lucky adventurers who wandered off with Columbus and never found his way home."

"Lucky?"

"Well, they got away."

"And your family?"

"Some left, some became Christians, some survived, some didn't."

"The story of my people is similar," Ana said. "Some became Christians, moriscos. Some left Granada, ran to the Alpujarra."

Rubén brushed the strands of grass from his trousers and grinned. He'd finally gotten her to admit where she came from.

They decided to take the long way down the hill through the new gardens toward the bridge to the Alhambra rather than stealing across the old royal pathway as they had earlier. But then they heard police sirens. "Is this a regular affair here in Granada?" Ana asked Rubén. "I was hoping that we'd had enough tragedy this week."

Rubén thought it was probably a traffic incident. Or a pick-pocket in the park by the Catedral. "It's a big city. Nothing to worry about. No te preocupes. No hay nada."

They were passing over the wooden footbridge, and the sirens were growing louder. Closer when they got back onto the Calle Real. Visible as they turned into the hidden space between the Carlos Quinto and the gardens behind the Court of the Lions. Two squad cars, an ambulance, a van and a team in hazmat suits. Doña Graciela and Inspector Drummond were off to the side, watching.

Hours later, after gas masks were put away and air quality tests were done and medical people and the police and the coroner had left, Ana was on the patio of the Hotel Parador, a place that had once been a convent built on palace remains. She was sitting near the American investigator and Doña Graciela—it seemed right to think of her that way, as Doña Graciela.

The American had changed into tweeds and a cuff-linked shirt. A uniform for him, perhaps. He was having a serious conversation with Doña Graciela. The American was quiet until he thought of something he wanted to know, then he would ask a precise question. Doña Graciela would listen, lean toward him a bit as though she wanted him to repeat himself, and then, before he could speak again, she would purse her lips and answer. Both Doña Graciela and the American seemed completely unaware of Ana's presence. They were busy, and Ana could see they were beginning to admire one another.

Rubén had been sent off to pick up a copy of the preliminary air quality report from the crew in the hazmat suits. Doña Graciela and the Inspector had invited Ana to share a glass of wine, but neither had spoken to her since, and they certainly hadn't noticed that Ana was spending her time gazing across the Cuesta at the gardens of the Generalife—carved shrubs, tall pines and green, so much green.

Ana was trying to recreate the peace she had felt a few hours earlier as she dozed on that warm hill, but she couldn't do it. She kept thinking about the man who died. The way they described him, his age, his clothes. She thought she'd seen him. He'd been in the

Alhambra, but where? In the morning, near the lions? No. It must have been later when she was retracing her steps. Before she fell asleep in the Whisper Room.

Ana opened her photos and began to scroll through the pictures taken that day. He should stand out. He wasn't a tourist, wasn't using a camera, wasn't the man with the audio tour earphones. He was wearing khakis and boots. His hands would be rough, tanned, like a native Granadino.

She kept scrolling. No one like that was showing up in her photos. Except maybe in the one she didn't remember taking. Could he be the man in the robo shot, the one recorded when she wasn't paying attention? She couldn't see a face, just trousers and boots. Smooth, clay-colored walls. A corner. A garden through the window.

Where was this shot taken? It had to be in the Whisper Room where she'd curled up in the corner. The boots, the dust on the toes and clay on the heels—they were the feet and legs of a workman. The clay-stained pantlegs and boots were remarkably like the ones that jutted out from under the gray sheet on the gurney the emergency crew had carried out of the palace.

Ana touched the screen and a strip of pictures appeared, a telltale video mini-roll. She was always doing that, shooting a video when she wanted a still. But nothing was moving in Ana's shot. Each frame was just like the one before it, and the man's face never came into view. It wouldn't be of much use, anyway, even if it was the man who had died, except perhaps to pinpoint the time of death.

"Decidedly uncomfortable," she heard the American say. "I asked him if the water line was checked routinely, and he became quite edgy. It was his work, he said. Then he told us he had an appointment."

So, the dead man was going to meet someone. Ana thought Doña Graciela and the American were piecing the story together, hoping to make sense of the death before making the requisite visit to his family.

"I don't know who he was going to meet, or why," the American continued. "Or if that person was the one who dragged him deeper in. There was no trail beyond the body, so the police gave up on the notion that someone might have left Don Marco and run deeper into the tunnel to escape the fumes."

Ana tried to avoid turning toward the American as he talked, hoping he would continue.

"I want to get back inside," the American said. "I want to see everything more clearly through my digital microscope. Maybe someone left Don Marco and went back into the workshop area, sweeping away footprints on the way."

Just then, Rubén came through the Parador into the dining patio with a sheaf of papers. He looked Ana's way briefly, but when he started to smile, he bumped into a service tray and stopped abruptly. Quickly, he worked his way around the waiters and several tables full of diners until he reached Doña Graciela, Drummond, and Ana.

"It was chlorine," he told the older pair. "They think you were lucky. Que suerte. The stuff can react with fluid in your lungs, the mucous, and then, suddenly, ¡muerto! Es letal."

"Lethal," Graciela repeated to Drummond and coughed.

"Internal hydrochloric acid," Drummond added. "Most likely what killed him."

"Fortunately," Rubén said, "by the time you two arrived it had dissipated to a mild irritant. The health department said we can open for the evening view of the Alhambra because the gas is completely gone."

"We're not going to open until the Patronato makes a decision," Graciela said.

Drummond was scanning the reports. "So where did the chlorine come from?" he asked. "An accidental belch from the city water supply? Not at all. It was powdered chlorine normally used in water treatment. They found traces under the body." He passed a page of the report to Graciela, directing her attention to the document's explanation.

"We left so quickly," she said. "We had no time to look."

"Are you sure someone's not still in there?" Rubén asked Drummond.

"No sign of anyone," Drummond said. "The second person would not have lingered."

Ana joined the conversation for the first time. "Best not to spend time with a corpse." Her comment had a jarring effect. "I mean no disrespect," Ana said. "I tend to think in folktales. I was thinking about a prince who falls asleep with a group of people and doesn't realize they're all dead until morning."

"She knows the 'Rasā'il,'" Rubén explained. "The epistles of the architects."

"You mean the philosophers?" Graciela said. Then, addressing Ana, she asked, "You know their epistles?"

Doña Graciela's comments sounded like corrections to Ana. What Ana meant to say was that she knew a story about death and melancholy, about lingering in melancholy, or not lingering. But it was clear that she had already intruded. "I know many old stories," she explained. "Some are from the epistles. Stories are my work."

Drummond broke the tension by asking a waiter for tapas—a plate of ham and chicken croquettes, a liter of water, a dish of olives. "We were all in the Alhambra today," he said. "Why didn't any of us see who Don Marco was about to meet?"

Ana felt she'd already upset Doña Graciela by calling Don Marco a corpse, so she wanted to be careful about entering the conversation again. She tried backing into it by saying, "I have something that might help. Not a real photo. Just one of those phantom things that smartphones snap on their own. Legs and boots. But I think they're his—the man's. It's actually a movie."

Graciela held out her hand and Ana passed the phone. "The video only shows his trousers and boots. And it doesn't move. My phone took it on its own, I guess I left it turned on while I was resting."

Graciela knew the boots and the khaki trousers. "A movie?" she asked. "I'm trying to identify the spot."

"The Whisper Room," Rubén said. "I found her asleep in a corner."

Graciela held the phone up to her ear. "Will there be sound? Can I increase the volume?"

Ana touched the sliver of metal that ran along the side of the phone and a bar of white extended across the screen. "Keep pushing the top button."

Graciela held her finger in place until the bar signaled full volume, then she held the phone to her ear, waiting reverently for sound. Finally, Don Marco's voice slipped into her ear, and when the sound ended, she started it again, and then again. After listening a final time, she handed the device to Drummond. "Tell me what you hear," she insisted. "I don't want to put ideas in your head. Just listen, please, before I say anything at all."

Drummond took the phone. He could hear the gravel in Don Marco's voice. It was him all right. In Spanish, of course. "Pretty sure I hear the word 'muchacho.' Then a growl on the middle phrase like Don Marco is holding back, like restraint turns it into a snarl. It sounds like, 'No opción,' or maybe 'No tenía opción.' And then there's a phrase, 'Usted me dijo.' Don Marco is saying he had no choice."

Drummond passed the phone to Rubén, who listened several times, nodding at each repeat. He started to pass it back to Ana, but took it back from her, lifted it to his ear and rolled the sound one more time. His face showed no emotion.

"Remarkable," Rubén said, handing the phone to Ana. "You've captured the essence of the Whisper Room. Just like the sultans."

Ana took the phone. For her, understanding was easy. She got every word. "The muchacho?" Ana asked Rubén. "Is he talking about the muchacho from yesterday? Your friend, Ander?"

Rubén was looking at Ana but he said nothing. He turned and spoke directly to Doña Graciela. "I'd like to examine those pages we were reading this morning. Could I see them again?"

"The papers in my office?"

Rubén had already left the table and was halfway across the patio.

Graciela asked Drummond to catch up with Rubén and tell him to wait in the lobby. She was going to have the tapas wrapped up. They were all hungry, and she needed to sign the check.

Ana didn't know if she was expected to accompany the group or not. "You want me to come? With my photos?"

"If you don't mind, yes," Graciela said, touching Ana on the shoulder. "I'd like to hear the recording again. Now is not the time for us to separate."

CHAPTER TWENTY-ONE

Back in her office, Graciela double-locked the door behind her guests. She plugged in the tea kettle before slipping her feet out of her boots and back into the black pumps she'd been wearing before the ordeal. The phone on her desk was blinking. There was a message from the chairman of the Patronato. The Alhambra would not open for the evening.

Graciela called security and ordered the doors shut and barred. Police would be combing the hill. She silently walked with Rubén to the Picasso print on the back wall, took it down, and tapped her code into the safe's keypad. She pulled the heavy door open and removed the box where she had sequestered the documents of surrender. Rubén carried the box to the table.

"Abu 'Abdallah's documents," she said.

Ana, keeping a respectful distance, asked, "May I look?"

Graciela pointed to a stool. "Push it up to the table," she said.

Ana moved the stool sat down.

Graciela found Ana's reticence rather timid for a New Yorker. Her every move revealed an ingrained habit of reverence. But for what? For Graciela's position? For the identity of the Alhambra and the history it contained? Perhaps for the last Emir, whose final words about his castle were pressed into paper inside that box?

Graciela could hear the water boiling, so she went back to the kettle and poured some of it into the black Wedgewood pot she'd brought from London. With a gentle twist of her arm, she washed hot liquid up around the inside wall until the china felt warm on the outside. Then she emptied the pot and set it on a linen towel. She opened a canister of dark aromatic tea and measured out seven scoops into the pot. The kettle hissed and whistled until Graciela lifted it to the teapot and poured boiling water over the tea leaves. She placed the lid securely and tied the corners of the towel over the top so no heat or oxygen would escape while the tea was brewing.

Drummond had been watching her.

"A little coat for our pot until it makes perfect tea," she said. The strain she felt was obvious to everyone, but her glance at Drummond revealed relief that he was there.

"You had an inkling of this level of intrigue?" he asked.

Graciela suggested Drummond take one of the leather chairs by the windows. He settled in quietly, mulling over a list of questions that needed answers. Had the foreman been murdered or was he accidentally overcome by the chlorine powder? How did the powder get under his body? If he was carrying the powder, was he planning to murder someone else? Did the accidental recording in the Whisper Room tie him to the first killing? Did it prove Ander's death was no accident?

Graciela took the chair across from Drummond. "The person Don Marco is talking to—I have no idea who that would be," she said.

Drummond sensed that Graciela wanted to tread carefully and not involve their young acquaintances unless it was necessary, but he knew that the recording on Ana's phone could not be kept from the police.

"The fellow who knew about the secret way through the hill is dead," Drummond pointed out. "The foreman whose job it was to keep track of that fellow and check the waterways is also dead. And we are holding critical evidence that we must soon hand over to the police." He suggested Ana download a copy of her photos before the police arrived, keep them safe on Graciela's machine or email them to herself as a backup.

Ana heard Drummond's warning. It was disturbing that she'd recorded Don Marco's last conversation with someone who may well have caused his death. She moved to Graciela's computer and uploaded a copy of the video and her Alhambra images as well. She'd had a good morning measuring and meditating, and she had no intention of surrendering the only copies of photos she'd taken, scenes in the Alhambra that explained the beliefs of the brethren in architectural clarity. She sat now in the soft high-backed chair behind Graciela's desk, quietly considering the meditation she had paced off earlier in the day. Here, she felt part of her family at last, a daughter of her father and her father's fathers in a way that she had never imagined possible.

Drummond asked Graciela for permission to dial the number of their mutual friend, the magistrate. There was no longer any chance of keeping the lions out of the gaze of the police.

Rubén had taken some of the treasured papers to the copy machine. Once copies were made, he placed the originals back into the box. Graciela walked with him to the safe and watched as Rubén placed the box gently inside. She closed the heavy door, replaced the Picasso, and nodded to Drummond, who began to press numbers into the phone.

When a woman's voice answered, he put the call on speaker. In quickly paced Spanish, the receptionist acknowledged that Drummond had reached the office of Julio Villanueva, investigative magistrate of the Autonomous Community of Andalucía. "I'm so sorry, she said, "but the magistrate will not be back in the city until tomorrow. Do you want to leave a message?"

Graciela gestured to end the call. They would have to deal with the homicide officer, the one who'd gone back to headquarters before the four of them had moved to her office.

"I'll call the policía directly," Graciela said. "I imagine the Capitán will simply come, take Ana's phone, and go away. I hope. I've had quite enough for today." But she knew this was not the end of her day, she still had to make a stop at the home of Don Marco. The policía would have been there by now, no doubt, but Don Marco's wife would be expecting a visit from Graciela.

Rubén was back at the table, bent over a sheaf of yellow pages he'd been sorting the day before. His body leaned so close to the notes that it seemed to enclose the pages in a tent of privacy.

Graciela moved to the counter where she kept her tea pot and the china cups and saucers that gave her a sense of calm. There had been afternoons in the museum in London when she thought she might have collapsed under the immense sadness of her widowhood. In those moments, the scent of a cup of well-brewed tea, the touch of the smooth china, cool to her lip just before she sensed the heat of a sip of tea—that's what had pulled her back.

What comfort could she offer Don Marco's widow now? Graciela couldn't imagine that Don Marco would have told his wife about the scenario that led him to the underground and the chlorine, or to the place above the hill where Ander had died the day before. How could Graciela explain anything without implying something else? Don Marco's wife knew him as a man who did simple work, yes, but work that had meaning. His every humble day was dedicated to preserving the history of Spain.

Graciela's tea was ready. She poured the deep brown liquid over milk. One cup for her, another for Drummond. The young ones could take care of themselves.

Drummond thanked her and took a long drink. His throat was still rough from the noxious air earlier that afternoon. It was odd, the way this investigation was turning out. When surrounded by artifacts of unfathomable worth, there was always a chance for crime, even a chance that the client who commissioned him to investigate might be involved in some nefarious plan. But he hadn't expected murder, or double murder.

He went back to the chair near the windows, sat down and stretched his legs out. Who had Don Marco been speaking to in the video? Who had told Don Marco to do something about the muchacho? If Don Marco had killed the boy, it appeared to be on the orders of the person who was present in the Whisper Room as the video was recorded.

Unfortunately, there was no image of the person who was with Don Marco. Drummond looked at the young woman sitting at Graciela's desk and thought about the Capitán who would soon be on his way up the serpentine hill to Graciela's office. How discreet could he expect the officer to be? How many others would soon know that the young woman had recorded Don Marco's last conversation with the person who may be his murderer? And once the word had spread about a recording, how would he and Graciela—and Rubén, of course—keep Ana safe?

Rubén looked up from his yellow papers as though he had been reading Drummond's thoughts. "And when the news is known…" he said "…what happens then?"

Graciela answered his question. "As soon as the Capitán finishes talking with Ana, you'll drive with Ana to Córdoba." She handed Rubén an envelope containing seven hundred euros.

Rubén looked at the money and slipped the envelope into his pocket without discussing the contents.

"It will give you a chance to follow the all the threads you've been tracing," Graciela said.

"And there's more to discover," Rubén said. "The Catholic Kings must have known the lions were important to Boabdil."

"Where will you look?" Graciela asked.

"In Córdoba's castle—the old headquarters of the Inquisición. I believe the records are still there."

"Good thing you're taking Ana with you," Drummond said. "You've earned a few days away from all this trouble. She should see Córdoba. Take her out to the old city, Madinat al-Zahra. That's where you were headed when we first met, isn't it?"

"Will you come, Ana?" Rubén asked.

"Of course she will," Graciela answered.

Ana smiled. "The recording. You're all trying to be so very calm and nice, but I'm in trouble, aren't I? I have a feeling that you're planning this journey as an escape rather than a vacation."

Rubén folded his papers and stood. "I've never been convinced there is a difference."

CHAPTER TWENTY-TWO

Drummond was comfortable in the leather chair near the windows. He'd poured himself another cup of tea, placed it on the coffee table next to his chair, opened his notebook, and read through his notes. Two men were dead—one young, one old. One was found with legs askew on the hillside below the Alcazaba, the other was dragged through dusty clay and chlorine. Both deaths were made to look accidental.

At the same time, he had become involved in two protection schemes—yesterday's plan to safeguard a Cuban scholar who had found the first body, and today's effort to watch over an American student who had accidentally recorded a conversation that connected the murders.

The Alhambra's director—Drummond's client—had wanted the police kept at arm's length from the investigation to avoid adverse publicity. Now, Doctora Graciela Corzal was at the helm of a scheme to smuggle the Cuban and the American out of Granada. She knew Ana's recording had to be shared with the police, but she had no intention of informing them about Ana and Rubén's flight from the city.

Trickery like this filtering into the business of artifact authentication wasn't that unusual. Crime was crime, and the practice of forensics was a routine he'd practiced all his life. He wasn't surprised that he was carrying out forensic examinations of everything and everyone including his three companions.

Rubén and Ana were close by, sitting cross-legged on the floor of Graciela's office. Ana had removed a small square book with animals pictured on the cover from her bag. Rubén had stuffed a few of his papers into a gray, cloth-bound volume. Graciela was back at the round table where they had worked earlier in the day.

They had retreated to this space so no one could hear what Ana had accidentally recorded in the Whisper Room. They might have stayed in the ancient security of the Alhambra with its layers of protection, but it had not proven to be secure for the two who had died in the last twenty-four hours. So they had hurried across a dry moat to the stone-pillowed walls of the Carlos Quinto, the building with a square exterior and a circular center open to the sky. The edifice had no twists, no turns. No strategies for survival, except a circle of tremendous pillars around the patio, projecting the intimidating power of Carlos V and his empire. How vulnerable was their sanctuary?

Rubén's voice floated across the room carrying the cadence of poetry, and Drummond found it rather pleasant. Ana sat on the rug next to Rubén. Her stillness was either meditation or shock. It couldn't have been easy for her to ignore the danger she had wandered into. Graciela was rustling through papers as she wrote a letter, perhaps to Don Marco's wife. The Capitán would not come for Ana's recording until he'd completed his report on Don Marco's death.

Graciela folded the sheets of stationery and sealed them in an envelope. She rose and moved to her desk where she opened a file folder containing lists of names. She circled a few, then a few more, following a trail of names connected to the water flow. It was clear to her that the flow had been altered a while ago. Now she was looking for someone who could have directed a change, perhaps crisscrossing the lines so that the Lion Fountain was being supplied with chlorinated city water, but as Drummond had said, not enough chlorine to cause asphyxiation.

It was the powdered chlorine found under Don Marco's body that added a new set of questions to the mystery. Why the extra powdered chlorine? Was it needed to boost the cleaning power of the city water? Had Don Marco carried the chlorine that killed him? And if he hadn't, who had? Was it the same person who had changed the water flow? Would that name be obvious on her lists?

Drummond walked to the counter, rinsed his teacup and wandered over to Graciela.

"Were you expecting this sort of turmoil?" he asked again

"The fountain has often inspired turmoil," she said.

"This much? Did you ever expect homicide?"

"This was exactly the sort of dangerous drama I had hoped to avert by hiring you." She turned the list of names face down on her desk. "The arguments about the fountain originated long before Boabdil, and they have never subsided."

"Not exactly a direct answer."

"Yet it is precisely the truth," Graciela said. "Ask Rubén about the early days, about Samuel ha-Nagid, the Jewish scholar who was famous for his diplomacy and military acumen. Samuel also wrote poetry, and he knew how to manage water."

Drummond was well aware of the fountain's early days. He knew about Samuel ha-Nagid, the general who had been governor, the man who had built a city in Granada long before the Alhambra. "He was trusted," Drummond said.

"Trusted deeply by the Berber King Habbus and his son Badis. And Samuel ha-Nagid trusted them as well," Graciela said. "Eventually, ha-Nagid's son, Yusuf, took over. He constructed a grand home on the red hill, and it may have been Yusuf who brought the lions here."

"Those were the days of cooperation," Drummond said.

"Yes. It seems the Moors and the Jews often found it safer to trust each other than to depend on the goodwill of political rivals. But cooperation can be contentious. Yusuf was not a talented diplomat like his father. He usurped some extremely compelling land in Granada, and he diverted water from the Albaicín. In the end, he was assassinated."

When she said the word assassinated, it sailed through the office like a weapon and brought Ana to her feet. She moved quickly toward them until Drummond guided her to the small refrigerator under the counter. He took out several bottles of mineral water. Ana opened hers and took a long drink.

Rubén was right behind her.

"I wish we could go outside," she said.

Rubén took her hand in his. "Not right now."

"I'm fine," she said. She seemed to have calmed down. "Really. I'll go back to my animal fables. They're good for me."

Drummond asked Rubén to sit with him near the windows. He wanted to keep an eye on the plaza below, but he also wanted to hear about any compelling detail that might explain what was happening. "I believe I'm still missing something."

For Rubén, the compelling thing about Yusuf's fountain was its resemblance to the Fountain of Solomon. "Just like Soloman's, except oxen were replaced by lions," he said, his voice soft but unwavering. "In Córdoba, there was a great admiration for Soloman, by all the people, and there were a number of animal gardens."

Drummond was aware of Cordoba's artists and their penchant for carving stone beasts to move water. "I know about the black amber lions and the beasts with jewels for eyes," he said, "and the elephant on the hill above the old city, controlling the irrigation of the farmland."

Rubén nodded. "And poets who wrote about the fountains as if they were beakers of divine elixir," he added. "Ibn Gabirol for one. I was just showing Ana his work. You know him?"

"Of course," Drummond answered. "The philosopher. Avicebron, the Christians called him. I read him in Latin."

"He wrote his poems in Hebrew originally," Rubén said. "He

was a great poet, and he was Yusuf ha-Nagid's teacher. So he knew the grand house on the red hill."

In Rubén's view, history would place Ibn Gabirol's poetry about the lions in a time chronologically before the Moors took over the red hill. He insisted Gabirol's poems were poetic evidence, just as the bricks and blocks of the oldest buildings on the Alhambra site were forensic evidence.

"We could go tonight to the Alcazaba," Rubén said. "and take a look at those stones—old, dark, bulky. They're evidence that Yusuf's castle was here on the hill years before this red palace."

Rubén handed Drummond a book with Ibn Gabirol's poem about a magnificent garden with a fountain at its center. "It's in English," he said.

Drummond read the lines aloud:

And there is a full sea, like unto Solomon's Sea,
    though not on oxen it stands,
But there are lions, in phalanx by its rim,
    as though roaring for prey—these whelps
Whose bellies are wellsprings that spout forth
    through their mouths floods like streams.

When Drummond had finished his recitation, Rubén waved his copies of the surrender manuscripts and said, "The story of Solomon was sacred to us all. Did Boabdil view the lions as reminders of Solomon's Sea? Was that his intention? Is that why the surrender document demands that los Reyes Católicos take care of the lions? I think it is."

Drummond said nothing. He found it best not to enter a conversation that involved a demonstration of belief. Rubén was convinced of his theory, transfixed by it, and Drummond was happy to leave him in that place. It was a better space than the one Drummond had imagined earlier for his young colleague—

precipitously near two deaths that had occurred at the Alhambra in the last twenty-four hours.

Graciela had been looking over the list of employee names while listening to Rubén's theory. "I can agree that the Lions are older than the courtyard where they stood," she said, "but until there is proof, I must remain neutral about their provenance. In my position at the Alhambra, I must always be open to new evidence, but no matter what, I am the guardian of the lions. Rubén, make sure your important papers are somewhere safe before the Capitán arrives."

She walked the counter and put the tapas on plates. She added crackers and hard cheese. "As soon as Ana is done with the policía," she told the group, "Rubén will drive to Córdoba. Eat now. There will be no time later for a meal."

The Capitán arrived much later than he had predicted. He had come without his assistant, who was still tied up with paperwork. He glanced at Graciela and said, "I understand you have evidence to turn over. Do you have it here?"

Graciela gestured toward Ana and said, "This young lady, Ana, fell asleep in the Whisper Room, and while she was sleeping, her mobile phone accidentally recorded a conversation Don Marco had with a third party. That video recording is the evidence."

The Capitán took out a notepad and asked Ana for her passport and a summary of what had happened in her own words. He made notes as she spoke, and then asked her to play the video. On his instruction, Ana played the video three times.

"You are a tourist here?" the Capitán asked Ana.

She nodded.

"How do you know this group of people well enough to be enjoying a casual afternoon in the office of the director of the Alhambra?" he asked.

"We met last evening," Ana replied. "At the Hotel Guadalupe. That's where I was staying here in Granada. They planned to have tapas and invited me to join them, but then Don Marco's death intervened."

"So, you do not know each other well?"

"No," she admitted. "But we became friends."

"I'm afraid I will need to take your phone, but it will be returned to you as soon as possible. In the meantime, please do not leave the country, and stay in close contact with your new friends until you hear otherwise."

The Capitán put the phone into a plastic bag and dropped it into his satchel. He looked at Rubén and then at Graciela. "The video is minimal, but are you are able to identify the voice as Don Marco's?"

"Yes," Graciela said. "I also recognize the trousers he was wearing when Inspector Drummond and I found him."

"And you are continuing your vigilance in regard to the gentleman from Cuba?"

"He is under my direct supervision, yes," she said calmly.

"One more piece of advice, Inspector," the Capitán said, nodding toward Drummond. "Both you and the directora have had a close encounter with chlorine gas, which could suggest a homicide. It is in your best interests to remain silent about the contents of this video."

Drummond took the nod as one more acknowledgment that he and the Capitán were in this dangerous investigation together. "We understand your concern," he answered.

"Every one of you understands?" the Capitán asked the group.

"Indeed," Drummond answered. "And we trust Granada's police will be equally discreet."

CHAPTER TWENTY-THREE

D iscretion. Maintain it. Easy enough for Ana. She'd always lived that way, so it wasn't hard for her to carry out Doña Graciela's plan. Doctora Corzal would visit Don Marco's wife as expected and take the American Inspector with her. Graciela would use Drummond's rental car because Rubén and Ana were to take the Peugeot and head to Córdoba.

Since the Peugeot was in the lot across the street from the Guadalupe, Ana was able to go to her room to gather a few overnight things for the trip. In less than ten minutes, she was passing through the lobby when she heard Rubén's voice in the bar saying, "Extremely sad. We're going to dinner now, but I'm sure we'll see each other later."

Rubén was talking to the French professor and the woman Ana had met the day before. The professor was holding a glass of wine. The woman had a handkerchief in her hand and seemed to be dabbing her right eye until she saw Ana. It was then she began waving the handkerchief.

Ana had been counseled not to do anything that might attract attention. The woman had been inquisitive, and Ana wanted to avoid having to explain how she and Rubén had come to know one another, so rather than join them, she waved back and headed toward the car.

Rubén caught up with her in the parking lot. "The professor is distraught about Don Marco. He knew the man well."

By the time Rubén and Ana had left the red hill and driven across the city, the sun had almost disappeared and the Sierras were a line of unyielding shadows stacked along the horizon. An occasional outline of snow was drawing a hard white edge on the mountains against the dark blue sky, but Rubén and Ana were heading into warmth, toward the flat land where weather reports predicted temperatures of 104 and higher. Until today, Ana had been converting temperatures on her cell phone, but now that she didn't have her phone, she'd have to start thinking in centigrade, 40 degrees.

"The Peugeot is moving nicely around these curves," Rubén said, more to himself than to her. Humming, actually. The car had him charmed. "Me encanta este auto."

"No hay Peugeots in Cuba?"

"Son muy viejos," he said. "So old, only los cubanos know how to fix them."

"You drive Doña Graciela's car often?"

"Not until now."

"It seems very nimble," Ana said. Rubén was driving fast, and Ana wondered if it was because he enjoyed the car on the mountain road or because he thought they needed to get out of Granada in record time.

"Perhaps I am the quick one," Rubén said, smiling.

Ana gazed out the window, checking the mirror on her side of the car. Would there be someone following them? If so would Doña Graciela and the American know who it was? And why did she keep thinking of Inspector Drummond as the American? Weren't they all Americans, except for Doña Graciela?

"How much trouble do you think I'm in?" Ana asked.

"Let me see. Look this way for a moment..." Rubén was grinning widely. "No more than normal for a woman whose roots lie deep in Andalucía." His voice was playful, but Ana knew he wanted to draw her eyes off the mirror and her mind off the possibility of a chase.

"Have I revealed my roots?"

"Sí y no," he said.

"And the 'No'?"

"You haven't told me that your family comes from the Majriti line—the line of Maslama ibn Ahmad al-Majriti, the man from Madrid. We also call him El Cordobés—not the matador, of course."

"Of course," Ana said. "And you're right, I haven't told you this."

"'Majriti' because he was born in Madrid, 'Cordobés' because he lived and worked in the sturdy environment that was the Córdoba of our dreams."

"And the 'Sí'?"

"You come from a nest of mathematicians. You speak English and Spanish, but you think mathematics. You have the math gene."

"And how does this tie me to your man from Madrid?"

"He was perhaps the most brilliant mathematician of his time. Besides that, he was an expert at interpreting the stars, and he hung around with the esoteric group that used animal stories like the ones you and your family tell."

Her family did tell those stories, but she wasn't ready to let Rubén know he was right. "You think I'm kin to Aesop and the Brothers Grimm as well?"

"Not at all," Rubén said. "Obviously, my assumptions are based on circumstantial evidence. But you spent your day in the Alhambra working through its geometry. The man I speak of is pivotal in the development of geometry, triangulation theory…"

"Trigonometry?"

"Sí, sí, sí. You know the fellow. He has a name something like yours…"

"You're very entertaining, but you haven't pulled me away from my worries," Ana said, looking in the side mirror again.

"Well, do some gazing at the stars, like your most venerable grandfather would expect you to do."

Yes. That's what might make Ana comfortable. Relax into the dark sky and let the stars take her thoughts.

"You want to know why we're rushing to Córdoba?" Rubén asked. "Will that make you stop worrying so much?"

Ana didn't answer right away. She wasn't convinced that Rubén knew why they had run off in a borrowed car with a plan to drive half the night to Córdoba instead of taking the morning bus.

To fill the silence, Rubén said, "It's because of my grandfather, not yours."

"Hardly our grandfathers," Ana said.

"Grandfather back a few generations."

"And a few hundred years."

"More like a millennium for you," Rubén said, "if you're finally admitting to being the daughter of the Majriti."

"I'm admitting nothing."

"Even your very secretive nature reveals what you hide."

"And so we are off to Córdoba, not because someone might notice that I recorded Don Marco's last conversation, but because of the pages you copied and slipped into your shirt pocket? Probably Boabdil's letter of surrender."

Rubén nodded. They had started at the higher, cooler level of Granada, descended with speed and ascended again on circular switchbacks, round and round the hilltop toward an old castle at the top. Floodlights kept the medieval structure in clear view for all the navigators of the night. Ana had seen it from the bottom of the mound when they were driving through the fields of olive trees. The castle, Ana knew, was built by the Moors on top of an old Roman fort in the thirteenth century.

"Fernando took this castle from the Moors," Rubén explained. "Fernando the first—father to the son who also took a castle from the Moors."

"Castles in Spain," Ana said. "Do you dream of castles in Spain?"

"My dream is that inside one very specific castle, in the very specific city of Córdoba, which—yes—does happen to be in Spain, I will find the records of a very Spanish institution. And in those records I will find some interrogatories that leave me little doubt about what the Catholic Kings thought was so important about the Fountain of the Lions that they did not want it mentioned in the articles of the surrender of the Alhambra."

"You know this about Isabela and Fernando?"

"I know that they—or someone close enough to one of them to control their documents—did not want it made public that Boabdil had prevented anyone from moving the lions from the courtyard."

"The records are in Córdoba?"

"Yes. They are still there—in what used to be the headquarters of the Inquisición."

In the darkness, the landscape appeared repetitive. Dark, bumpy hills. Field after field of olive trees. Another old castle. Windmills. More dark bumpy hills. Sheep sleeping on the grassy slopes.

"You're falling asleep," Rubén said. "That's not allowed. You must keep me awake by telling me more of those stories about the animals."

"Did I tell you how much you and your friends reminded me of the crow and the rat and the tortoise escaping from the hunter?"

"You mean when we we left the Alhambra after Ander's death?"

"At that moment, I was sure the police officer was the hunter chasing you and your companions."

"Sí, sí, sí… And what do you imagine now?" Rubén leaned lightly on the steering wheel, his head turned toward Ana just enough to let her know he wanted her to fill in the blanks.

"You're really interested? You actually see value in the stories beyond their being a wake-up potion?"

"Sin duda. I really do. Who do you think we are now?"

"You—you're still the crow. Doña Graciela and the American—both of them are chewing on the nets that had ensnared us all day. But Doña Graciela might fit another character too. She's getting us to Cordoba like the tortoise ferried a monkey across the pond in another fable."

"Seems you think we're all in some jeopardy," Rubén said before swerving to avoid a small animal.

"Just like that creature on the road," Ana said. "The little thing sped up and made it across the road before we could do him any damage."

"I was hardly a hunter. He ran in front of me. I swerved."

"I feel great kinship with that little beast," Ana said.

"Probably a rat of some kind, in any case."

"It was rat who saved the ring-doves. The whole story begins with the ring-doves, but soon the ring-doves fly away and it becomes the story of the tortoise, the crow, and the rat who chews through the net the hunter uses to trap the gazelle. Now he's gone, I think. There is no one behind us."

"No one?" Rubén asked.

"A long way back, there was another car. But it's been gone for a while."

"Thanks for letting me know," Rubén said. "So, after talking to the Capitán yourself, do you still think he is the hunter?"

Ana no longer thought he was. The Capitán had no agenda other than to solve two local deaths. For him, the fact that the deaths happened on the grounds of the Alhambra had nothing to do with it. "The Capitán doesn't appear to be into history," Ana said. "He's very much a present tense sort of soul."

"So, what else happens in the story?"

"Like I was saying, at the beginning of the story, a flight of ring-doves is snared in a net and a crow is watching. The crow sees the birds get gnawed free of the net by a rat, and the crow is so impressed by the rat's generosity that he makes him a friend for life. Then a tortoise and a gazelle join the group, and the gazelle—who is enjoying new-found friends—steps into another trap and calls out for help. That's when the good rat and the others free the gazelle. So, all the animals are in a parade of sorts now, a very fast parade, running down the path toward the safety of the forest. Except, of course, for the birds, who are flying above the pack of friends. They're going swiftly and are almost free."

"And?"

"And that's when they notice the tortoise is missing."

"Captured?'

"Not right away, but shortly after the others are out of sight. The tortoise couldn't move fast enough. Swiftly and silently came the hunter's net once again."

"Pobre tortuga. Es el fin? Is she gone?"

"What do you think?"

"I don't know."

"You should know. Fables have rules," Ana said. "Stories are set in motion. What comes after the capture?"

"The rat chews another hole in the net?"

"Yes! Of course. But first, the hunter has to be lured away from his prize so that the others can come and break la tortuga out of the mesh. It's the gazelle who does it now. The fast one."

"Shelomo Ibn Tzaqbel."

"What are you saying?"

"The gazelle, I know that gazelle. She runs through medieval Hebrew poems."

"In my story, the gazelle attracts the hunter's attention and the hunter goes off after her. But she's so fast, the hunter has to run for miles trying to catch her."

"That's Ibn Tzaqbel. '… race to hunt gazelles across the herb-filled hills…' Same hunter, same gazelle!"

"Maybe." Ana liked the idea of a universal gazelle, but she wanted to finish her story. She was almost to the end.

"Remember, the hunter is chasing the gazelle, and while the hunter is distracted, the rat and the crow and the birds all pull apart the net so that the tortuga can slip away. The end."

"That's it? The end?"

"More or less. The rest of the story is about the importance of helping your friends."

"But is it your end? You still haven't told me who you think the hunter is, since you no longer believe it's the Capitán."

"Honestly, I have no idea. Who would want to kill your friend? And Don Marco? If they weren't strange accidents, who would kill them?

"Don Marco may not be as innocent as that little rat that crossed our path back there."

"I think there must be a jackal. Somewhere, there is a dishonorable jackal in this story. A jackal out for himself."

They were driving north now, skirting the town of Lucena. "El-iossana," Rubén called out when they passed the road sign. "Eliossana, God may save us."

"You mean Al-Yussana?" Ana countered.

"Don't let the Lucentinos hear," Rubén said.

"The Lucentinos are fully aware of their history, I'm sure, because this is a history that I know too," Ana said. "Our friend Boabdil was captured here when he tried to take the town back from the Christians."

"It was a Jewish town, with a rabbi elected by the whole village—a rabbi who was the judge in criminal and civil court. Many famous scholars lived here."

Ana thought they should pause to breathe the air that the old ones had once inhaled. This might bring the story back to life, as her teacher had done by following in the steps of a hero.

It was almost two in the morning by the time Rubén squeezed the Peugeot through the narrow streets of the Jewish quarter of Córdoba and back onto a paved avenue that edged along the Guadalquivir. Just before they reached the old Roman bridge, they turned onto a cobblestone street and passed the edge of the Mezquita-Catedral.

A woman was standing in front of the wrought iron fence that rimmed the Mezquita. She was posing in front of the arched door for a photograph. Her shirt blended with shards of rust color that radiated from the arch above her head. The man with the camera was on the other side of the street, framing her with as much of the building as he could. In the photo, his distance would turn the woman into a miniature figure deposited there to show the grandeur of the old Mosque.

The city had only recently grown quiet. A few late diners still wandered along the pavement next to the Mezquita that glowed in the combination of moonlight and floodlight. Pointed turrets rose above great squares of stone, deep gold against a blue-black sky.

Back in Lucena, Rubén had launched a competition to name the poets and philosophers from the region, especially those who had been there before the Christians. The game was not yet over.

As Ana stepped out of the car in front of the Maimonides Hotel, Rubén pointed toward the bridge and said, "This was the Romans' Spanish capital. Seneca lived here."

Tall glass doors opened at the front of the hotel and Ana walked into the Maimonides. It was a small, elegantly designed place. Marble floors, stone arches and pillars mimicking those in the Mezquita across the street. There was a dining room with white tablecloths that could offer a quiet meal. Would they linger there in the morning over coffee before heading out to find Rubén's evidence? Ana doubted it.

Rubén was impassioned. He'd been driving through the night—more than three hours, and at top speed. He should have been tired, but arriving in Córdoba had sparked new energy in him. At the front desk, he showed the night clerk a letter written by Doctora Graciela Corzal, director of the Alhambra, identifying him—and Ana Madrizon—as representatives of the administration of the Alhambra and asking the hotel to extend the Alhambra's long-established credit to the two travelers.

The night clerk quietly read the letter out loud. "Señorita Ana Madrizon and Doctor Rubén Torres are visiting Córdoba at the request of the Alhambra, conducting official business for the Alhambra." The clerk looked up and nodded at Ana and then at Rubén before he went back to reading the note. "I have reserved two rooms for them. Please locate them on the same floor as close to one another as possible."

The specificity of Doña Graciela's request caused Ana to flush. She hardly thought the last request was necessary. Spain was such a proper place, what would this man think?

"Indeed, Doctor Torres, I have secured rooms 309 and 311. They each have a balcony, so you will be able to enjoy la procesión from the quiet and privacy of your chambers."

"La procesión?" Ana asked in Spanish. "Cuándo?"

"Pasado mañana," the clerk said, and then repeated himself in English, "Day after tomorrow, Señorita. Corpus Christi."

What had she done, what rule of pronunciation had she transgressed that the clerk understood that English was her primary language?

Rubén said it was simple. She wasn't expecting the feast day, and she was wearing American shoes.

"American shoes?"

"Your accent is fine. It's as good as mine—but the pair of shoes you're wearing now are crying Yanqui just like your sandals did yesterday!

Ana was wearing a pair of Munros, comfortable but dressy enough for Spain. "They're not Nikes," she said, as they headed up the elevator to the third floor.

"They don't make Nikes in the States," Rubén said, obviously proud that he was still managing a line or two of friendly banter after a second sleepless night.

CHAPTER TWENTY-FOUR

The night air was giving Drummond a chill, and he wanted to stop at his hotel for a sweater. Graciela considered going inside with him, but she decided it was best for her to stay in the Citroen. Leaving an unattended car was prohibited on the Alhambra grounds, even in front of the hotel. Perhaps it would have been wise to book him into the charming old hotel to start with, steps from the palaces, but he'd been intent on spending at least one night downtown in the Reina Cristina. He said it made him remember Lorca's poetry, not that there had been time for anyone to contemplate Lorca.

Graciela knew Drummond was trying to be polite by offering her a ride home and appearing eager to see the neighborhood on the hill where Don Marco and his family lived. But Graciela knew his chivalry was anchored in concern about Don Marco's chat in the Whisper Room with someone who seemed to have ordered the artesano's death.

After their quick stop for a sweater, Drummond maneuvered his Citroen along the serpentine streets of the Albaicín where the Moors had lived before the Alhambra was built. He was doing a competent job vying for road space with taxis carrying tourists to the flamenco shows in the caves. "Gypsies still live in those caves?" he asked.

"The caves are like stage sets now," Graciela said. "The dancers live in the city. They ride up to the top for shows, go back down afterward."

"Should we take in a show?"

Graciela told him she'd locate a performance that Drummond would find less touristic. "Those newsprint photos hanging in the caves were shot decades ago."

Suddenly, the efficient but not-so-smooth Citroen jostled her up against the door as it squealed its way around a turn. This was not the kind of ride she was accustomed to. Her Peugeot had a way of gliding up hills. "Here!" she said. "We are here."

Don Marco's house was one of the few old homes that hadn't been extended, expanded, and gentrified. In fact, it looked shrunken, maybe cut in half. Drummond lodged the Citroen in a tight space between a garden wall and the street. "Should I wait?" he asked.

Graciela wanted Drummond to come inside. This was a courtesy call, not an investigatory interview, despite what they'd learned from Ana's recording. The courtesy call would not take long, and Drummond might notice some aberrant detail. His ear might catch a tone. "Of course, we will respect her sorrow," she said and rang the bell.

Señora Elena Goya de Gutierrez seemed smaller and thinner than Graciela had remembered. She did not appear to have been crying, although her dark blue skirt was wrinkled at the hemline as if it had been twisted repeatedly. When she and Graciela performed the expected embrace and the señora's hand rested on Graciela's shoulder, the widow's touch was strong, but her palm felt damp, perhaps from anxiety. Had she been ill?

Graciela and Drummond were led through the small but tidy living room, past the photograph that Graciela knew had been a source of pride for Don Marco and his wife, up a circular staircase, and onto the roof terrace. The señora gestured to a table where she had set a pitcher of iced apple tea and a set of amber tumblers.

"I knew you would be here, Doctora," she said. "They told me that it was you who found him."

For Graciela, it was still not easy to move away from the memory of the dark bundle she had seen on the ground below the Court of the Lions. She introduced Drummond and mentioned that he too had found Don Marco.

"I heard that you attempted to get him away from the gas… back to the fresh air," Doña Elena said.

"We deeply regret that we were not able to help your husband," Drummond said. "I am sorry for your loss."

Drummond was being courteous, but his statement reminded Graciela of the odd way Americans had of apologizing to the bereaved for a perceived emptiness caused by death, as though absence were all one faced after the loss of a loved one. It completely ignored the hideous passions that traveled with death—anger, hatred, despair, all mingled to form a monstrous presence rather than an absence. Spaniards were more accustomed to anguish, more willing to acknowledge pain as palpable agony—an uninvited, terrible guest filling the empty chair.

Doña Elena was twisting the hem of her skirt again. "So much grief in our community," she said. "First, we lose Ander. Now this."

Graciela leaned forward, surprised. "Qué pena," she said. "I was not aware that Ander's people were here in Granada." It wasn't like her to have missed a fact like that. She should have contacted the boy's family too. But she'd been concentrating on the lions and had neglected to ask the most fundamental question. And who would she have asked? Ander's supervisor, Don Marco?

"His family is in the north, but he lived here." The widow extended her hand toward the horizon.

Graciela knew she'd broken a rule of propriety, and the small transgression had amplified anxieties that had been growing for her all day. She was pleased when Drummond entered the conversation.

"Where has Ander been living?" he asked.

"Just here. Across the street. He was renting a room that is sometimes available to the apprentices."

"You knew the boy before he moved south to Granada?"

"No, but he came with good references from respected artesanos." The señora explained that Marco had taken a great interest in Ander, especially recently. He'd spent his free time with the young man, making sure Ander understood how important his work had become. "Marco was not just the boss. He was the teacher, you see, and last night he was deeply upset over the boy's death."

Graciela nodded and glanced briefly at Drummond, who asked, "Did your husband have any idea about the circumstances of the boy's death?"

"A horrible accident," Doña Elena replied. "The boy had been working on his own, just as Marco had warned him not to do—away from Marco and the others who knew the dangers of the Alcazaba. He was alone when he fell from the wall." She turned to Graciela. "The young scholar who works with you. He found Ander, didn't he?"

Graciela nodded. "He is also deeply upset by Ander's death, just as we all are saddened by the loss of your husband."

The widow's voice was high and cracking. "What is happening, Doctora?"

The monstrous grief that Graciela knew had been hovering throughout the afternoon was with them now.

"In these last days, Marco has been so tired. Did no one notice? He's been coughing through the night," the widow said. "Is it no longer safe for anyone in the Alhambra?"

Graciela had been asking herself the same question, but she wasn't about to reveal that she'd been concerned enough to send Rubén and Ana off to Córdoba.

The scent of strong, sweet tobacco drifted onto the terrace and a tall muscular man in the clothes of a laborer appeared in the doorway. He stubbed out a cigarette on the floor before taking a seat at the table. "Is there no one in charge of the safety of your employees, Doctora?" he asked.

Graciela had never met this man, and she wasn't happy to be meeting him at that moment.

The man continued his complaint. "My brother-in-law told me he was working too many hours. He felt like he was only breathing through one lung. Isn't the Patronato responsible for this?"

His question was moving dangerously close to a legal boundary Graciela was not prepared to confront. This was a condolence visit, not a grievance session.

"This is my brother, Tomás," the señora said. "He has come from Cádiz."

"I have been talking to the policía," Tomás said. "They will not confirm this was an accident."

Graciela took a deep breath. She had no intention of becoming entangled in an argument with a stranger who was assuming authority in Don Marco's home. Layers of irony were settling between them as they sat side by side at the tea table, and she did not want to be portrayed as the woman who had lost control of the Court of Lions.

Don Marco had been a trusted employee, an artesano she'd known and respected, a victim whose apparent admission of involvement in Ander's death had been accidentally recorded by a young American. Don Marco had not been accused of murdering the boy he'd been advising and supporting, but Graciela couldn't find a way to absolve him. What she needed to uncover was who had started this scheme, who had Don Marco been whispering to, and what did they have to gain from Ander's death.

But who could she ask? Certainly not la Señora Elena Goya de Gutierrez. Don Marco's widow had no idea her husband could have played a role in the death of his apprentice, or that his own death might have come at the hands of someone who had lured him into a scheme to reroute the water supply to the lions. At least, Graciela didn't think the señora knew any of that.

There was no use continuing this conversation. There were no more than a few formal words for Graciela to say in the home of a victim who might also be a murderer.

"We will speak again soon, Señora, and of course, the Patronato will be in touch as well." She placed her hand over the strong but wrinkled hand of Don Marco's widow, nodded, and stood, signaling to Drummond that it was time to leave.

CHAPTER TWENTY-FIVE

Ana stood at the hotel breakfast buffet, glancing from the juice tray to the hot table where a tourist was waiting for a tortilla Española. She strolled along the bar for a close look before selecting a spare repast including strawberry yogurt, a bowl of blueberries, two spoons—the first for yogurt, the second in case she decided to stir her coffee—and a latte in a tall double-surfaced drinking glass. The layer of air between the inner lining and the exterior shell of the glass made it easy to grip, even when full of coffee and scalded milk.

She carried her tray to the table and sat down. Rubén was standing in front of a blue china bowl filled with a mound of boiled eggs, using his body as a screen to keep the other guests from noticing him take a half dozen. Thin slices of pale yellow cheese attracted him too, and the hard-crusted breads and baskets of oranges and apples. He gripped several slices of cheese with the silver tongs and held them over his bag momentarily before putting them on his plate. He took two more servings of cheese and three small loaves of bread, the cheese going on the plate, two of the three bread loaves falling into his bag. Typical student behavior, Ana thought. Rubén may have finished his Ph.D., but his status as an underpaid research assistant working far from home on a post doc kept him attentive to provisions.

Rubén sat down next to Ana and suggested she consider stocking up on a few extras in case the day's activities made it impossible for them to stop for lunch.

"You seem to have plenty in your bag already," Ana said. "You can take the man out of the university, but you can't take the university out of the man."

Rubén shrugged. "Cubans are ready for everything. We never know."

Ana left again and came back with two small glasses of juice and placed one in front of Rubén. "Grapefruit," she said and sat down.

"Today you are going to need more than berries and yogurt," he told her. "You need to take a few things so we can work through the lunch hour."

"I expect the castle will close down in the middle of the day," she said, sipping her coffee. "They won't let us stay there over lunch."

"The Alcázar closes at two o'clock. We can find a quiet place in a park to enjoy a picnic while we consider the documents we hope to find this morning."

It was already thirty-nine degrees, almost a hundred for Ana who thought in Fahrenheit, and she was not anxious to spend the hottest part of the day in the open air. "Forty-one this afternoon," she said. "Your documents might survive, but I won't." Ana pointed to his bag. "What have you packed for us besides bread and cheese?"

"Doña Graciela's letters," Rubén answered. He had always called the director of the Alhambra "Doctora" or "Profesora," but Ana had slipped "Doña," into their conversations, a term of respect she must have absorbed from her mother or grandmother. Now, Rubén found himself using the word. "One letter for the hotel, another for the museum in the Alcázar. A third in case we come into conflict with local authorities."

"We expect to be arrested?"

"Not at all. The letter is purely precautionary. Inspector Drummond's idea, I suspect."

"And what else?"

"Copies of the articles of surrender, a notebook, several pens, my camera, four hard-boiled eggs, two oranges, and—as you saw—two small loaves of very delicious bread. I will wrap the cheese and add it when we've finished breakfast."

Ana was hoping the day would offer time for her to do what Doña Graciela had suggested—stroll along the streets where red flowers hung on white-washed walls, walk across the Roman bridge, see the water wheels, visit la Mezquita, and tour the ruins of the old city.

"La Mezquita is right across the street," Rubén said. "We'll go there on our way to the Alcázar de Los Reyes."

The Castle of the Christian Kings had been the headquarters of the Inquisición. It was the spot where Rubén had said he believed he would find the secret documents.

"Ojalá," he said. "The kings used to live there in the Alcázar—Isabela y Fernando—while they were campaigning against the Moors... and the Jews, of course. We know that Columbus visited them in that building. Perhaps my grandfather was with him. The Alcázar was given to the Holy Office, and it was used as headquarters for the Inquisición until sometime in the 1830s."

That was a long time ago. Ana wondered if the documents had been moved.

"I believe they're here, in Cordoba," Rubén said. "In a room that's climate-controlled—all the documents of the era."

"Doña Graciela has seen what you're looking for?'

"No."

"Still, you know what you're looking for?"

"Not exactly. But I have an idea. I'll know it when I see it."

A s the two stepped into the street where a worn brick wall of the Cathedral Mosque loomed in front of them, Ana said, "La Mezquita first." It was a statement rather than a question. Ana was determined to gain entrance to the Mezquita before Rubén entangled her in his document search at the castle.

She walked quickly along the north side of the edifice to the open gate next to the bell tower-minaret. Rubén followed, as she had hoped.

"The Alcázar is nearby, a two-block walk, no more," Rubén said, reaching into his pocket for the six euros needed for entry to the Mezquita. "We must not be tempted to overstay. We can spend an hour here but no more."

Once inside the Mezquita, Ana understood Rubén's cautionary comment to her. Pillars confronted them, a forest of granite and jasper and marble topped by double arches of red and white stone. The arches flared at the top of the pillars as they rose like giant pines from the marble floor. The Moors had been great recyclers. They had made use of what the Romans and Visigoths had left behind and had improvised when they had run out of something. If the jasper pillars were too short, open arches were added, one arch on the shoulders of another, to invite the spirit into the heavens.

Ana listened as if there were secrets in the air. She was filled with reverence for the people who had built this place. There had once been over a thousand columns here. After the renovations, only eight hundred fifty-six reached for the sky like the trunks of petrified sycamores, but to Ana they still numbered a thousand. She thought of the great minds drawn to the city as if pulled by a magnet. People like Ibn Rushd. The world owed him so much.

"It was because of Ibn Rushd that Europe found science and philosophy," Ana said. "Ibn Rushd led Europe to Aristotle."

"You mean Averroes?"

"Same guy, different name."

"I know. But for some reason, the Europeans called him Averroes," Rubén said.

"Córdoba was a superpower back then," she whispered.

"With the help of Maimónides," Rubén whispered back, "Moses ben Maimón. Not since Moses has there been so Moses a Moses."

Ana said, "And tolerance abided," but she was wondering how free those years had been. "Was it really fashionable to think and talk about each other's ideas?"

"They still had secrets," Rubén said. "Think about the old ones—your grandfather and his friends, the free thinkers who brought their ideas to Spain."

Ana didn't think the people Rubén called "old ones" were actually her grandparents, even though she'd been raised on the mathematical theories of Pythagorean neo-platonists whose works had been translated into Spanish by someone whose name resonated with her own—the man from Madrid. But she didn't feel resonance the same way Rubén did. Rubén acted as though he had nightly séances, as though he and Columbus's interpreter shared a time and space they could enter at will from both the fifteenth and twenty-first centuries.

Why should Ana think Maslama Al-Majriti, the man from Madrid, or any other person associated with that secret group of friends was her grandfather? She'd never even seen a list of names of the intellectuals who had met in Basra and in Spain to talk about numbers, geometry, astronomy, politics, animal stories, and the music of the spheres. "Secrecy was their shield," Ana said. "They didn't agree with the people in power, so they met in secret and kept things under wraps."

"Your people lived in Spain centuries ago, and one of them was a man who translated a major book. Your animal tales show up in it. And your name is reminiscent of his. But you and your family, you're still one big secret."

That was true. Secrecy was part of her family's handling of stories. The animal tales were laced with secrecy, even when they were passed on to Ana to study as folklore. So, under it all, maybe she was a representative of a secret intellectual cadre.

"The list of Córdoba's enlightened citizens is quite long," Rubén said, "and we'll find your people. We'll get in touch with them while we're here,"

Secrecy was at the heart of her work. But yesterday afternoon in the Alhambra she had experienced something more. Today, again, while standing in the Mezquita contemplating the number of pillars, her father's words—words she hadn't heard in years—came back to her. "Do not confuse a number with a thing numbered." Had he been quoting the epistles of the sincere friends?

Something else had also captured her that morning as the sun streamed into the spaces above her head. The proportion of column to arch, of white stone to red stone. The harmony of granite and marble and jasper. The phrase "beauty arises from harmony and proportion" was running though her mind.

Rubén's voice intruded. He was standing beside her, talking to her, and she hadn't been listening. "But Córdoba was not perfect," she heard him say. "They burned books."

"A crime," Ana said, pretending to have heard everything she had missed.

"The Almoravids destroyed al-Ghazali's work. And, of course, there was the destruction of Madinat al-Zahra. Maimón and Rushd had to abandon Cordoba," Rubén said. "They moved south to Granada where tolerance and money were fading as well, but some could still be found."

"And for this reason, you believe the lions were brought from Córdoba to Granada? Perhaps to be used again in another garden?"

"Exactly. Very likely," Rubén said. "When the sultans gathered materials to build the last Moorish palace in Spain, the most abundant building component they had was their nostalgia for Córdoba."

"It was never as beautiful as we want to remember," Ana said. "My family came through Córdoba as well. My grandmother used to tell us stories from the days before the escape to the Alpujarra."

"Before Córdoba became home to the Inquisición," Rubén said. He folded the circular he'd picked up as they entered the Mezquita and put it carefully into his trouser pocket. "Time to move on, to the Alcázar of the Inquisición. The answer to my question will be there."

"And the question?" Ana asked. "Is it clear to you yet?"

"It is. What did the Catholic Kings expect to find in the fountain of the lions? What was the secret of the animals? What caused the deaths of Ander and Don Marco?"

"That's three questions," Ana said.

"Sí," Rubén answered. "Por lo menos, tres."

CHAPTER TWENTY-SIX

Shoes scuffed over cobblestones, languages rolled across languages, a guide's clear voice demanded eyes on the umbrella. Morning sounds cut deep into Drummond's sleep and woke him. It was eight o'clock. His plan was to go back to the chamber beneath the Court of the Lions with Graciela. He'd come to Granada to look at the lions as valuable artifacts, but she'd also asked him to work with her until police cleared up the deaths of Ander and Don Marco. So he was going to spend the morning piecing together yesterday's impressions.

It had been quite a while since he'd conducted investigations into the pitiless scraps of perversion that accompanied murder. He'd left that work when following a trail of deviance had become too attractive to him, when every smear of it had become too difficult to shower away. And now he was back at it again, gathering up the slivers of existence that remain when a life has been lost. Lingering bits of evidence. Signals left by the victim. Stains and specks shed by the perpetrator.

Treading through the details of these deaths seemed less honorable than searching for evidence of artistic swindle. Less clean than uncovering details of authenticity. But why? Why should pulling threads to unveil fraud be the more virtuous pursuit? It had become clear to him this morning that swindle was also a feature of homicide, that inauthentic details could always be found in the staging of a murder.

Somewhere in this case, he would find a person who was able to enter into private spaces, who had sufficient authority to control a man like Don Marco, who could convince him there was no choice but to dispose of his protégé Ander, and who could manage the use of deadly chlorine. Someone would be feigning innocence.

He would have to study the characters he'd met in the Alhambra's private spaces as if he were looking at them through his digital magnifier. He would need to focus until he could perceive the inauthentic fragments and then close in on the guilty party.

Drummond dressed quickly and made his way down the staircase and past the desk to the courtyard café at the center of the hotel. He found a small table under an arbor of grape vines and next to a fountain that had been built into the garden wall. He was quickly brought orange juice, a basket of bread, strawberry yogurt, a plate of cheese and thinly sliced ham. Then came two silver pots, one filled with coffee, the other with hot milk. As he drank his coffee, he jotted down a list of places that required privilege for access, people he'd met in the last hours, and events that had involved the places, the people, and both.

The first place he noted was the hill below the wall of the Alcazaba. The people were Ander and Rubén, the police, Graciela, Professor Lenhard and himself. The event was murder, although there was still a chance the first death was an accident.

Who could have pushed—or startled—Ander over the wall? Who had authority to be there? Graciela would be entitled to be anywhere on the grounds. Rubén most likely had permission of a sort, and he had called the police. Drummond was there as Graciela's consultant, and she had not been surprised to see Professor Lenhard—and, of course, the victim. What was it that Ander had wanted to show Rubén? His analysis of the first place had not yet provided clarity.

Other places: the Courtyard of the Lions at night. If he, Graciela and Rubén all had been given authority to be there, who was left?

Was Lenhard there again? Almost. Lenhard had just been outside. And the Capitán. Though Graciela was trying to keep her concern about the lions under wraps, authority over homicide could hardly be withheld from the police.

Another place—the public walk to the Guadalupe Hotel. Drummond had been there, of course, and Graciela, Rubén, Lenhard, the police, and the American girl he now knew as Ana Madrizon. Ana had been watching them, perhaps following them. Waiting. She was a tourist. What authority had she been given to be part of that scene? None. Except that the entire scene had taken place on public streets within a public accommodation and well within the reach of Ana Madrizon's curiosity. Perhaps it was this curiosity that reminded him of the young agents he had led years before. Their curiosity had been fueled by unfettered energy, just like Ana's. She had kept her curiosity secluded behind an attitude of deference, but the energy was there. Drummond could feel it.

The next place on Drummond's list was Graciela's office during the night when Rubén had found the articles of surrender. Anyone else? It depended on whether Rubén was telling the truth. But Drummond couldn't think of a reason for him to lie. Rubén was obviously favored by Graciela. She would have given him permission to be there working at her desk, just as she had done on many occasions. And Rubén hadn't noticed anyone else in the office overnight, had he? The keys—they were the problem. Where had Graciela placed them, or misplaced them? Had she left them on the desk as Rubén insisted? If Graciela hadn't left them there, and Rubén hadn't, who could have?

Drummond continued through the places and sounds of the day before—the Courtyard of the Lions, the chamber below, the tunnels, the hidden space where Don Marco lay, words recorded in the Whisper Room, the strange turn of scenes at the home of Don Marco's widow. Was the señora as ignorant of her husband's affairs as she seemed? Was the rough-hewn fellow playing the role of family bouncer actually the brother of Don Marco's widow? Was the suggestion that Graciela and the Patronato were at fault the result of authentic grief, or was it a ruse to bounce Graciela out of Don Marco's home?

And what about Graciela herself? Was she responsible? She had drawn Drummond into a search for authenticity, and he had remained at her side as death attached itself to the growing puzzle. Had she tricked him into staying on? No. He would not accept that, even though it was obvious that he was no longer impartial. He'd become attracted to the Alhambra, to its history, and to the very compelling woman who was its director. She could have died from the chlorine gas herself the day before. In his opinion, she could not be guilty.

The longer Drummond spent ruminating, the more clearly he believed that whoever had been responsible for the poisoning of Don Marco and near-poisoning of Graciela and himself had managed to convince Don Marco to take the chlorine in his own hands. Drummond recalled a pail against the wall—a red pail of cleaning supplies a few feet from where Don Marco's body was found. Was the pouch of noxious white powder sealed in such a way that Marco neither suspected nor detected danger until it was too late?

If Marco had been working with the powder on a daily basis— purifying water or cleaning waterways—he might have become overly familiar with the substance. Drummond had come across that kind of accident among people with swimming pools. They grew so accustomed to handling chlorine they overlooked its toxic nature.

Neither he nor Graciela had been affected until they were at Don Marco's side attempting to revive him. The timing made sense once the police found the bag of chlorine powder under Marco's body. And since there was no trace of footprints going back to the work area or forward into the hill, Drummond doubted anyone other than Don Marco had been there at the moment the toxic dose was released.

Drummond was growing tired of his own exercise. It hadn't offered him the illumination he'd hoped for. He signed the check for his breakfast and phoned Graciela to see if she was ready to go back to the site of Don Marco's death.

When Graciela answered Drummond's call, she was already on her way to meet Capitán Castañeda. Earlier that morning, she'd given the security guards permission to admit the Capitán and his forensics team, and now that he had been inside the Nazrid palace for a while, the Capitán had requested that she come to meet with him at her earliest convenience.

"That means now," she told Drummond when she met him in the plaza. They moved quickly through groups of tourists. The board of the Patronato had voted to cancel visiting hours for the weekend despite Graciela's suggestion they leave things open during the day to avoid sparking a public outcry.

The Capitán was waiting outside the Nazrid Palace when they arrived. Standing there at the edge of the plaza, they were the most interesting scene available to the crowd, and some of the tourists were taking photos of them.

The Capitán nodded to Drummond and said, "The Inspector has begun a career as a homicide detective? Or perhaps, more accurately, he has returned to his former career."

Graciela answered, "Inspector Drummond has agreed to help the Alhambra through this difficulty. I presume you are comfortable with his joining us?"

"It's a minor issue," the Capitán said. His forensics team was curious about a brass keyhole indented into the rough wooden seat of a bench near the point where Don Marco died. "Do you know anything about it? I have been told you are the holder of the key."

"I do have the key to the safe-keep," Graciela said. "Let's go inside. I'll find it in my bag."

As they moved through the great halls and across the Court of the Lions, Graciela pointed to benches tucked here and there against the walls. "Safe-keeps are everywhere," she explained. "Identical locks were installed in the early 1920s, a rare demonstration of concern for the time. When I became director, I called in all the keys. One universal key in my possession seemed sufficient."

They stopped at the small door just inside the arches of the Abencerrajes and Graciela unzipped her leather bag and pulled out her keys to sort through them. When the familiar brass key failed to appear, she searched for it again. It was smaller and thicker than her other keys, so it should not have been hard to find. She arranged the keys in the palm of her hand and counted them. Then she held them out to Capitán Castañeda.

"Do you see a small brass key on this chain? Take a look, would you please? My eyes are tired this morning."

The Capitán studied the keys. "There does not appear to be anything wrong with your eyes, Doctora. Are you sure it was on this set of keys?"

Graciela took the keys back and shook them. Had the small key been on the keychain yesterday when Graciela thought Rubén had taken them to open her cabinet? She never imagined someone coming after that particular key. There was nothing of value—nothing at all—in any of the safe-keeps. Who would have taken that key?

"Perhaps we could pry it open," Drummond said.

"Forensics considered that, but of course they could not imagine desecrating a national monument to gain entry. Are the keys routinely in your possession, Doctora?"

"Routinely," she said.

The Capitán pressed on. "Always?"

"Apparently not, but the majority of the time."

Graciela moved toward the doorway to the workspace where Don Marco had died, but the Capitán had positioned himself squarely in front of the entry.

"I would appreciate your telling me about the time your keys were not in your possession," he said.

Graciela was going to have to explain the loss of her entire set of keys the previous day. "There was an incident on Thursday evening, or Friday morning—after Ander died."

"Where?"

"At the Guadalupe Hotel—for just a moment."

"A moment? That's it? At the Guadalupe Hotel?"

"And my office."

"Two times?

"It could have been two times, or it could have been a single incident."

"Another incident in which your Cuban assistant was involved, Doctora?"

Graciela wondered where Rubén had been when Inspector Drummond retrieved her bag? She wasn't sure. But later, of course, he was in her office, and she thought he might have spent the night there. He said her keys were on her desk.

"Yes. Rubén was with us when we noticed that my keys were not where they should have been."

"Please summon him now if you would. Where is he?"

Graciela shook her head, and Drummond took it as a sign for him to end his silence and take some blame, admitting that Rubén had been sent to Córdoba.

"I must claim responsibility for a decision that will displease you, Capitán," Drummond said. "My concern that the young American student's life would be in danger…"

"You mean Ana Madrizon?" the Capitán asked.

"Yes," Drummond answered. "I was concerned her life might be in danger if someone found out she had recorded Don Marco's admission in the Whisper Room. I took a somewhat parental role and sent the young pair off to Córdoba. I convinced Doctora Corzal to lend them her Peugeot to make the trip. Today's discovery of the theft of the key lends credibility to my concern."

"There was no need for concern, Inspector. No one knew that the American girl heard the admission, or that she recorded it, or that all of you heard it when she played the recording for you. A good deal of time passed, I might say, before you contacted the policía."

"Has anyone inquired?" Drummond asked.

"About what would someone inquire? If nothing has been said, what inquiry is there to be made?"

"Perhaps a simple inquiry about the girl being in the Whisper Room? From someone at the hotel, perhaps—a friend who might have seen her there?"

"No, nothing."

Drummond was doing his best to be polite. "Capitán, were there by any chance any inquiries about the rest of us who heard the recording?"

"You are overly cautious, Inspector. I wonder why you haven't all run off to Córdoba. You and your professor friend who followed me around this morning asking about Doctora Corzal. If you'll pardon me, Doctora, that gentleman is oddly attentive."

Graciela took a light breath. Professor Lenhard had been doting on her for years. This was hardly the time to engage in a discussion about his scholarly romantic crush. There were so many other things to think about. It hadn't been her idea, but now she was pleased the Patronato had halted renovation and closed the Alhambra until this dreadful situation was resolved.

She'd been concerned that Rubén had fallen victim to tales of treasure hidden somewhere in the Alhambra by the last Emir, and now it was obvious that the quest for treasure had taken two lives— and the game was continuing. All the workers were at risk.

The Capitán was in the right. She and Drummond and Rubén—and even the unlikely young woman from New York—had misjudged their responsibilities. They'd been playing at detective work instead of letting the policía take charge. And look at what had happened.

"We have closed the Alhambra," Graciela said. "We will be attentive to your needs. You can count on our full cooperation."

The Capitán did not seem pleased that full cooperation was pledged at such a late date. He scolded Drummond for his outrageous impertinence, and Drummond agreed that his behavior had been anything but commendable. The scolding and the apologies continued until the forensics team completed its work. The Capitán agreed that Graciela could contact Rubén in Córdoba by phone and order him to return immediately.

"He is, after all, still a suspect, and there is a possibility he could do something far more drastic," the Capitán said. "I could easily notify the policía in Córdoba and have both the Cuban and the American girl detained. My enormous respect for Doctora Corzal and my sympathy for Inspector Drummond's exaggerated and misplaced concern for the girl are the only reasons I have not arrested all of you."

Drummond accompanied Graciela back to her office in the Carlos Quinto and stayed while she contacted the public relations office to set the official reason for the closing—tragic accidents. When that task was done, she spoke with several directors of the Patronato and scheduled a time on Monday for them to make a public statement. "By then, we will have cleared this up," Graciela responded to a voice on the other end of the line.

She started to call Rubén but hung up before the call went through. How foolish, she thought. How could she call him? The policía had both cell phones—Rubén's and Ana's. "We won't be able to reach them unless they are in their rooms at the Maimonides," she said.

It was Drummond's notepad that Graciela had used to pencil the hotel number the night before. Once again, Drummond handed it to Graciela. She called the desk clerk who told her both Doctor Rubén Torres and Señorita Ana Madrizon had been gone since early morning. Now, all Graciela could do was leave a message at the front desk.

CHAPTER TWENTY-SEVEN

The line of tourists snaked its way through myrtles, jasmine, and azaleas, past a woman sitting on a patch of grass behind a row of red geraniums. She had a baby at her breast and a basket at her feet. "Por favor," she repeated, "Por favor." Rubén dropped two coins in the basket.

"The economy," he said to Ana. "It is not an easy lifestyle, begging. I give what I can."

They were moving very slowly in the mid-day heat and Rubén asked Ana to hold his place in line as he went back to the woman and handed her two of the hard-boiled eggs he had sequestered from the buffet at the Maimonides. The woman tucked them into a large pocket then looked Rubén in the eye and said nothing.

Ana was moving her feet quietly, each step bringing her closer to the arched window in the stone wall where a bald man was taking money and handing out paper tickets. She smiled when Rubén returned.

"Still counting pillars?" he asked.

"Numbers are more than numbers," she said.

"Another piece of wisdom from the Rasā''il, from your ancestor's epistles?"

"Now you call him my ancestor, rather than my grandfather?"

"It's hot. If I continue to cause you irritation, you might grow impatient with me. But tell me more about numbers."

"Have you heard that God existed before the universal intellect, just as one existed before two?"

"Not in those exact words," Rubén answered. He had separated the euros Graciela had given him into small packets of bills and tucked them into his trouser and shirt pockets. He gave the remainder, still in the official business envelope of the Patronato, to Ana. Now he was close enough to the ticket window to pull out one packet and separate a ten-euro note. He showed it to Ana as he approached the man selling tickets.

"Dos, por favor," Rubén said. Two—coming after one like universal intelligence coming after God. He wondered if Ana would be in a metaphysical mood for the rest of the day.

The ticket seller looked at his watch, "Es el mediodia," he said, gruffly reminding Rubén that he would lock the gates at two-thirty. Everyone would have to be out of the Alcázar within two and a half hours.

"And the office of the municipal museum?" Rubén asked. "Which way?"

The man gave Rubén his tickets and a map printed on office paper. He pointed at the sketch of tile-roofs that began on the garden side of the Alcázar and ran from the tower toward the Guadalquivir River. "Por la Torre de la Inquisición. Preguntele al guia." Ask a guide.

Ana offered Rubén thanks for the ticket, although both knew that Doña Graciela was the one who would eventually need to be thanked.

"El gusto es mio," Rubén said.

The gardens were inviting, and it was possible they could have entered the round Torre de la Inquisición from an external door, but Rubén saw no doorway that would connect to the second-floor rooms on the sketch. He decided to go up the stone staircase to the second floor and follow the path along the top of the wall that ran toward the point where a modern stone structure had been wedged into the back side of the old tower. It reminded

Rubén of additions jammed onto the side of brick houses in Havana to make room for more tenants.

In the corner where the outgrowth of rooms was connected to the tower, a doorway opened onto a narrow interior hallway that ran under a series of white arches. At the end of the hall was a sign with the words "Municipalidad de Córdoba." A woman sat just inside the door, her hair pulled back from her face into a tight bun. She looked up from a ring binder, nodded at Rubén, smiled politely at Ana, and asked if she could help.

Rubén offered her the letter that Graciela had addressed to the Directors of the Municipal Library of Córdoban Documents. "We are scholars who work with the Patronato of the Alhambra," he told the woman. "We have been told that some documents important to our research are here in the library section of the Alcázar museum. We'd be most grateful if you would allow us a few moments to read those documents."

The woman arose from her desk and walked to one of a series of doors that Rubén could see from the small, square reception area. Rubén scratched his temple and pursed his lips. He'd experienced this before. The quick departure by a minor employee only to be followed by the entry of a bureaucrat of slightly higher status. This routine was usually the beginning of a great deal of organizational ladder-climbing and a series of negative responses that rarely ended in a helpful decision. It was happening again, but this time it was worse. They were moving laterally, working their way across a chain of access that advanced around the reception area but never moved them to a higher level of authority.

They were finally invited through one of the doors into the office of Doctor Rafael Montoya, a tall, thin man wearing dark trousers and a pale yellow shirt. His suit jacket was arranged on the back of his desk chair. He was older than Rubén, but younger than Doctora Corzal. There were a series of photographs of the Alhambra on the wall.

Montoya invited Rubén and Ana to take a seat in front of his desk. "I understand you are hoping to see material from the Reconquista, am I correct?"

"Señor Montoya," Rubén began, but he was interrupted at once.

"Doctor Montoya."

"Doctor Montoya." Rubén bowed his head slightly to convey humility over his mistake. "We are hoping you will let us peruse articles of royal correspondence from that period."

"I am afraid I do not have the authority to grant you access."

Rubén removed Graciela's letter from its envelope. "Doctora Graciela Corzal de Moreno, as you see from this letter, has suggested that the library of Córdoba holds the documents that are so essential to our study."

"And what, exactly, are you studying?"

Rubén did not expect that question. He was amazed at his lack of preparation. He had no answer.

Ana touched his arm. Was she signaling that she was ready to take over? He wasn't convinced she was prepared either, but she'd already begun speaking before he could stop her.

"The convergence of folktale and historical record," she explained. "It is a project that has tremendous import across the disciplines of folklore, archeology and literary forensics. Our work has caught the interest of scholars here in Spain, as you see from the interest of Doctora Graciela Corzal de Moreno, and from North and South America. I am from New York University. Rubén comes on a postdoctoral grant that supports the work he's done in Havana and Buenos Aires. So much depends on your being able to help us."

Montoya was staring at Ana. Rubén couldn't tell if he was impressed or if he wasn't sure what Ana had just explained. Then Montoya pushed his chair back and stood up. "I'm sorry to disappoint you," he said.

The man seemed so sincere that Rubén was curiously ready to believe him until Montoya continued on a path that led to yet another denial of access.

"Most likely we do not have what you need," Montoya said. "I doubt the material in the Alcázar's library would be of help. You are doing imaginative work, and our files contain only the most tedious and mundane. The royal quotidian. Trivial discussions of such things as the Queen's dislike for the sounds emanating from the water wheels and her instructions that they be dismantled."

"La Reina Isabela was interested in the flow of water?" Rubén asked.

"Other than the water wheels, I couldn't say. I don't believe that has been studied."

The logical follow-up question on Rubén's part would be to engage Montoya in a conversation of the Royal Monarchs' disassembly of the fountain in the Court of the Lions soon after they moved into the Alhambra, but he didn't want to lead the interview toward the lions or the murders.

He waited for Montoya to speak, which did not happen. Montoya remained quiet. Was it purposeful? Was Montoya hoping they'd jump into the silence and reveal the exact object of their quest?

Rubén and Ana said nothing. Montoya sat down again, leaned across his desk, and finally spoke, "Even if we did have the material you were seeking, permission would have to be secured from the Holy Office, which retains ownership of all documents created during the time of the Catholic Monarchs. We are only the shepherds of these works here at the municipality—not the owners. And I am one of the least of the shepherds."

Montoya stood again and moved from behind his desk, a signal Rubén took to mean that the conversation was over. But Montoya wasn't leading them to the door. He was walking to the photographs on his wall. When he reached them, he paused and looked at Rubén and Ana. "I understand, of course, the importance of your quest. When Andalucía catches your imagination, as it caught mine when I took these photographs at the Alhambra, it is next to impossible to extricate yourself. Nonetheless, I am afraid the municipality is not the proper venue for your request. You must carry my apology to Doctora Corzal. She is deeply respected here in Córdoba."

So, Montoya was acquainted with Doctora Corzal. Rubén wanted to know more. Was Montoya merely aware of her work? How long had they known each other? Did the photographs signify that Graciela had given him some privileged status, or had they perhaps collaborated on a project?

"I have long admired her scholarship and her dedication to the preservation of the treasures of Spain," Montoya said.

Rubén sensed an opening. They had been dismissed by several other minor bureaucrats, and Montoya had let them know that he had no greater stature than the officials who had already turned them away. Yet they were still in his office, and Montoya was still talking to them. The respect that Montoya said he had for Doctora Corzal might be just enough for Rubén to wedge his foot in the door.

"Perhaps you could tell us where we could find the proper venue," Rubén said.

"In Rome," Montoya answered. "The Vatican."

"And what exactly would we need to send to Rome?" Ana asked.

"A list of the individual pieces you want to see. A specific list."

"Document by document?"

"Author and recipient if it is a letter. The date of each as well if it is a decree. And, of course, a brief assessment of topic for each document—key words. You are, no doubt, acquainted with the importance of key words to the librarians who will have to do the preliminary searching to make the documents available to you. You'll need to be precise. Hopefully, you will supply the same key words as those used by the Vatican."

"Doctora Corzal would be deeply appreciative if you could help us with that very issue," Rubén said. "If you could, perhaps, you might give us the opportunity to peruse the catalogue I'm sure you maintain for the materials. That is, if you could allow us to take a few moments in the library. It is here, correct? In these offices? Just down the hall? If we could jot down the sorts of specifics that would be of use to Rome?"

And that was it. For the first time, and with ninety minutes left until closing, Rubén heard a sweet sound emerging from Montoya's lips. "Sí." He could let them see the digital catalogue—what there was of it. This was a new endeavor—something Montoya had started rather recently. One of his projects as director of digitization. Montoya could not let them see the actual files, but the project that he was proud to have begun was only a few doors away. He would let them have a look at the digital catalogue—a very quick look.

"You will see something that does not exist elsewhere," Montoya said as he led them to a room that had not been visible from the entrance hall. The room had been used as an antechamber of sorts in years past, he explained. At one time, it had led to the Tower of the Inquisición.

As Montoya held the door for Ana, Rubén gave the locking system a quick look. It was reminiscent of the interior doors in his university residence hall in Buenos Aires. Obviously, the entry had been reconfigured under budget constraint. The doorknob was polished brass, and the pre-hung door was not heavy. Very convenient.

Inside the library, Montoya settled Ana and Rubén at a long table with three desktop computers. The room was completely unremarkable in every way except size. It was five times larger than Rubén had expected, running behind the administrative cubby holes for the entire length of the municipal offices. Closed shelves and drawers lined the walls, and Rubén was sure the documents in question were behind the wooden doors that concealed the shelves and inside the drawers that carried no mark, no clue to the nature of the papers they held. There was only one break in the shelving, a space that included a second full-sized door much like the one that they had just entered.

Montoya explained that he had been assigned the responsibility to digitize the library. "Eventually," he said, "when I finish my work, scholars like you will be able to see these old papers on the internet from anywhere in the world. You won't have to see them in person."

"Like the Dead Sea Scrolls," Rubén said.

"But less interesting," Montoya said. "I have only begun the cataloguing, and I am in the process of attaching the Vatican's key words." He sat at one of the computers and opened the program he was using to queue the documents. "So, you see, your request for keywords is perhaps the only one I can fulfill. 'Alhambra' is, of course, one of the keywords, so I will enter it. There! You see? Here is the list of documents that are in some way connected to 'Alhambra.'"

The list was extensive—too extensive for the time they had. "Can we focus more closely, maybe by supplying a year or two? Can a year be a keyword?" Rubén asked.

"Yes, of course." Montoya tapped in "1492" and the list shortened from 11,000 to 2,672 documents.

"Are most key words in Latin?"

"Latin key words are at a minimum in my system. You are searching for material that relates to Spain. The Vatican is aware of the new millennium." Montoya smiled, pleased at his own good humor.

Ana asked if he might be willing to allow them try using the marvelous catalogue he had created. And maybe, for the sake of speed—since they were now down to seventy-five minutes—perhaps he could log onto a second computer for her to use.

"As I have said, I cannot offer you access to the documents, but you can look at my catalogue if it will help you prepare a request to the Vatican."

His humility was overstated, in Rubén's opinion. Montoya had connected thousands of documents to words that could signify subject, author, date, and recipients of the documents. He was obviously proud of his accomplishment and willing to share it with anyone who would acknowledge the brilliance of his work.

"I have not found such a research system, from the north to the south of the American continents. You are most kind to let us see your project."

"Magnificent!" said Ana. "Amazing."

"Few have any idea that this system exists, so no one will be concerned you are using it," Montoya said. But he also told them he could not leave them alone in the library. The security camera had malfunctioned a few weeks before and budget cuts were making it difficult to do repairs, but protocol was still protocol. He called the dark-haired woman who had been at the reception desk and asked her to join them.

"Señorita Alvarez will stay here with you. She'll be helpful in case you have additional questions," Montoya said, then checked his watch. "You may work for another seventy minutes. I myself must return to the schedule for the day."

Ana was given the computer station on the side of the table closest to Señorita Alvarez. Rubén was across from Ana, most of his torso blocked from Señorita Alvarez's view. Ana started immediately by brainstorming a list of words that might lead to documents she thought would be helpful. She jotted them on a page of her small notebook and began keying them in.

Rubén concentrated on the information on his desktop. He wondered if Montoya had included additional information in his catalogue—more than just topics, dates, names of authors and recipients. He was sure there would also be a reference for each listing that described its location in one of the cabinets that lined the walls of this room. A code, perhaps. A letter or series of letters. Perhaps a compass point—"N" for "Norte," "S" for "Sur," "E" for "Este," "O" for "Oeste."

He keyed in "Alhambra" and "1491" then scrolled down the list of documents that came up. He noticed they all had a series of numbers listed in the bottom left corner. The documents with the earliest dates ended with the letter "N."

Señorita Alvarez had read and reread the pages in a folder she'd brought to occupy her time. She stood, stretched, and sat down again in the uncomfortably hard plastic chair where she had been perched. She stood up again and stretched, then walked over to Ana to ask if they could work a bit faster. She had a report to print, and she needed to return to her desk.

Ana had been distracted by the impatient gestures and thought it would speed things up a great deal if Señorita Alvarez could leave them for a few minutes to complete her printing task. "We promise we're worthy of your trust. We're too busy here to do anything malicious."

Señorita Alvarez smiled, but she walked back to her chair. When she opened her folder and began to read her documents again, Rubén suggested that he and Ana could be locked in from the outside. "That way, you'll be sure that we are here at our stations, doing what we have permission to do, and you'll be able to do what you're expected to do as well."

That seemed to satisfy the assistant's desire to comply with her administrative responsibility. She left the library, pulling the door shut so that it made a hard thump before she turned the key locking it from the outside.

"Are we locked in?" Ana asked.

"For the moment," Rubén said. He was looking at the camera mounted above them on the ceiling and wondering if it was truly out of order. Wasn't that too coincidental? Could he trust that there was no surveillance of the documents in the anteroom to the Tower of the Inquisición?

Without thinking about what they would do if they really were watched, he decided to take the risk. Back at the computer table, he reached into his bag and extracted a key chain that included a small eucalyptus-colored device. He pushed the edge and a USB key emerged. Within minutes, he had copied Montoya's catalogue and slipped the drive back into the bottom of his bag.

The bag had been with him in Buenos Aires and on the trip up the continent from Argentina back to Havana. He had mended two rips in a side pocket with silver duct tape, and he tore off a small piece, wrapping it around his little finger. As Ana glared at him, he put his forefinger to his lips. Montoya had said the camera was out, but he'd said nothing about sound recording devices.

Rubén rose silently from his chair and walked quickly to the door positioned at the center break between the rows of library shelves. Again, he saw a brass doorknob. And again, a prehung door with an air of nonchalance rather than security. What kind of bureaucratic committee had decided to replace a five-hundred-year-old door in a library full of rare papers with a prehung plywood imposter? Had someone decided to do away with any architectural sign that might remind the municipality of the former use of the antechamber to the Tower of the Inquisición? Had someone purposefully designed this space so that it appeared inconsequential?

If that were so, the design had worked. The door looked so insignificant that Rubén couldn't help but turn the brass knob. It was almost unintentional. He just turned the knob, and the door opened onto an unlit staircase that spiraled up to the top of the tower and funneled down into the earth. When he heard Ana gasp, he pulled the duct tape off his finger and slipped it over the latch. Then, he shut the door in one smooth, quiet move. He could hear Señorita Alvarez turning the key as he settled back into his chair.

An hour later, Rubén was standing at the front desk in the Maimonides Hotel. He had given the clerk his safety box receipt so he could retrieve his laptop, and now he was waiting for Ana, who had stopped at the restaurant next door.

Ana entered the lobby carrying café con leche with ice for each of them, a box holding two slices of tortilla Española, and a small sack of pastries for dessert. They took the elevator up to Rubén's room where they set out their lunch, including the bread and cheese from breakfast. Ana's notes, Rubén's laptop, and the key chain with the flash drive were set out next to the food.

"You stole the catalogue," Ana said. "No wonder you wanted a letter from Doña Graciela for the authorities. We're fortunate we didn't have to use it."

"I didn't really steal the catalogue. It's still there. I just made a copy. And you can't help but be happy that I have it," he said as he opened it on his laptop. "Now, let's see what we have and what we still need."

"You think they'll let us back in without permission from the Vatican?"

Permission was too slow a process for Rubén. "We've done rather well getting this much," he said. He'd begun to list what he thought he knew: there were letters to Isabela and Fernando—and some to Isabela alone from Tomás de Torquemada.

"The Grand Inquisitor," Ana said.

"And Isabela's trusted advisor. I still wonder who had the greater influence, the advisor or the advised."

"I've always seen it as a ghastly synchronicity."

Rubén refined his keyword searches to include "Alhambra," "1491," "surrender," and "Musulman." The catalogue information for the documents appeared on the screen. Then he typed in "fuente," "leones," and "hidráulico."

"What's that last one," Ana asked.

"The water system," Rubén explained. "The royals were fixated on water systems. Remember how Montoya said Isabela had water wheels disassembled?"

"Actually, he said she was bothered by the sound."

"Exactly. Why would she be bothered by the sound? She was fixated on the water—the whole fluidity thing. They were always looking for signs of alchemy."

"Or gold," Ana said.

Rubén refined his search further. The documents he wanted would be dated between November 1491 and January 1492. In the end, the catalogue pages connected to four letters of correspondence and three other documents came up repeatedly on the purloined software, all connected to Torquemada and Isabela, and all bearing dates in December of 1491.

"Precisely what we need," Rubén said. "These are the ones we want to see."

He was sure he'd cracked the location code as well. Everything, except the one letter that looked like private correspondence from Torquemada to Isabela alone, had the letter "S" at the end of the catalogue number. "Sur."

"They're somewhere on the South wall," Rubén said.

"And the last one?"

"A puzzle. The last one appears to list a letter that isn't directional. 'T.' Isn't that what it looks like to you?"

Ana saw the same pattern.

Rubén broke off a piece of bread, split it open so that he could insert a slice of cheese, and said nothing more until he'd finished eating it.

Ana was looked at the titles, authors, and dates of files that had surfaced in Rubén's search. She penciled them on the page beneath those of the files she'd found in her work. She was using her eyes instead of relying on computer matching, so she went over the entries twice.

Back in the library, Ana had been keying in ideas that Rubén hadn't employed, all related to the notion of numeracy and her father's mystical practices: "one"—which existed before the universal intellect; "four"—the creator had made most things in fours; "seven" for opportunity; "ten"—the perfect number; and "the thousands"— which had reminded her father of the animals. She had typed them all in both numerals and words. Next, she had meditated on how they might be related to what Rubén had found and to three other documents that had come up repeatedly on Rubén's laptop, all connected to Torquemada and Isabela and all bearing dates in December 1491.

"Your mystical mathematics," he whispered as he typed in Ana's entries. "We're going to find something, believe me! We'll figure it out before we go back in." He was pacing now.

"And how do we do that?"

"Figure it out?"

"No. How do we go back in?" Getting to the bottom of the mystery was attractive to Ana, but she was not comfortable with breaking into the library of the Inquisición.

"The door to the library has one of those flimsy locks I used to open with my ID back in Buenos Aires. And the door from the Tower is identical. I left that one unlocked."

Ana had no desire to rob a library that belonged to the Vatican and was under the protection of the city of Córdoba. She looked at her watch. It was almost six o'clock. They had stayed inside where it was cool, but they had been working all afternoon on three hours of sleep, and she was drained.

Doña Graciela and the American, Drummond, had tried to cover their anxiety, but Ana was sure they'd been convinced she might be in danger because of her Whisper Room video. She was certain that was why she had been sent to Córdoba in the middle of the night. Now, she'd become involved in a data heist carried out by Rubén. And even though she shared his passion for the Alhambra, his quest was exhausting her. She needed to rest.

"We can have dinner later," she told Rubén. "Then we can talk about the 'T' and what the letter means."

She gathered her notes, along with the pastry that Rubén had not eaten, put them in her backpack, told Rubén she'd meet him in a few hours, and went to the room next door. Once inside, she locked her door and stretched out on the bed.

CHAPTER TWENTY-EIGHT

Raphael Montoya did not see himself as a quarrelsome man. He'd taken the director of digitization position without complaint, even though it was beneath his professional capability, and he'd expanded its scope to include the library cataloging project. Anyone could see his accomplishment, even that Cuban and his American friend. Montoya had gone out of his way to accommodate them, to fulfill a request from Doctora Graciela Corzal de Moreno. She must not have noticed who would be handling her request. She would never extend the same courtesy to him. But he had been gracious.

The pair had expressed their appreciation of the electronic cataloguing, accessed it for seventy-five minutes and then had left. Montoya was, by his own assessment, a perfect host and very easy-going person. But some things were so annoying they could not be ignored, like the security cameras being out of order. Why did the city have cameras at all if the budget could be slashed so deeply that even Vatican documents could be sacrificed to cost cutting? In the long run, doing things cheaply resulted in making things costly.

That's why he had decided to purchase a new camera system at his own expense. He had the money. And until the system could be installed, an audio system picked up conversations in the library. The audio quality was unremarkable while the Cuban and the American girl were working. They had convinced Señorita Alvarez to abandon her post temporarily, but from the sound of it, they hadn't done anything other than carry on their heroic task of trying to discover working keywords. Besides, they had no access to the actual documents. They were safe, in file drawers armed with an alert device he'd patterned after his home alarm system. When the alarm was on, a message would be sent to his phone whenever a drawer was opened.

He hadn't believed the girl's story about an academic project involving scholars and writers from three continents. And if the famous Doctora Corzal was involved, the project would benefit no one but her and those directly attached to the Alhambra.

The favoritism shown for Granada fatigued him. Other historic sites were suffering. The whole country was suffering. He could see the writing on the walls. In a few more years, if things kept going the way they were, Spain would be near bankruptcy.

Montoya glanced at the photos of the Alhambra on his own walls and began to laugh. Of course there was writing on the walls. There was writing on every wall in the Alhambra.

Montoya believed that he should be in charge of that place. He should have been named director years ago, not Graciela Corzal de Moreno. He'd been sure the Patronato would select him over her. He was well-liked from the moment Jaime Silva took over after the Doctora's husband had died. It had been a joyful decade for Montoya. He had accomplished so much while Graciela Corzal was off studying in England. He'd spent weeks and months—years, really—in the castle. His photographs of the interior had been used as visual guides by the Patronato and their visitors. He was certain he was favored for the position until the day Silva retired and Doctora Graciela Corzal de Moreno assumed the throne.

If Montoya had been hired in place of her, the Alhambra would face no trouble in its quest to be a Wonder of the World. The Alhambra needed his financial acumen, his family's wealth, and his knowledge of intimate concerns that had passed between the monarchs and their most holy advisor, Tomás Torquemada. Montoya's eye for detail was missing. Isabela and Fernando had a vision when they took over Granada, a vision he was convinced Graciela Corzal de Moreno would never grasp.

A call came in, and he answered it before the second ring. It was Mademoislle Trouchon in Granada.

"Sí, Sí, Sí," he said. "I am so pleased that you are calling, Mademoiselle."

"Have you heard about the trouble at the Alhambra?" Trouchon said. "One of the workers, a young artesano, has been thrown to his death, and the supervisor of the artesanos, Don Marco, suffered a tragic and fatal accident. The site has been closed."

"Don Marco?" Montoya remarked.

"A most dependable man."

"Why didn't I know about this? Have they arrested someone?"

"There is a person of interest," Mademoiselle Trouchon said. "A Cuban. Professor Lenhard gave him a room in the Guadalupe to keep an eye on him. Your room, perhaps?"

"Have you talked to the policía?"

"They don't know where the Cuban is, this Rubén Torres."

"Here. He was just here. In the library seeking documents. And an American girl as well."

"Have they gone?"

"Moments ago. Should I call the policía ?"

"No," the French woman said. "In fact, we should use the telephone as little as possible for the next few hours. We'll speak in person this evening. Professor Lenhard and I will drive up to Córdoba in time for dinner."

Montoya's hand was trembling. "Until this evening then," he said.

Of course, the Cuban and the girl were on a fraudulent mission, and Graciela Corzal had sent them. He should have confronted her young partisans. If only he'd known about the Cuban. But in the end, Montoya felt he had acquitted himself well. The pair was gone from his domain. And beginning now, the library was officially closed to them and all outsiders for the weekend.

Now, at least, he would have a chance to speak to his contacts in person. He must find out what happened to Don Marco. During the time before Graciela Corzal had taken over, Montoya had worked with Don Marco, and they had been meeting recently along with Professor Lenhard to work on a special feature for the Wonder of the World project.

Which of the apprentices had been killed? No doubt it was one of the youths who had been helping with the project, probably one who had been receiving a stipend from the fund. Montoya had invested so much in the project—his time, his money, his genius.

Did the policía really believe it was murder? Was Graciela Corzal attempting to link him to the tragedies? Had she learned about his work with Don Marco?

Montoya was shaken. He went out to the reception desk and told Señorita Alvarez that he would not return after lunch. It was already past three o'clock.

Señorita Alvarez reminded him the offices would be shut down until Monday, so no one was staying on, not for long. Most were gone already. Preparations for the celebration and the climb had been completed. The festivity committee would be handling the climb in the morning, and in the event of an emergency they knew how to contact him.

They certainly did. Montoya's superiors had made it clear he was to be on duty all weekend and available during all activities at the Alcázar throughout the Corpus Christi celebration.

Señorita Alvarez continued talking. "I've made copies of the instructions the council drew up for the climb and I sorted the flags for the winners. I'll drop them off with the security patrol at the archdiocese on my way home."

The climb. Somehow, he had pushed the climb to the back of his mind, although he couldn't imagine how he could forget such a disagreeable event. It was another one of those schemes to turn history into some sort of local carnival rather than offering knowledge of the past for the edification of a global audience.

"Is there no way of avoiding this chaos again, Señorita Alvarez? We've tried hard to discourage this behavior in the past."

"No way," she said with a sigh. "Once the Mezquita-Catedral bells ring in the morning, they'll be climbing."

"Such a foolish risk, like the running of the bulls. Insanity! Why are tourists attracted to this?"

"Maybe because a good number of them make it to the top every year," she said. "They want the red silk flag. It's a trophy scarf."

"Spain has more to offer than a scarf. It has history, castles, gold. You'll soon see."

"The Cruz Roja will be standing by, although I hope no one falls." Señorita Alvarez smiled at Montoya. Was she sympathizing with him, or did she find the climb exciting?

Montoya paused for a moment in the doorway. "Make me a reservation for dinner at the Caballo Rojo. For three. Not before ten o'clock. I'll be meeting people from Granada."

"The young pair who were here earlier?" she asked. "They were so polite. I rather enjoyed them. Hard workers."

He stared at her with disbelief. "Not at all," he said. "I'll have dinner this evening with scholars. Adults. Serious people with important missions. I've had enough of schemers today."

Montoya retraced the steps he'd taken the day before through the garden, past the poppies and cedars, out onto the street to the café for a small plate and a glass of wine, and then a short walk to his apartment. He'd been home about an hour when he couldn't wait any longer for information about the rude young pair that had been sent to spread chaos into his life. He placed a call to the policía in Granada and identified himself immediately as the director of digital resources at the Municipal Museum in the Alcázar del los Reyes.

"I must speak to the detective investigator supervising events at the Alhambra."

"I'm very sorry," a voice said, "but Capitán Castañeda has not yet arrived."

It was a familiar voice and Montoya took it as a sign of good fortune that he recognized it as a veteran member of the patrol, an old friend, one who did not seem to mind hearing from him.

Montoya mentioned a disturbing report of two homicides in the Alhambra. "Can you verify the information?"

"Two homicides? I must tell you that I am not authorized to do that sort of verification," the officer said. "You will want to talk to the Capitán. But there is news all over town that some fulano has closed the Alhambra down because of tragic accidents." He advised Doctor Montoya to ring back in an hour or two. The Capitán would have returned from the Alhambra by then.

CHAPTER TWENTY-NINE

The Capitan returned shortly after Montoya's call and was informed that Señora Elena Goya de Gutierrez, Don Marco's widow, was waiting for him. She had been crying and her voice was slipping out flatly through her lips, as though it had no air behind it. Out of respect, the officer had established her in the anteroom outside the Capitán's office, rather than make her sit in the screened-in area at the front of the station.

As she was led into the Capitán's office, she said, "If I had not been so happy, he might still be alive." Her face was flushed. It was her fault, she was certain. She had been pleased when Don Marco began to bring home extra money. It meant she could finally help her brother Tomás. His company had closed, and he was working for himself, for anyone who needed a strong man who could fix things for no money, for nothing, really.

With the extra money, Doña Elena and Don Marco could finally have the things they wanted—a new television, a bicycle for their grandson. They were going to spend a few days at the sea next month, it was all reserved. But recently something was making him sick. He talked about his lungs. Lately, his breathing sounded bad. She was worried about his heart.

She told the Capitán about Marco meeting with people she called managers—a gentleman who knew the legends of the Alhambra, another who spoke with an accent and was well regarded by everyone. Recently, there had been a woman too. They came to the Albaicín to talk about the project.

Elena wiped her moist eyes with a handkerchief and said, "Important work, this woman said. Something about finding the legends, finding the proof."

Doña Elena smiled for a brief moment before she went on to explain that Don Marco had been appointed to hold special meetings with some of his apprentices. He had been given funds for the apprentices, and there was extra pay for Don Marco too. It was all proper. The money was from the Patronato, he told her.

"But since his body was found, I've begun to doubt everything. I can't sleep with that money in the house. I don't want it."

"Were these extras always paid in cash?" asked the Capitán.

Doña Elena nodded and handed the Capitán a shoebox she'd been holding in her lap. "Except the last payment. You will see there is one check in there. Marco didn't have time to cash it."

Capitán Castañeda opened the box. There were three stacks of euros. Between two of the stacks protruded the corner of a check. The Capitán closed the box and asked Doña Elena if he could record her story. It wouldn't take long. An officer would accompany her home. But she said there was no need to take her home. Her brother was waiting for her, in the café across the park.

CHAPTER THIRTY

Rubén had been walking through the Judería, a Jewish neighborhood that still looked much the same as it had a thousand years before—cobblestone streets, flowers cascading over whitewashed walls, patios with tile fountains. He'd became entangled in the quarter, crisscrossing his own path. He passed a stationer's shop twice before he noticed a map of the neighborhood in the window. Inside, the scent of cedar boxes full of parchment pages mingled with candles and lamp oils.

He purchased the map and almost as an afterthought, he bought an eight-by-ten envelope made of soft, handmade paper and a roll of tape. With the map in hand, he easily found his way through the narrow maze of streets to the old Synagogue, standing where it had since the fourteenth century. Hebrew script and mudejar reliefs still lined its walls, though they'd been covered up for several centuries when the Synagogue was used as a hospital and school, and then as the headquarters of the shoemaker's guild. Resilience was how his ancestors had survived in Spain, the way his family had survived in Cuba. Making do. Fitting in. But never letting go of the past.

He'd found a restaurant with a dining room built into one of the old patios and a menu that seemed affordable. The clerk at the hotel had suggested the Caballo Rojo instead, but when Rubén stopped in and rode the elegant glass elevator to the Caballo Rojo's third-floor dining room, the elevator opened onto a line of waiters in tuxedos.

Diners were seated at tables covered in heavy white table linen drap-
ing to the floor. The Doctora had given them money, but she would
hardly expect then to spend it on luxuries. He decided he and Ana
should have dinner in the small café in the Judería.

    Two hours later, they were seated at a table near the back of
the café. They started with white wine, the day had been too warm
for red, and then they shared a plate of beets, carrots and dark olives. "Good bread. Good fish. Fresh salads," Rubén told Ana. "Your
mother would approve."

    Ana wasn't sure her mother would approve of anything she'd
been doing since she and Rubén had stolen away from Granada. It's
not that she was shocked at her own behavior. New Yorkers weren't
shocked by anyone's behavior. But she'd been surprised when
Rubén copied the database from the library's computer and slipped
a piece of tape over the latch on the door to the tower. She didn't
mind helping him figure out the keywords system because it seemed
as though Doctor Montoya wanted the keywords discovered. But
Montoya couldn't have known that Rubén intended to slip back into
the library on his own.

    "You're planning to steal the originals?" she asked Rubén.

    "Steal is such a value-laden word," he answered. "I simply
want to read them."

    A waiter brought two shallow bowls of gazpacho, then fish and
rice for Ana and a thin beefsteak with fried potatoes for Rubén.

    "When do you plan to do this?" Ana asked.

    "In the morning. There's a miraculous event tomorrow. While
you were having your nap, I came across a poster inviting people to
the competición de la torre, the competition of the tower!"

    "Tomorrow morning?"

    "Por supuesto," Rubén said. "As a guest of the city of Córdoba,
I'm invited to climb the Torre de la Inquisición. Can you believe it?
Tomorrow morning, at precisely seven o'clock. There's a prize if
you make it to the top of the torre."

"But not the prize you're hoping to win," Ana said.

"Perhaps I will win two prizes," he said, smiling.

"You might be caught trying to break into the library."

"I won't break in. I left the door unlocked."

"You might not make it. You might fall," she said, though she didn't really believe he would. From the start, Rubén had reminded her of the crow. She imagined looking up and seeing the top of his shiny, black head as he tip-toed around the rim of the tower.

"It's in my nature to climb the torre," Rubén said. "I'm named for the tower. What's more, I know what the letter "T" stands for in the catalogue code. Most of our selections have letters representing one of the four directions, but I'm certain the document marked with the letter "T" means it's on the wall that is shared with the torre."

"But that would also be "N" wouldn't it? Or is the tower on the South wall? In any case, why the repetition?"

Rubén shook his head, then shrugged. He wasn't worried about it. "I typed the word 'torre' and the reference worked in the keyword program—just like your numbers did. I was directed to the same catalogue entries."

"That's because you're truncating," Ana said. "Using only the part of the word. Just like I did with the numbers. It's one of my favorite research tricks."

"What do you mean?"

"You just explained it. The torre is in your nature because you're Rubén Torres. By leaving off the letter 's,' you have truncated your name. What if the same thing is going on with the document? What if 'T' is not just for 'torre,' but also for 'Torres?' Only not Rubén Torres, but Luis Torres? What if your ancestor is in one of these documents?"

"That's it!" Rubén said, suddenly waving at the waiter for the check.

"I'll get the food," Ana said, wrapping his steak, the last of her fish, and a handful of olives into a napkin. "Let's run the keywords again."

CHAPTER THIRTY-ONE

G raciela was rummaging through her email for any message Rubén might have sent, evening was settling on the horizon, and there was still no word from them. Drummond was pacing around Graciela's office, not expecting either of the young travelers to call. It was likely Rubén and Ana had checked back into their hotel and then gone out for tapas.

"We should get something to eat," Drummond said. He could use a glass of wine, and a private moment or two with Graciela. She'd hired him to diagnose the authenticity of lion number nine, and he'd all but completed that task. Did she understand he was overstaying his prescribed duties? Of course she did. But was he interpreting Graciela correctly? Was she the one who wanted him to continue investigating the curious deaths or was he simply fascinated by the case? Or by Graciela?

"I think I'd like to go home," she said. "I am very tired. But I don't seem to have my car."

"I'll drive you," Drummond said.

"Are you disappointed about having no dinner?" she asked.

"Of course," he said.

Graciela continued to hunch over her computer reading through emails. "So many requests for comments, and we agreed that none of us would speak to the press tonight." She leaned in closer to the screen. "This message is from Lenhard," she said. "He's asking me to open the

Alhambra tomorrow for his docents. He says this group has invested a great deal in their visit to Granada. What does he mean by that? He must be aware that the Alhambra is closed." She pressed the print command and pointed toward her printer. "Take a look at the list he's attached."

Drummond lifted the list from the printer. Lenhard had used a corporate letterhead—"Castillos, SL—Madrid, Granada, Paris"— and he offered ten names that he hoped would be granted special entrance into the Alhambra during the shutdown. The only one he recognized was Mademoiselle Trouchon, the woman Lenhard had been looking for when they met him earlier that day.

"May I have this?" he asked.

"That's why I printed it. I need more help from you if you're willing to stay."

"You've always said Lenhard was harmless."

"That may be so, but he's beginning to annoy me," Graciela said. "Can you continue our investigation?" She shut down her computer without replying to Lenhard's email.

"So you regard it as our investigation?"

"I would like it to continue that way," she said, smiling as she picked up her purse.

They made their way to the Citroen and down the hill to her home without saying much until she offered him a glass of wine. This time it was Drummond who declined. He was focused on another task now.

He was wondering about Lenhard's mention of investments. Had the investments made by people on Lenhard's list been financial in nature? If investments had been officially recorded, where could he find that data? He was driving toward the Granada city offices, but he could see the building was closed, everything but the police department. Did he dare ask Capitán Castañeda? They had promised Castañeda that police business would be left to the police, but the names on Lenhard's list were hardly police business, just a group of touring docents. Would the Capitán be of any help?

Drummond spotted a café across from the city offices. If he took a table outside, he could watch for Castañeda while he thought about his next move.

He parked near the café, grabbed his laptop, and found a simple wooden table on the patio. The little restaurant would have been more pleasant if Graciela had agreed to accompany him. He missed her company, the way she thought about things—always investigating, doubting everything and everybody, playing an intriguing game of certainty and disbelief. She seemed to exercise her skepticism all the time, even when the situation involved people she believed in, like Lenhard. And when she'd declined Drummond's invitation to have dinner, could that have been part of the game too?

The deaths of a very young man and a very old man had settled over them like a fog. Mortality was filling any space there might have been for social pleasantry. And there was the worry over the safety of the American student and Graciela's Cuban apprentice. Drummond checked his phone to see if there was a message from Córdoba. Nothing. Rubén and Ana had not called.

The waiter was standing at his side, and Drummond asked for the beef steak, a salad and bread—the crisp, crusted bread he found in every Granada restaurant. And of course, a half carafe of red wine and a glass of mineral water.

Then he pressed the home number of his friend who had been out of touch, Investigative Magistrate Julio Villanueva.

After three rings, Villanueva answered. "Hardly a coincidence," he said. "I just finished speaking with Doctora Corzal. She told me about the deaths, which I already knew about. But she also mentioned you were examining names listed on a request for a special visit to the Alhambra during the shutdown. This is a request from someone known as a friend of the Alhambra, is that true?"

"Yes, it's that independent scholar who's been hovering around Graciela. I believe he's from Alsace."

"Hovering around the Doctora? Is there an issue with that gentleman?"

Villanueva's use of the honorific instead of Graciela's first name reminded Drummond he was violating decorum by calling her Graciela. He'd been working closely with her, but he didn't want to appear as a suitor. "Other than his being omnipresent?" Drummond asked.

"Yes, other than that," Villanueva replied.

"Only that his request included a comment that these visitors had made substantial investments in Granada. On a Saturday evening, is there a way I can track investments?"

"Is it possible the investments are in real estate, land, businesses, or other assets in that realm?"

Drummond laughed. "Any investment is possible, isn't it?"

Villanueva said there were public archives of land and business transfers online.

"Can I get into the archives this evening?"

"Actually, you can. We have two online systems—the Land Registry and the Business Registry. They're public. Anyone can consult them."

"So, I can search them tonight?"

"I believe you call it 'twenty-four-seven' in the States. I will send Doctora Corzal what you may need to get into the site, but it may take an hour or so," Villanueva said. "But please be careful, both of you. And your young friends in Córdoba. You're not the policía, not oficiales here in Spain, none of you."

"I've been reminded of that by an officer named Capitán Castañeda. Has he mentioned the circumstances to you."

"Yes," said the magistrate. "We spoke."

The call ended and Drummond sipped his wine. It was tart, perhaps a bit young, but it was inexpensive. And the beef was tender enough to be satisfying. He was finishing his meal when he noticed a man approaching. There was a cigarette in his hand and the scent of dark sweet tobacco that came with him reminded Drummond who he was. Without asking permission, the man took a seat at Drummond's table.

His only greeting was a nod before he pointed toward the city offices. "She is inside, over there with the policía. My sister, Señora Elena Goya de Gutierrez."

"She's been arrested?" Drummond asked.

"No, she has come to the policía on her own to surrender the money."

Drummond was confused. "What money?" he asked.

"Bonus money that Don Marco was given by the Patronato. I told you, the Alhambra was making him work too hard."

"Do you know what that work was?"

"It was obvious," Doña Elena's brother said. "Everyone was talking about it—the dead boy included. Finding proof that the legends are true. That Boabdil hid his gold in the Alhambra."

"Are you sure it was money from the Alhambra?" Drummond asked.

Doña Elena's brother removed a small box from his shirt pocket, took out one waxy match and lit his cigarette. He inhaled deeply and exhaled a long stream of smoke, which passed to the left of Drummond. "I do not doubt my sister's word."

"Cash?" Drummond asked.

"Most of it," the man said.

"Was there any paperwork that let her know it was from the Patronato?"

"A bank check." He looked at his watch. "By this time, she's given it to the policía."

Drummond noticed the man run his hand over his shirt, as though he needed to feel the presence of something in his pocket. "Anything else?" Drummond asked.

"I told her she will get in trouble if she shows it to the policía."

"But she has already given everything to the them, right?"

The man's whole body shook as if it were saying, "No," but his voice said, "Sí."

Drummond let silence fall between them as he took a long slow swallow of wine. He motioned to the waiter, requesting a glass for his companion. The waiter poured wine from the carafe into a new glass and re-filled Drummond's as well.

The man finally broke the silence. "They were working him too hard, and their promises were worth nothing, not even the one on paper. And here you are now, waiting, ready to add to her worries," Doña Elena's brother said.

Only hours before, Drummond had been suspicious of this man, but it seemed now that he was simply protecting his sister. "I don't want to cause your sister any trouble. I was sitting here across from the police station because I thought I needed to have a chat with Capitán Castañeda about a totally different matter. Fortunately, I have managed to resolve my question without speaking to the police."

The man's hand was resting now on his shirt pocket.

Drummond asked, "Do you recall any names on the paper, or the check?"

The man quickly moved his hand to the table. "A name like the Alhambra. Maybe Alcázar. Acazaba. Or Palacio. One or the other."

"Castillo?" asked Drummond.

The man inhaled deeply, then said, "Quizás," and took a drink of wine.

Drummond was anxious to get in touch with Graciela. He slipped money under his plate and stood. He no longer needed to be there. He asked the man to let his sister know she could contact him through Doctora Corzal at any time. The man held his cigarette between his lips and reached out to shake Drummond's hand.

Drummond took the back road to the top of the red hill and circled around to his parking spot at the converted convent, now a Parador where Graciela had secured a space for the Citroen. His inn was a hundred feet or so deeper into the Alhambra grounds, just up the gravel street. A warm light glowed in the lobby, and three young women sat behind the reception desk chatting. Drummond paused on his way up the staircase, when he realized the woman who'd welcomed him the day before was speaking to him.

"Los leones," the woman said, "el noveno. The guards were in the courtyard, and they tell me el noveno has stopped gushing water at his assigned time."

Drummond called Graciela as soon as he got to his room. She'd already heard about the problem with el noveno. The lions, including el noveno, were all emitting a slow trickle now, nothing more.

"Lion number nine as well?" Drummond asked.

"He is as quiet as the others. No beautiful stream of water at his appointed hour."

CHAPTER THIRTY-TWO

G raciela had been tempted to stay awake to see if el noveno did anything unexpected in the next few hours, but she decided to rest while she could. The guards had promised to alert her if the fountain exhibited any changes. She'd begun to worry more about the humans. Drummond was facing an all-night session tracking the names of the docents that Lenhard had sent on Castillos, SL letterhead. Rubén and Ann might call from Córdoba at any time. And now it seemed that Don Marco's widow was talking to the policía about money Don Marco had received from a mysterious source for doing something extra. The lions were calm in comparison.

She sent Drummond the codes he needed to use the Land and Business Registries online, made herself a cup of hot peppermint tea and took it to her bedside. Before each sip, she breathed in the warm peppermint steam she knew would make her sleepy.

When her cell phone sounded, she thought it was her alarm and sat up in bed, fumbling for the clock, until she realized the sound was coming from her mobile phone. A call at this hour had to be from Rubén, but the voice she heard was low, and the language was accented with a heavy Alsatian breathiness.

"Forgive me, Doctora," said Lenhard. "I have heard that the Alhambra has been shuttered and I sent you an email earlier, but you did not respond. Now I am concerned about your welfare, so I called out of concern. I would be there in person, but I have been called away to Córdoba."

"I'm fine," Graciela said. "The Alhambra is fine. Thank you for your concern, Professor." She had no doubt Lenhard would be seeking her out in person if the Alhambra were open, but at this hour? From Córdoba?

Lenhard spoke again. "I must admit that I called because I am hoping for a small favor as well, one that is very important to me. My docents are still there in Granada, and I am hoping that you might accommodate them by giving them, and Mademoiselle Trouchon, the briefest of access to the Nazrid Palaces today."

Lenhard and his request again. She hadn't heard from Drummond since she sent him links to the registries. Had Drummond found something related to the docents? Had his search somehow alerted Lenhard?

"Doctora, if you could unshutter the Nazrid Palaces ever so briefly, you will do me a kindness of paramount worth," Lenhard said.

She quickly sorted through her messages. No. Nothing from Drummond during the night.

Her feet were on the cool tile floor now and her eyes were growing accustomed to the dark. She stood and walked across the room to the dresser where she routinely placed a bottle of mineral water in an ice bucket in the event she became thirsty in the night, as she often did. She poured a glass, while Lenhard's appeal continued.

"Perhaps Mademoiselle Trouchon alone. She could take some photographs for the docents, and then meet them in the plaza to plan a visit for Monday. Then they wouldn't experience such deep disappointment. She can be there in a few hours, and she will take full responsibility for the docents while they are near the palaces."

This version of his request seemed even more peculiar than the first. Was Mademoiselle Trouchon suddenly called to Córdoba as well? She decided not to ask. Lenhard had to know it was impossible to grant him privileges.

"I understand your difficulty," Graciela said, "but it's not conceivable at this moment."

"Again, my dear Doctora, my profound apology for my audacity in calling at this hour, but I am still hoping you will help me. You have always supported my scholarship. You have always made me at home in the Alhambra. If Mademoiselle Trouchon leaves within the hour, she will arrive in Granada by mid-morning. I beg you to help me with this problem. Isn't there any chance?"

Graciela slipped on a silk robe and went into the sitting room she used as her home office. She unlatched the heavy shutters and pulled them open. Outside, there was little sign of day in the dark blue night, only the slightest aura of gray beginning to spread across the horizon.

"No. I have to say 'No,'" she said firmly. "That decision is no longer in my hands. You must understand."

"The events have been disturbing, to cause you to close things down so tightly and to disallow valid exceptions." Lenhard was whispering now. "Upsetting to you and your American visitor. Especially the last situation."

The last situation? Did he know about the last situation—the missing key and the Capitán's admonition? Or was he talking about Don Marco's death?

"Such a tragic accident for Don Marco," Lenhard said. "You and Inspector Drummond finding his body, so soon after the fatal discovery by your protégé. This must cause great concern."

"This is a very inconvenient time for a call, Professor." Graciela was in the kitchen now, heating a kettle of water for her morning tea.

But Lenhard whispered on. "And the death of the boy. So troubling that the authorities don't see the death as accidental."

"What authorities? The policía?"

"Yes. They confided in a colleague of mine here in Córdoba. He's been told the circumstances of the boy's death were more complicated than we believed."

"What circumstances? What colleague?"

"I would prefer not to say. There has been tension in the past."

Ah, so Lenhard had been speaking with the foolish castle fellow. "Montoya?" she asked.

"He's in charge of digital projects at the Library of the Inquisición. How good it was to see him today. I was feeling an immense guilt at not keeping a watch on your young Cuban gentleman, until our friend Rafael Montoya told me of the talented young man's visit to his library—along with the American girl. I wasn't aware they were working on such an important project for you. And under your sponsorship. This encouragement of young scholars is another reason you are held in such high esteem."

For a moment, Graciela was relieved to hear the young ones were safe. She almost asked Lenhard to go to the Hotel Maimonides immediately and instruct Rubén to call her right away. But Lenhard had gone silent. Was he quizzing her, waiting for her to acknowledge Rubén's and Ana's presence in Córdoba? She couldn't really interpret it any other way.

The plan that she and Drummond had conceived was to conceal the young pair's whereabouts, and now she felt it paramount to hide their location from Lenhard as well. She was uneasy with his phone call, and with this stall in the conversation. After his effusive beseeching, his silence seemed oddly intrusive.

She broke the quiet. "You have no responsibility for Rubén, Professor."

"May I presume the Capitán is no longer concerned about him?"

"There is no reason to worry about Rubén, or the young woman."

"You do seem worried, Doctora. I wouldn't have any trouble finding them. This city is smaller than it seems."

There was a sting in Lenhard's suggestion that he could easily find Rubén and Ana. His call was obviously something more than the scholarly crush she had tolerated far too long.

"It is extremely early in the morning," she told him. "Too early for this chat."

"Doctora, why can't you offer Mademoiselle Trouchon access to the Alhambra today? Allow her a very brief visit."

"I cannot. Perhaps you can invite your docents to Córdoba," she said, determined to conclude the conversation. "We could then arrange something for them next week."

Graciela ended the call without waiting for a response. She poured boiling water over English Breakfast Tea leaves in her small tempered glass pot. Lenhard's pre-dawn call had left her distressed. And how was she to think of this intrusion by Montoya, who had been creeping into her worries for years.

Montoya's theory was a quixotic infatuation with the past. Did he really believe Spain's hidden riches would finance its reincarnation as a world power? So he'd gone digital. Maybe that world was working for him, offering him a new gravitas. She hadn't been paying attention to Montoya's career moves, and her inattention had led her to drop Rubén and Ana directly onto his path. But why had Montoya been in contact with the policía in Granada? Would his animosity toward Graciela be a danger to Rubén?

She put her phone in her pocket and assembled the teapot, a few slices of lemon, and a china cup and saucer on a tray and walked through the library onto the balcony where she would have a view of the Darro and the Alhambra. The sun had now come up. The morning air was cool. The day would be easier to face once she had done her morning meditation, so she sat quietly, breathing in and out, timing each inhalation, each exhalation, allowing herself to sip her tea.

But her worries returned. Had she failed to hear a call from Rubén? She checked again, but there was nothing. Was Lenhard's conversation a sign that Rubén was involved in even more trouble? She was hoping Rubén and Ana would spend time in the Mezquita and the old Synagogue, that they'd take an afternoon walk along streets where the world's most significant scholars had once gathered. She should have known he'd involve Ana in his obsessive search for documents that related to the surrender. What made her think they'd break away to enjoy Córdoba and leave the mystery of the documents behind?

Quickly she dialed the Maimonides Hotel and spoke with clerk at the front desk. He rang the rooms assigned to Rubén and Ana, but no one answered. He suggested they might be at breakfast. The dining room was open early for Corpus Christi. Graciela asked about the notes that she had left the night before. The clerk reported the notes were still in their assigned mailboxes. They had not been collected by either of the guests.

"Should I leave them additional messages?" he asked.

"No need. The first message is enough."

He suggested Graciela call back later in the morning. "The afternoon might be better. Festivities will begin at the Alcázar very soon. Your friends may be there for the competition of the torre."

"The torre of the Inquisición?" she asked.

"Yes, of course. The young people try to climb up the torre."

Rubén wouldn't try to make the climb himself, would he? Unlock access to the library documents the way he'd managed to unseal her private files?

She made one more call, this one to Walter Drummond.

Drummond had been working most of the night, using the URLs that Villanueva had supplied to Graciela to check the list of docents. Yes, searching these registries was possible, as Villanueva had said, but also time-consuming. Name by name, Drummond searched for real estate connected to the docents. None of them had purchased land in Granada in the last six months. Or the six months before that.

It was almost dawn and Drummond's last hope was to get a wider view of this scheme by entering the corporate name—Castillos—the name on the letterhead bearing the list of docents. "Castillos, SL." Was that the name Don Marco's brother-in-law had been trying to remember? What had he said? Palacio? Alcazaba? Alcázar? But he could have been searching his memory for Castillos.

Drummond typed "Castillos, SL," into the Business Registry, requesting information on land purchases made by the company. Again, he was careful to follow the advice Villanueva had sent through Graciela, "Remember, the computer is a literal creature. Take no short cuts. Pay attention to the question. Answer exactly, and then wait. The Business Registry will take a bit longer, up to an hour, to supply you with the information you want."

As he waited, he could hear scattered voices below his window—was it tourist time already? Were they talking about the deaths as they walked on the street below. About the Alhambra's closing? Were they aware of the centuries of artifice on this beautiful red hill?

Above his bed, an overhead lamp was encased in an eight-pointed wooden star punctured with tiny geometric shapes. His ceiling had the look of the stalactited dome inspired by Pythagoras in the Sala de los Abencerrajes, the room in the Alhambra with the rust-stained basin that may have belonged originally to the lions.

With a faint beep, the list of the board of directors of Castillos, SL, appeared on his screen. The docents' names were not among the members of the board, but Lenhard's name was there, as was Mademoiselle Trouchon and Raphael Montoya. Next came a list of Castillos' corporate land purchases, mostly small plots. Shops on the cordera running up the hill from the city to the Alhambra. Parcels across the Darro stretching into the Albaicín. A few larger plots of commercial land downtown, and three that stretched south toward the Alpujarra, the mountainous terrain where Boabdil had sought refuge.

Drummond decided to go back to the site that tracked personal purchases. He had checked for the names of the docents, but he hadn't looked for individual real estate purchases by Lenhard, Montoya, and Trouchon.

And there they were. Lenhard and Trouchon had been purchasing contijos—country houses with significant land spreading out toward Lobras and Timar. Montoya had acquired a number of smaller parcels nearby, specks of land marking a path up El Fuerte, the mountain that held the stone remains of an eighth century Moorish Fort on its shoulders and a labyrinth of cinnabar/mercury mines in its belly. And then there were properties in the city of Granada close to the Alhambra. Both Montoya and Lenhard had been accumulating holdings near the Cerro del Sol, the mountain that had been mined by the Romans. But the veins of gold in that mountain had never been depleted by the Romans or the Moors or the French. Were these the investments Lenhard had been so concerned about?

Drummond heard his phone chiming somewhere under his bed clothes. The ringing stopped before he could find the phone. It was Graciela's number, and he called her back. She was apologetic for telephoning him at dawn, but Rubén had not contacted her, and Professor Lenhard had made a most peculiar call at a very odd time. He'd apparently gone to Córdoba and had spoken with Rafael Montoya from the Library of the Inquisición about Rubén and Ana.

"Montoya, the eccentric literalist? I just found him on the board of directors of the Castillos bunch, the company listed on the letterhead that Lenhard sent you."

"Montoya has met Rubén and Ana and seems to have some details about Ander's death."

"How would Montoya know?"

"Apparently he was talking with friends in the policía."

"In Córdoba?"

"In Granada."

"Did Lenhard specify what details the Granada Police gave Montoya?"

"No. I felt he was playing with me somehow."

"And he called before dawn to initiate this game of his?"

"He wanted me to open the Alhambra today for Mademoiselle Trouchon and her docents. Or Mademoiselle Trouchon alone. He was quite insistent."

"How quickly can you dress?" Drummond was already out of bed. He pulled on a clean pair of khaki slacks and a fresh white shirt. Before he closed his laptop, he wrote a quick email to Julio Villanueva, the investigative magistrate, and attached the information he'd found about Castillos and the individual purchases made recently by Lenhard, Trouchon, and Montoya. Then he packed his laptop into its case, pulled it over his shoulder, and headed down the staircase. It was time to set off for Córdoba with Graciela.

CHAPTER THIRTY-THREE

The scent of rosemary was overwhelming, drifting into Ana's room through the French windows she'd forgotten to close before falling asleep. It was just before six in the morning. Rubén would already be standing in line, anticipating his turn to climb the Tower of the Inquisición.

Why hadn't he made sure she was awake? He could be so annoyingly protective.

She stepped into a white sundress and grabbed a brown striped shirt from her bag in case she needed long sleeves. She didn't know exactly how people of Córdoba celebrated Corpus Christi, and she didn't want to offend anyone celebrating a religious festival.

Her notebook was on the bed where it must have fallen out of her hands as she fell asleep. She dropped it into one of the large pockets on her dress, then pulled her hair into a ponytail high on her head, and grabbed her sunglasses and messenger bag. Her Yanqui shoes would have to do.

A breakfast buffet had been set out for early risers, with small lunch bags filled with hard boiled eggs, bread, cheese, and dried fruit. Ana took two of the bags. Rubén would be as hungry as she was.

Outside, long branches of the aromatic plant covered the streets. She'd never seen rosemary like that. It was deep, spread like hay, and the sweet scent was powerful. Ana's mother kept rosemary trees and little tarragon bushes in her kitchen so she could break off sprigs when she was cooking. She would lift each tiny branch to her face and breathe in. But they were meager tendrils compared to the boughs of rosemary that were scattered across the cobblestones in Córdoba. Rosemary grazed her ankles as she walked through the herbal carpet toward the Alcázar.

There was a line at the entrance like the day before, but this one was moving more quickly because there was no entry fee. No one had come to see the Alcázar or to visit its museum or talk to bureaucrats working inside. Everyone was there for the climb and the festivities in the gardens.

Ana made her way slowly through the grounds and around the trapezoidal sets of myrtles toward the long narrow pool she'd seen the day before. She had hoped to stroll alongside that pool with the jets spilling from the sides and spouting from the center, but yesterday there was no time to linger. Today, however, she could set her own pace.

She entered through an opening in the dozens of tall tubular evergreens that loomed into the air and she walked the length of the path. There was no use trying to find Rubén until after he had made his climb. Besides, she was sure she'd give him away if she hovered around him before he executed his plan.

Ana came out of the enclosure near the elevated statues of Isabela and Fernando posing with Columbus. Was Isabela really bothered by water? Her stone statue didn't look at all distracted by the reflecting pools surrounding her in the gardens. Maybe it was just an obsession with moving water, or an apprehension about who or what the water's mover might be.

The Tower of the Inquisición was behind a square pond bordered by waist-high wrought iron fencing and lollipop-shaped trees. This garden was full of fantasy. And there, leaning into the wrought iron railing was the woman from the bus tour, the one traveling with Professor Lenhard's group. When the woman saw Ana, she smiled. Maybe too wide a smile, the kind policemen and psychiatrists wear when they're approaching someone standing on a ledge. The smile didn't fit the woman. She'd always appeared to be both restrained and demanding. Like when she came rushing over to sit at Ana's table in the restaurant after the professor left abruptly to follow the police car. No "Pardon me." She simply seated herself at Ana's table and took over.

The woman's smile began to dissipate as she approached Ana this time. "I am pleased to have found you," the woman said. "We've been concerned about you since we saw you leaving so quickly the other night. You and that young man the professor was sponsoring in the hotel, but he's nowhere to be found. We were afraid we would hear tragic news. There has been so much of it."

"We're here," Ana said. "And we're quite fine. We've come to visit Córdoba—for the festival."

Ana caught a glimpse of Rubén at the base of the tower, about to climb to the top. Ana hadn't understood that he was going to scale the stone exterior. She'd imagined contestants running up and down interior stairs, knocking into each other in the process. But now she could see ropes dangling from arrow slits at the top. Stone bumps and dents on the tower exterior could be used as footholds by the climbers until they could catch a rope and pull themselves up. But how did Rubén plan to be unnoticed long enough at the top to escape into the library?

The woman was offering to buy Ana a café con leche. There was a bar set up for the festival in the gardens, and Professor Lenhard wanted to meet there. "Come join us," the woman said. "Our friend, Doctor Montoya, has a table. I believe you've already met him."

The woman took Ana's arm and led her toward the temporary café. Ana didn't pull away. She didn't want to act as though she had something to hide or make a gesture that could cause Doctor Montoya to doubt the story she'd told the day before. Ana thought it best to go with Mademoiselle Trouchon for a while and provide a distraction that might keep her from noticing Rubén, who was just now reaching one of the ropes.

O nce Rubén had a rope in his grip, he had no trouble ascending to the top of the tower. He had done this sort of climb often in the Andes when he was in Argentina. He loved mountain climbs, but he loved training on climbing walls just as much, and this tower was more like a training wall than a cliff in the Andes.

As he made it to the arrow loops that circled the crown of the tower, his feet struggled to find more stones that jutted out around the outer edge. He touched one, then another, and breathed a sigh of relief. Now he could look around for the protrusion in the tower where the staircase joined the tower's crown. There it was.

He held on, one hand at a time, as he moved to the left. Uno, dos—he was at the first loop. Tres, cuatro—Ana's perfect "número cuatro." He leaned into the loop and there they were—the stairs, the beautiful stairs.

There was an edge of stone around the inside of the tower, just enough edge to give him a foothold. He rotated over the rim, rested one foot on the ledge, and let his other foot slide down to the landing space. He rested there a moment, steadying himself. Then he turned and looked toward the sky and listened. No one was in pursuit. No one had noticed his exit into this auxiliary route to the interior.

He descended the spiral stairs until he came to the door. Once there, he put on the pair of document gloves he'd carried in his pocket and turned the knob. It was unlocked as he had left it.

Rubén walked across the library to its north wall and opened the first cabinet. It was unlocked. Inside, there were wide, flat drawers with dates labeled across the front of each. So, he'd been right. Everything was logically arranged. Nothing was locked. Why lock cabinets and drawers if no one is allowed to go near them without a dispensation from the Vatican?

Rubén felt a slight shiver at the notion that no one had ever transgressed as he was transgressing. At least, hardly anyone. Decades ago, someone must have managed to remove the articles of surrender that rested now in Doctora Corzal's safe. Was that someone her mentor?

Montoya had only begun the cataloguing the documents, but the keywords Rubén and Ana had been working with had each come up with codes in the bottom left corners of the references. If Rubén was right, the codes would lead him to the proper drawers, and he'd be able to sort through them one by one until he found what he wanted.

The top drawer was labeled 1481 to 1485. The middle one, 1486 to 1490. Rubén crouched into a comfortable position in front of the bottom drawer, 1491-1495. This was the drawer he needed. The keywords all led him to documents there.

In that drawer, messages about water were plentiful. He found notes from Torquemada to Isabela, all bearing dates in December 1491, and all warning that there had been conversations about water between Boabdil and the famous Jewish translator Luis Torres. Both had been under surveillance and they'd been caught talking about water, about fountains, about Solomon. There were accusations of alchemy, of moving a substance from liquid to solid, from water to silver. And there was something else Torquemada clearly didn't understand, something about "thousands."

Rubén had hoped to find a document clearly stating that Isabela believed there was gold in the pipes that led to the lions. But he found no such document. Nothing was clear. The letters read like pieces of evidence being readied for an auto de fé. Apparently, Luis Torres had been required to summarize his conversations with Boabdil, and Torquemada had given the Queen a list of the topics the two had talked about—the fountain, water, poetry, and "thousands" of something that was unclear to Torquemada.

Was this a reference to Ana's mystical thousands? Was it tied to the fountain, to the lions, to alchemy? Or could it be presumed that the Inquisitor had treasure in mind? Perhaps. But Torquemada had not revealed a specific reason for forging a new version of the articles of surrender.

Outside, officials were announcing the last set of climbers and counseling those who were still enjoying the view from the top to collect their victory flags and begin their descent. Rubén's time was up. He would have to be ready to emerge from the inner workings of the tower as the last climbers reached the summit.

He took four documents, flattened them, and slipped them into the hand-made envelope he had purchased from the stationer the previous day. He closed the drawers and shut the cabinet. He took off his shirt and taped the envelope to his back, running the tape around his chest three times. Then he buttoned his shirt and tucked it into his trousers and escaped onto the staircase inside the tower.

When the last of the climbers hit the summit, he planned to join them and claim his victory, a personal victory—proof his grandfather had been under the scrutiny of the Inquisitor. But he hadn't found any secrets about Boabdil's gold. He was leaving without a map to the treasure that had so tempted Ander and Don Marco and led to their deaths.

Rubén stood on the top step from which he could reach one hand to grip the edge of an arrow loop, and then he moved one foot to the stone ledge that he'd used on his way onto the stairs. He took a deep breath, gave his body the boost he needed to pull himself over, and he was there—ready to join the other climbers in line for their victory flags.

Ana was walking with the French woman along the marble path next to the four largest reflecting pools. Mademoiselle Trouchon was holding her forearm the way Ana's aunt used to when she'd been sent to hurry Ana home for dinner. Had Doña Graciela sent Mademoiselle Trouchon to fetch Ana as if Ana were somehow off schedule? No, it was more likely that Mademoiselle Trouchon was just a bit peculiar, and Ana could tolerate her behavior as long as a café con leche would keep her and Doctor Montoya from disturbing Rubén on his quest.

Mademoiselle Trouchon led Ana to a granite patio on the promenade between the last two pools. It had been set up as a garden restaurant with small bistro tables and chairs, a bar with stools, plates of pastries and trays of liqueurs. The dark red machine behind the bar was hissing steam from hot milk and filling the air with the scent of freshly roasted coffee beans.

Doctor Montoya had stationed himself a few tables away from the bar. It looked as though he had secured a table, his briefcase was there on a chair, but he was standing. Ana thought he was talking to someone on his phone, but when she moved closer, she saw that that he was tapping and swiping the screen. When Montoya saw Ana, he shook his head and sat down.

"Bad reception," he said to Ana.

They were a curious pair of companions, Doctor Montoya and Mademoiselle Trouchon. It was surprising they even knew each other. Although Ana could see it as a rather ordinary occupational match—a docent and a digital librarian, both interested in antiquities. And there was excitement circulating around Doctor Montoya now, a kind of electrical charge that had been absent the day before in the library. He was carrying himself like a celebrity, and Mademoiselle Trouchon seemed impressed.

"Doctor Montoya is in charge of this feast day," she said.

"Only the activities here on the grounds of the Alcázar de los Reyes," Montoya said, smiling. "The procession belongs to the Church and the faithful."

"And the rosemary," Ana said. "Where did all the rosemary come from?"

"Tradition. It's part of the Corpus Christi tradition. Pleasant, isn't it? I was about to order coffee and breads, but I see you've come equipped with your own lunch." Montoya pointed at the hotel lunch bags Ana was carrying. "The Maimonides is taking good care of its guests."

Montoya tapped the logo on one of the lunch bags and smiled, and Ana realized she had given away the name of her safe lodging in Córdoba.

"Did you tell me yesterday that you had family here in Spain?" Montoya asked.

Ana didn't recall talking to Montoya about her family. "I don't believe so," she said.

"We had no time for pleasantries, but your accent has a familiar sound. Not like most New Yorkers. Perhaps it was your surname that caught my ear. Is it the sound of Madrid that I hear in Madrizon?"

Ana felt the edge in Montoya's voice. Was his sharp comment aimed at the family he thought she came from centuries before?

"Doctor Montoya has been telling me about your work," Mademoiselle Trouchon said. "I hadn't realized you and Professor Lenhard's young Cuban charge were both interested in looking into the Holy Office documents in the Alcázar."

Ana was sitting with her back to the tower and had no idea where Rubén was, but the French woman was acting as though Rubén was Lenhard's responsibility.

Montoya spotted a man in uniform and walked quickly over to talk to him. He didn't notice that he'd left his phone on the table. Did Ana hear a light buzz from it? Maybe once or twice, then nothing more. She wasn't sure that she'd heard anything—the festival was getting noisy.

When Montoya returned, he wore a transient smile, one that came and went so quickly it was almost imperceptible. But it made Ana feel queasy.

"There has been no judgment on the second death," Montoya was speaking to Mademoiselle Trouchon, and he seemed out of breath. "At this point, both incidents are listed as misfortunes, although they may have a suspect and seem to have evidence the first was not entirely accidental."

"Evidence?" Ana asked. She wondered what evidence Montoya was talking about. Had Ana's recording been released? The Capitán had promised not to make that information public.

"I'm sorry, how thoughtless," Montoya said. "I imagined you knew the whole story, being the insider at the Alhambra that you are."

"Doña Graciela?" Ana asked. "Is she all right?"

"She is fine," Mademoiselle Trouchon answered. "The Professor spoke with her early this morning. But she is concerned about you. Imagine, even with all the trouble at the Alhambra, she worries about you." She looked as if she expected Ana to speak, to reveal some secret she'd shared with Doña Graciela.

"The Alhambra is closed," Montoya said leaning back in his chair to sip from his demitasse of espresso. "It could not be left open. Our Wonder of the World has become a public danger."

Mademoiselle Trouchon touched Ana's hand. "You see why we were concerned when we couldn't locate you."

"Or your somewhat famous Cuban colleague," Montoya added. "Did you write your letter to the Vatican?" He tapped his spoon on the table for emphasis when he said the word "write" and leaned toward Ana.

His intensity made Ana take a deep breath. "We've done a great deal of work, Doctor Montoya. You'll be pleased with the requests we're sending to Rome."

"So, your trip is going well," Mademoiselle Trouchon said. "Professor Lenhard and I were not aware you knew Rubén Torres before you arrived in Granada."

"We met for the first time in Granada," she said, then turned to Montoya, hoping she could cover any flaw in her story. "The internet is vital to scholarship, as you pointed out to us yesterday. An essential tool for international collaboration. But I am equally curious. Have you and Mademoiselle Trouchon known each other long?"

"For many years," Montoya said. "Through our association with Professor Lenhard. He has long offered significant support to those of us concerned about Spain and her history."

Montoya stood and began to wave toward the Alcázar. "I see our young scholar! He is apparently an athlete as well. He comes to us carrying the red silk flag of victory!"

As Rubén walked toward them, Montoya waved a bright blue handkerchief. It caught Rubén's eye and he waved back. Before he joined the group, Rubén picked up a bottle of spring water and drank it at the bar, then he went to Ana's side and arranged his chair so no one could see the slight bulk on his back.

When the waiter came, Rubén asked for a café con leche and another bottle of water. He looked for a paper napkin to wipe the perspiration off his forehead, and Montoya offered him the blue handkerchief. "Please, Doctor Torres, use this. You are learning that scholarship is strenuous work."

"The exhausting practice of the intellectual life," Rubén said, then laughed.

"Exhausting for Ana as well," Mademoiselle Trouchon said, laughing as she spoke. She seemed surprised by the levity of her own remark. She patted Ana's arm. "Your travels alone must have been draining. I noticed you napping the other day in the Courtyard of the Lions."

Ana pulled her arm away, letting it fall to her side, then turned to Rubén, who glanced first at Mademoiselle Trouchon then at Montoya.

"You saw Ana drifting off to sleep?" Rubén asked. "When?"

"The other day," Mademoiselle Trouchon said. "The day after you had come to stay in the Guadalupe."

"Asleep in the Court of the Lions? Amazing," Montoya said. "Who could sleep amidst that beauty?"

"No one falls asleep near the lions," Rubén said. "Certainly not Ana Madrizon."

Mademoiselle Trouchon insisted Ana had fallen asleep in the Alhambra. "Of course, it may have been another spot," she said. "Everything is so wonderfully connected."

Ana knew there had only been one occasion when she'd fallen asleep in the Alhambra. She didn't know how long she had slept before Rubén woke her up, but who could have seen her except someone who was in the Whisper Room? Ana stood and turned to Rubén's to see if he understood the significance of Trouchon's off-handed remark.

"You're looking a bit pale," Montoya said to Ana. "Are you ill?"

Rubén rose to his feet and tossed three euros on the table.

Montoya said, "We should take her back to the Maimonides."

The only words that Ana could force out were, "No, gracias."

"There is no need," Rubén said. "We are expected back in Granada, so we must be going. No doubt, we will see each other soon." He took Ana's hand and backed away, keeping any sign of the envelope under his shirt out of view. "Doña Graciela is expecting us. Forgive us, we must leave you now."

Montoya picked up his phone. He'd missed a message from his alarm system. He stood and shouted at Ana and Rubén as they mingled into the crowd. "I need to speak with you. I need to know what you were doing on the tower climb. Did you find a way into my library?"

"I'll send you a copy of our note to the Vatican soon," Rubén called back. He and Ana had to move. Fast. They walked briskly away from the promenade to the path beside the reflecting pools until they were near the Alcázar wall.

Montoya's phone was buzzing again. "Another alert," he whispered to Mademoiselle Trouchon. "He's taken something. He must have taken something."

Rubén and Ana were on the street near the old water wheel, hurrying toward the Mezquita when they began to hear the coronets and drums. Rosemary covered all the streets. People were coming toward them seven abreast, row after row of marchers carrying banners. First, a coterie of elderly women, and behind them, a cluster of priests in white cassocks and black capes, then a band of young seminarians in robes, and behind them priests in ivory vestments. A Monsignor moved quickly through a company of Spanish soldiers, all in black berets and knee-high boots, some with red drums strapped to their shoulders, others carrying machine guns.

Rubén and Ana wound their way into the parade, snaking through the local authorities, the military personnel, and the priests swinging incense. Ana was close behind Rubén until her shoe caught on a cobblestone and she tripped into a gray-haired woman who was holding a Rosary Society flag in one hand and a black leather handbag in the other. The woman's purse was jostled onto the ground.

"Perdón. Lo siento, so sorry," Ana said to the three women who circled around her, scolding her inattention and lack of decorum. Ana bent to pick up the bag and the woman's things that had been scattered into the rosemary. The elderly woman pointed at the compact in Ana's hand and asked for it. She didn't see that Ana was holding the woman's phone as well.

Ana handed over the compact, and the woman faded back into the procession without her phone. Ana called out "móvil," but the woman had already disappeared into the crowd. Ana didn't intend to keep the phone, but she was sure she'd find a way to get it back to the woman later. Besides, the phone could come in handy in an emergency. And wasn't she in one now?

Between the drumbeats, someone was yelling, "El Cubano, el Cubano," and Ana could see that it was Montoya on the other side of the street. "El Cubano tiene mis documentos."

Few heads turned as Montoya passed through the crowd shouting about a Cubano. Rubén had become a part of the crowd near a shop with children's flamenco dresses hanging from the ceiling. He was singing along with the military band and the seminarians.

What made Montoya think a Cubano would look different from a Cordobés? There wasn't anything about Rubén's appearance that would label him a Cubano. How could people know who Montoya was chasing?

Ana hadn't seen Mademoiselle Trouchon making her way through the parade, but suddenly Ana found herself looking directly into the face of the French woman. And just as had happened earlier, Ana was taken by the arm.

"Doctor Montoya believes your friend has taken some things from the library," Mademoiselle Trouchon said.

A line of well-dressed men and women paraded toward the two women, parting around them and continuing on toward the narrow streets of the Jewish quarter. "You see that we are standing amongst the authorities right now," Mademoiselle Trouchon told Ana. "Come with me and we'll sort it all out before Doctor Montoya calls them in."

Ana caught a flash of black hair, was it Rubén going into a shop across the street? Montoya had passed him and was working his way around the corner behind four rows of Church women and the military band.

"The best thing you can do is to come with me now," Mademoiselle Trouchon said as she pulled Ana out of the center of the street.

What could Ana do? It was clear the French woman had been in the Whisper Room and Ana needed to escape from her. But Ana also wanted to help Rubén escape with his documents. Should she stay with the French woman? Try to convince her Rubén had taken nothing?

"If you tell me what your young man is after," Mademoiselle Trouchon said, "Professor Lenhard might be able to help."

Ana could see acolytes advancing, and behind them the priests holding the corners of the Golden Altar of Corpus Christi. The procession had filled in the space between the shop that Rubén had entered and the cobblestone path on the other side where she was standing with Mademoiselle Trouchon. The French woman was squeezing Ana's arm hard enough now that it hurt, and Ana felt a chill. She should run, but how good were her chances of outrunning the French woman? Very good, actually. She could easily get away from a woman wearing a suit and heels. Ana could trick her, make her think she had something more valuable than what Rubén had stolen. The French woman could be lured off Rubén's trail.

Run like the gazelle across the herb-filled hills, wasn't that the line Rubén had recited the other night as they drove from Granada? Run like the gazelle across streets filled with rosemary?

Ana held the elderly woman's mobile phone in her free hand and waved it. "I have a recording on my cell," she said to Mademoiselle Trouchon. "It's from the Whisper Room. Don Marco's last words. I have it all here."

Mademoiselle Trouchon smiled at her. "You are under too much strain. Come with me now. We'll go inside, we'll find a cool place where you can rest. This has been too exciting for a young American."

"I am not under any strain at all," Ana said. "Don Marco's voice was recorded when you saw me sleeping in the Whisper Room."

"Don Marco believed Rubén Torres killed the young apprentice. You must disconnect yourself from Torres. He is a danger to you." The pitch of French woman's voice became more and more strident as she tried to force it above the coronets and the drums. "Come along, now."

Ana could tell this was a practiced act of concern. She wondered if it had worked on Don Marco. Is that how he had been lured into the scheme?

"Now!" the French woman said. "While I can still help you."

"The recording is here on this phone," Ana said.

As Mademoiselle Trouchon reached for the phone, she loosened her grip on Ana's arm. Ana pulled away and dodged around the golden shrine into the marching horns. The French woman tried to move around the priests and the sacred shrine, but Ana ducked behind a row of soldiers beating red metal drums, then another and another, and wound her way through a choir of nuns and a group of Church faithful until she found herself on the avenue that led from the Maimonides Hotel to the Patio de los Naranjos, the court-yard where the thousands of faithful had washed before prayer in the Mezquita.

.

CHAPTER THIRTY-FOUR

D rummond moved the Citroen across Córdoba's San Rafael bridge, skirting around the Alcázar to the wide avenue that skimmed the northwest edge of the Barrio de la Judería and the Corpus Christi crowds. It had taken a good hour longer than he had expected to make the trip from Granada to Córdoba because of traffic and fender benders. Every town was celebrating.

When he and Graciela had finally entered Córdoba, the procession was filling every street. They couldn't drive on the street that ran between the Mezquita and the Maimonides Hotel. They were advised to park outside the district on the Avenida del Aeropuerto and make their way on foot through the festivities. It would have been a hefty walk, so Drummond pulled into the taxi lane next to the medieval Synagogue and Graciela jumped out.

"I'll meet you at the Maimonides," she said, then folded into the Corpus Christi throng.

When Drummond found a parking spot on the Avenida, he tore a page from his notebook and wrote down "Maimonides" and his reservation number as the hotel had suggested. He set the note on the passenger side of the dashboard, locked the car, and headed toward the hotel.

Damn. He was angry with himself. That morning when they'd decided to drive to Córdoba, they should have departed immediately, instead of being drawn back into the Alhambra for one more look. It had taken too much time. They'd been surprised to find the Capitán there, and he'd been equally surprised to see them stepping down the stone steps to the orange crime scene tape.

"You are hoping to find something?" the Capitán had asked, more politely than Drummond expected.

"No hope," Graciela said, "Only a sense of unease."

The door was open to the space where Don Marco died, and just outside the door, a block of wood wedged between the seat of the bench and the compartment beneath it, the one that had been locked with Graciela's missing key. Graciela couldn't see if there was anything inside. "You found my key?" she asked.

"I am afraid I must apologize, Doctora. We have not found your key. I have taken the authority to use force." The Capitán then asked his crew to open the compartment and take additional photographs of a metal strong box that was tucked into a corner. "Please keep your distance," he said.

Graciela remained silent, standing off to the side. Drummond stooped down next to the photographer. He could see that the antique box had a fresh keypad soldered above the keyhole. Someone had lifted it into the twenty-first century, adding an electronic combination either to replace or supplement the antique lock.

"There is no way that we can tell what we have. You should not be here," the Capitán said, motioning toward the door. "You must be on your way."

Graciela needed another moment. She wondered if the Capitán had received any inquiries about the whole affair.

"Perhaps we have. Do you know a certain Rafael Montoya? An official of some sort in Córdoba?"

Graciela's voice came in a low whisper. "What did Montoya ask?"

"He asked about the deaths. And he asked about Rubén Torres and the young American. They visited him yesterday, with a letter of introduction from you. He referred them to the Vatican. Are they carrying passports, Doctora?"

"Didn't you confiscate Rubén Torres' papers? And the passport of Ana Madrizon?"

"Yes, but even so, you will understand if I ask the authorities in Córdoba to pay the young pair a visit?"

"Neither one of them presents a danger," Graciela said. "It's highly unlikely the young gentleman from Cuba and the American tourist will take sanctuary in the Vatican."

"I insist that you tell me where you have sheltered them." It had been a demand from the Capitán who then turned to Drummond and said, "Estimado Inspector, your reputation for unmasking fraud will be no protection against those who have ended two lives."

That had been the moment when Graciela accepted the Capitán's help. "The Maimonides," she said. "We're on our way now."

The Capitán's warning was still ringing in Drummond ears as he rushed the wrong direction through a street full of priests vested in the ivory and coral of the day. He hadn't told the Capitán about Montoya's connection to money that Don Marco had received. And he hadn't mentioned Professor Lenhard's pre-dawn call to Graciela to ask if the Alhambra could be unshuttered for Mademoiselle Trouchon. But he had sent those details, as well as the financial data, to Julio Villanueva, and now he hoped the investigative magistrate would have passed everything on to the Capitán.

Drummond pulled his phone from his pocket and called Julio Villanueva.

Villanueva told him the Capitán had departed for Córdoba. "With new information," he said. "The autopsy shows the young artesano had mercury vapor in his lungs."

"Can you tell me more?"

"It is a good thing Doctora Corzal told the Capitán where the young ones were staying," Villanueva said. "You'll see the Capitán soon. He'll tell you more, I'm sure."

Graciela was making her way through rows of Church faithful as she threaded around the old city, smiling and nodding and offering greetings. It was imperative that she maintain a respectful demeanor. It was expected. Wherever she went, she carried the Alhambra with her.

The Corpus Christi procession was not designed to pursue a straight line. Instead, it led the faithful around a continuous web of narrow streets. Graciela kept a steady pace but couldn't move as quickly as she wanted. She stayed along the side of the procession as it moved toward the pealing bells. Emiliano Alacín, one of the members of the Patronato, was standing among a cluster of officials. He huddled briefly with Doctora Corzal, and once assured that all was under control at the Alhambra, he promised to contact her later.

For a moment, Graciela thought she caught a glimpse of Rubén edging across the red tile roofs of the shops, but just as quickly the figure was gone. She could hear the bells hanging in the tower above the Mezquita-Catedral, and they were growing louder.

The next turn carried the procession onto a shadowed street. It was out of the sun, the air was cooler, and the tension Graciela had felt in her shoulders eased. She inhaled the rosemary at her feet and followed a path that appeared to lead the faithful toward a cave. But there would be no cave at the end of the block. The street would curve gently and the faithful would turn. Sunlight would be restored, and The Maimonides and the Mezquita-Catedral would come into view.

Behind Graciela, a man's voice called out, "Cubano, te veo," and when she turned, she saw Montoya—older and thinner than Graciela remembered. He looked tired and defeated until he saw her.

"Doctora Corzal! I'm sorry to inform you that your protégé is a thief."

Graciela stepped into a doorway between shop windows full of novelties.

Montoya followed her in three long strides. He looked quite worn. Graciela touched her hand to her lips, trying to quiet him, hoping he would notice that he was interrupting a significant moment for the faithful in the procession. Perspiration had soaked through his shirt and there was a streak of dirt across his cheek.

"Doctor Montoya," she said. "Have you been chasing Rubén?"

"I believe he's confiscated material from the Alcázar library, and to think it was at your request that I opened the doors to him and his American friend."

Graciela asked him again to lower his voice so as not to make a public scene.

"These are serious charges. Do you have proof?" she asked.

He said he had none, but he intended to check the library drawers right after he confronted Rubén. "Why would he be scaling rooftops if he were innocent?"

Graciela looked at this difficult man, dripping wet and hurling accusations without the slightest evidence—a man with theories like street tales, who had made inquiries into the deaths at the Alhambra and was shouting nonsense now in the middle of a religious celebration. Graciela set aside her own glimpse of a Rubén-like figure on the rooftops and said, "Doctor Montoya, I seriously doubt that you saw Rubén on a roof."

She followed the procession down the narrow street toward the Mezquita-Catedral. Montoya positioned himself a step or two behind.

About twenty meters ahead was a tall man with gray-brown hair, his khaki suit jacket straight on his shoulders, his smooth gait moving him without a tip or a bounce. He resembled Professor Lenhard. Could it be? Was he following her? How ridiculous. He was ahead of her. She was following him.

As she turned into the open sunlight, the Mezquita-Catedral was in full view, and there at the corner was Professor Lenhard in front of the glass doors of the Hotel Maimonides. He seemed to be blocking her entrance. Was it an attempt to make Graciela notice his importance?

"The Cubano is on the rooftop!" Montoya shouted.

Graciela stood rigidly still. How could Lenhard tolerate Montoya's behavior? But then, Lenhard had not been comporting himself as she had expected lately—making phone calls in the middle of the night, issuing disturbing demands, standing now in front of her like a general, while Montoya, that most unusual underling of his, was rushing up from behind.

"Doctora Corzal," Lenhard said. "I've determined this is the hotel where the your young assistant, the one you asked me to watch over, has taken up lodging."

"What leads you to that conclusion?" Graciela asked.

Montoya was excited to answer "The girl was carrying her lunch in a bag from the Maimonides. Not very clever, was it?"

It was not easy for Graciela to be polite at that moment, but she managed to ignore Montoya and tell Lenhard in a soft voice that she would be happy to speak with him later. She was expected inside.

"You must stay with us," Lenhard said. "You will want to hear what I have to say."

Graciela did not want to hear what he had to say. She wanted to go into the hotel, wait for Walter Drummond, locate Rubén and Ana, and get them back to Granada. "I am busy at the moment," she said and moved toward the door, but Lenhard was still blocking her entry.

"I must warn you that you have placed your faith in the wrong person," Lenhard said.

Graciela tried to politely extricate herself from this trap, but Lenhard continued to block the door. "Listen to me," he insisted. "It's important. Doctor Montoya has discovered that your young Cuban revolutionary has murdered one of your workers and stolen material that belongs to the Vatican."

"Professor," Graciela said. "Your behavior is not acceptable."

"In all the years you've known me, have I ever deceived you?" Lenhard asked. "I have not. I tell you now, you are in danger. You must come with us for your own protection."

Lenhard nodded to Montoya, who grabbed Graciela by the wrist and called out, "I have her!"

The glass doors opened and Drummond emerged from the hotel. He'd never met Montoya personally, but he was sure the fellow holding Graciela's wrist had to be him— one of the three points in the Castillos triangulation, and the one whose theories about the literal existence of riches in the castles of Spain may well have supplied motivation for all the machinations. Drummond stepped to Graciela's side.

"We must go," Graciela said to Drummond as she pulled her arm free. "This cannot continue here." She tilted her chin toward the passersby gazing at them.

The hotel doors opened again, and Capitán Castañeda came out. Graciela was surprised at the relief she felt when she saw him. She told him Montoya was trying to take her somewhere, and she had no idea where.

"They want to convince me Rubén has stolen documents and murdered Ander. They have no proof, but they believe that it must be so."

"A common problem in law enforcement," the Capitán said. "No one is to go anywhere other than with me." With a sweeping gesture of his left hand and the assistance of three officers, he motioned Lenhard and Montoya to a small nest of sofas and loveseats in the far corner of the hotel lobby. Graciela and Drummond followed.

CHAPTER THIRTY-FIVE

Ringing, ringing, ringing. The bells had been ringing without pause above Ana's head in the tower that ascended almost a hundred meters above the Patio de los Naranjos. Yesterday, the patio had been silent as Ana followed the paths through a grove of small trees. The minimalist design was exciting. But now, the openness was emptiness. She was exposed.

How foolish to have told the woman she had video on the phone. She had overplayed the role of the gazelle. Ana had made it to the Mezquita, but she was still running from the woman she believed had murdered Don Marco.

She looked around the courtyard for a doorway or an alcove where she could hide in case the French woman entered the Mezquita, an exit to somewhere safe. And there it was, right next to her, the alcove leading to the Puerta del Perdón, the ground level of the bell tower. There were steps going up the side of the tower, a narrow staircase snugly attached to the wall. If Ana went up the staircase, she might find a window where she could see the city streets as well as the interior of the Mezquita.

Ana tore off two pieces of face tissue and rolled them into balls to serve as earplugs in the bell tower. She climbed the staircase two steps at a time, so many stairs, she was breathing hard. She had to slow down. She climbed at a slower pace until she reached the landing where the twelve bells pealed above the city—three bells on each side of the tower. Above the bells there was another platform with arches on all four sides, open above waist-high walls.

And there it was—the view Ana had hoped she would find. This tiny space, these small windows, were extending her vision over every street, over all the people. She could see the entire city from the stone tower. The pillars of jasper, granite, and marble were hidden under the rooftop, so Ana couldn't see inside the Mezquita, but the view of the procession making its way along the streets below was exactly what she needed.

She looked across the street to the red clay roof of a restaurant and spotted Rubén on the roof, waving at her, trying to tell her something. He looked worried. She couldn't hear what he was saying because of the bells. So many bells.

 Rubén pointed at the Puerta del Perdón, moved to edge of the roof, and climbed down to the street. He moved through the procession, pushing his way through the faithful.

Ana walked to another open arch and stood on her tiptoes so she could see where Rubén was going. He was coming toward the Mezquita. And then he was at the gate, opening the heavy door.

Ana hadn't heard the footsteps clicking up the stairs behind her. She didn't feel the pressure on her back until it became a shove and the jolt knocked her hard against the wall. The lunch sacks fell out of Ana's hands, and her body collapsed below the open arch.

The French woman crouched over Ana, trying to find her phone.

"It's no use!" Rubén yelled.

The French woman paid no attention to his shout. She was rummaging through Ana's messenger bag.

Rubén had no weapon, but he grabbed Mademoiselle Trouchon by the arm and shouted, "Stop! Stand up or I will pick you up. And then I don't know what I will do."

The woman stood and backed into a corner as if she actually believed what she had been claiming—that Rubén was a murderer.

"I think you know I am strong enough to toss you out of the tower," Rubén said. "So don't approach me."

The French woman didn't move. "She fell. I was trying to help her. Look, she's waking up. I did nothing. She's fine."

Ana moved her hand toward a pocket in her white dress where she'd been carrying the phone she'd used to trick the French woman. Rubén took the phone, and when he remembered that it wasn't Ana's and they didn't know the password, he tapped in the global emergency number for help.

Graciela was sitting on a yellow leather chair in the lobby. Drummond had pulled a stool from one of the high-top tables in the Maimonides bar and settled in next to her. Lenhard and Montoya were sitting at opposite ends of a brown leather couch. Hotel guests were staring at them, and that bothered Graciela. The situation was impossible. Graciela expected Montoya to start ranting at any moment about Rubén and stolen documents. How long did the Capitán think he could keep Montoya quiet?

The Capitán was standing, a canvas bag at his feet and several police officers directly behind him.

Drummond attempted small talk with him, asking about the traffic from Granada. How had Capitán made it to Córdoba so quickly?

"We flew. To save time," the Capitán said. "And since all of you have landed in this hotel, I expect we will soon be joined by our elusive young couple and the French woman. May I call her your assistant, Professor Lenhard?"

Lenhard's voice was flat. "A colleague."

Graciela noticed Montoya grimace. "Mademoiselle Trouchon and I had coffee with the pair an hour ago," he said.

"That's helpful," the Capitán said.

"The Cubano is a thief!" Montoya muttered.

There. It was beginning again. A public scene, and Graciela didn't want any part of it. "Isn't that enough for the moment?" Graciela asked Montoya. She wanted a private place where the Alhambra could be disentangled from Montoya's conspiracy talk.

The desk clerk approached the group and asked if the Capitán would allow him to hand a phone message to Doctora Corzal. The clerk insisted it was an urgent call.

Capitán Castañeda unfolded the note and read it, then ordered several policía to the Mezquita, immediately. "Puerta del Perdón. That entrance is open today."

As soon as she read the note, Graciela began to pace, every muscle in her body wanting to leave the hotel and run with the policía toward the Mezquita-Catedral.

"Doctora Corzal," the Capitán said. "I must insist that you and Inspector Drummond remain here with me."

CHAPTER THIRTY-SIX

They could have been mistaken for tourists, these four travelers waiting in a corner of the Maimonides Hotel lobby, each with a different storyline filtering through the silence that gathered around them.

Walter Drummond recognized the tangle of contradictions that tied them together— Graciela was attempting to fulfill her unattainable burden of responsibility, Yann-Hubert Lenhard was righteous in his unacknowledged greed, and Rafael Montoya was struggling to hide the folly behind misdirected blame. And Drummond himself, he was guided by the imagined clarity of a complicit observer. How would these stories end now that the Capitán had taken control? Was all of this visible to the hotel guests who had begun to cluster at the reservation desk, anxious about the presence of police in the lobby of their hotel?

The Capitán spoke in a low but audible voice about a young American who was injured but appeared to be all right. She would be arriving at the hotel shortly with the Cubano who had called for help—and with the French woman, Mademoiselle Trouchon.

"Your colleague," the Capitán said with emphasis as he looked at Lenhard. "It appears she will be joining us in handcuffs." The Capitán then informed Lenhard and Montoya that they were witnesses to something he did not define. They were not free to leave.

Whispers at the reservation desk grew louder when Mademoiselle Trouchon was led in by the officers. Graciela Corzal turned
away, but her anxiety about the negative attention aroused by this
incident was obvious to Drummond. There was no way the Capitán
could maintain control right there in the lobby. This was not a casual
get-together.

"You will need to find a better location," Drummond told the
Capitán.

"Not until the streets empty out. I will not be transporting this
group through the procession to headquarters."

It was the hotel manager who stepped in and suggested they
move to a private space upstairs.

It took just one nod from Graciela, and they were all together
in a suite on the second floor with its own sitting room and kitchen-
ette—more than ample space for the group and three officers. Two
more guarded the door—one inside and one in the hallway.

"These are the policía of Córdoba," Montoya said. "You are
invoking the authority of the policía in my city? Much as I respect
your authority in Granada, Capitán, I do not believe you have any
authority here."

The Capitán lifted the forefinger of his left hand into the air. As
he did, an officer moved to his side. "I am serving at the request of the
judicial magistrate. As you will notice, Doctor Montoya, we find our-
selves stuck together in a mesh of sorts—people from different cities,
people of different cultures, people from distant countries. If you take
a seat, you will soon understand why we must us all be together."

The small sitting room was silent as Montoya backed up and
took an armchair by the window. Professor Lenhard was in a chair
next to him.

Rubén and Ana had just arrived from the Mezquita and Ana
reclined on the couch as Rubén spoke to the Capitán, showing him
the palm of his hand where he'd scraped himself on the red tile roof
trying to reach Ana quickly. His skin was torn and still bleeding.

"I need to wash it," he explained, pointing to the attached bedroom. A drop of blood dripped onto the couch next to Ana.

The Capitán seemed to hiss "prisa" as he nodded toward the bathroom.

Graciela was sitting on a wooden chair behind a small walnut desk, and Drummond stood next to her, near a counter where he'd asked room service to set out bottles of mineral water. He passed a bottle to each person, including Mademoiselle Trouchon, who'd been stationed on a chair as comfortably as possible with restraints on her wrists.

Rubén quickly went through the attached bedroom to the bath, shutting the door gently behind him. He rinsed his hands and took off his shirt. He used a razor from a hotel shaving kit to cut through the tape that bound the handmade envelope to his torso. He rinsed his hands again and took a hand towel with him. As he walked through the bedroom, he slipped the documents under the mattress. No one commented when he came back into the suite and sat on the floor next to the couch where Ana was resting.

When everyone was in a circle of sorts, the officer moved back and the Capitán returned to Mademoiselle Trouchon's side.

"Must the Mademoiselle be handcuffed?" Lenhard's voice was loud enough to give away uneasiness. "She has explained that the girl fell. She was at her side assisting her before the Cuban arrived and made his allegations."

"There are two unfortunate deaths that could be linked to the Mademoiselle, along with Señorita Madrizon's experience in the bell tower. I have a recording that was made accidentally the other day in the Whisper Room. If I play it for you, I believe you will better understand the problem. You will need to listen closely to hear what may have been Don Marco's last words."

Drummond was startled that the Capitán intended to reveal Ana's recording to a room full of suspects, but the Capitán turned to Ana and she seemed to be nodding approval.

The volume from the phone was low, and Lenhard and Montoya leaned in to hear the audio. The Capitán set the volume as high as it would go and played it a second time.

That time, the words "sin opción" came through clearly. And so did the voice of Don Marco barking, "Usted me dijo."

"Don Marco is saying someone told him he had to do something, he had no choice," Drummond said.

Lenhard responded cooly, "In truth there seems to be no way to know who that person was."

Rubén answered. "It would have to be someone standing with him in one corner of the Whisper Room, a place from which his voice would be inaudible to almost everyone in the room but perfectly transmitted to someone in the opposite corner. A person like Ana, who had fallen asleep there."

"There is nothing to tie the Mademoiselle to this recording or to Don Marco's obviously accidental death," Lenhard replied.

"That might be true if the Mademoiselle had not revealed to us this morning that she was there, that she saw Ana sleeping," Rubén answered.

A quick inhale from Mademoiselle Trouchon was all but covered up by Lenhard's voice. "Please, let us all calm down here. This is surely a recording made by a young American student whose imagination has been overwhelmed by the tragic circumstances of the last few days. We are engulfed in romantic notions of rooms in the Alhambra with secret powers."

The Capitán stooped to the canvas bag at his feet and removed an antique copper chest, setting it on a coffee table. "The desk clerk at the Guadalupe hotel has identified this as the antique box left for Mademoiselle Trouchon a week ago by a gentleman of the same height and stature as Doctor Montoya."

"Impossible!" Montoya said. "Outrageous that you would involve me in this spectacle. I would never leave a thing of that antiquity without packaging it for safety and privacy."

"Indeed," the Capitán said. "You had done an exquisite job of packaging. In fact, the desk clerk watched the Mademoiselle unwrap it."

Lenhard turned to Graciela. "This is unbelievable. I promise you, I knew nothing." He lowered his head and was shaking it slowly in a gesture of contrition.

To Drummond, Lenhard appeared to be feigning his innocence. "Perhaps we would believe you, Professor, if you and your associates had not been paying Don Marco and his assistants to divert the stream and meddle in the waters of the Courtyard of the Lions. It was not the city water alone that brought chlorine into the fountain."

"Gentlemen," the Capitán said. "Let me continue. There are more details to consider."

He told the group that Don Marco's widow had come to him to relinquish a quantity of money that had caused her concern. Her husband had been working on a project, and money had arrived every month for him and his apprentices. Also, there had been offers of land near El Fuerte.

"Doña Elena also talked about a chemical Don Marco would not bring home," the Capitán said. "He kept it doubly sealed, at the Alhambra. He didn't want to risk his wife's health."

Lenhard was growing agitated. "You have accused Mademoiselle Trouchon of heinous crimes, but you do not describe anything other than an unfortunate accident."

"It is the Cubano who should be detained," Montoya said, tapping his phone. "The Cubano has stolen documents of historic value to the Holy Office. I received an emergency phone alert from the library this morning. Secure file drawers have been opened in the archive."

"You received a call from the library when no one was there?" Graciela asked.

Montoya spoke with a tone of ridicule. "Doctora, you would do well to update your opinion of me. I am director of digitization for the Alcázar. I installed the networks in the Alcázar, and I know how they function. You and your friends think you can link me to some scheme by bringing in this old box. I doubt that you even know what's inside."

"So, let's open it," Rubén said.

The Capitán picked up Mademoiselle Trouchon's handbag and removed her passport, a leather case containing euros and change, a handkerchief, a ring of keys, a tube of hand cream, a notebook, a pen, and a single brass key that was smaller and thicker than those on the key ring.

Graciela recognized it. She glared at Trouchon."You broke into my office? You took that key?"

"Perhaps it will open the box," the Capitán said. "Shall we try?"

The Capitán attempted to open the box with the brass key. When the key didn't work, he said to one of the officers, "Turn this over to the bomb brigade. I apologize for not doing so sooner. I was sure it was an innocent container, but now I realize we should have exploded it back in Granada." His gaze shifted to Montoya. "Unless, Doctor Montoya, this package is yours. I'm sure you see that a newer digital locking device has been added to the chest. Perhaps this is the package left at the Hotel Guadalupe for Mademoiselle Trouchon?"

He asked Mademoiselle Trouchon if she knew the combination for this new lock, but she remained silent.

The Capitán gestured to the officer near the door as though he were calling for the explosives team, and at that moment Montoya stooped over the box and keyed in a four-digit combination that unlocked it. Inside the box, tiny flakes of sand or dust glimmered in the light of the chandelier that hung above. Not dust, but gold.

"This box belongs to me. It will not hurt anyone, I assure you. I will take it."

"Thank you, Doctor Montoya," the Capitán said. "But we will take care of your gold."

"Oro de tontos," Rubén said.

The Capitán handed the box to Drummond. "Inspector Drummond, you are the expert on authenticity. Would you call this substance 'fool's gold?'"

Drummond recognized an opportunity to disentangle the threads he'd been unraveling since he'd arrived in Granada, and no one was going to make him stop—not immediately anyway.

"I'm going to postpone the debate on the quality of Doctor Montoya's gold," he told the Capitán. "I want to talk about why I am here. I came to study the famous lion that returned from Paris with unexpected energy. When I discovered el noveno's inner workings were authentic, that they were the originals, I knew someone must be playing with the waterways that feed the lions."

"Was this what Ander wanted to tell me about?" Rubén asked.

"If supply lines were manipulated, a meddler could divert the natural stream at the source and el noveno's surges of water could be switched from one pipeline to another," Drummond said.

"But what about the chlorine," Graciela asked, "the white powder found under Don Marco's body, the powder that was ruining his lungs?"

Drummond explained, "Marco and his apprentices were cleaning the pipes under the Alhambra all the way back to the control point on the hill above the Darro."

Rubén was sure there was a point of entry on the hill, the spot Ander had discovered.

"If such a point exists, it was Boabdil who caused it to be," Montoya said with a smile.

"Sin duda," Rubén said. "There's no doubt. Ander and the apprentices all believed they were about to find Boabdil's gold. Ander was going to show me the location before somebody stopped him."

"As any reputable scholar should know," Montoya said with condescension, "though entry might be gained through the hill, treasure would reveal itself through the lions." Montoya rose and headed toward the counter until one of the policía stepped in. Montoya grumbled, "Tengo sed. I just want another water."

The Capitán gave him a fresh bottle to quench his thirst and Montoya went back to his seat.

Drummond suspected that Montoya's reaction was a sign that the tampering and cleaning was all in preparation for the contents of the antique box with the digital lock. The tubing to lion number nine—and eventually to other lions as well—had to be clean and dry so the gold dust wouldn't get clogged in the line. But even if Madame Trouchon had the key, when did she hide the antique box outside the passageway where Don Marco died?

Drummond turned to Mademoiselle Trouchon. "Not long before we found Don Marco, Professor Lenhard came looking for you. He seemed worried about you. Where had you been?"

Again, she did not respond. The only sounds were faint scratches from her restraints when she attempted to touch the pink marks on her wrists.

Drummond thought he knew the answer. He said, "I believe you had gone with Don Marco. You insisted he add more chlorine to make sure the tubes would be clear, but you didn't want him to see you hide the gold dust. You didn't even want Don Marco to know the full extent of your deception. Is it possible that you shut the door on him—accidentally, perhaps—while he was working with the chlorine?

"Did you close him in with the gas for just a minute or two so he wouldn't see what you were hiding? When you opened the door again, did you see that he had collapsed? Did you run? Try to get away from what you must have known was a tragedy?"

Lenhard spoke for her. "She was across the plaza in the restroom. I found her myself. She was not feeling well. I sent her back to the hotel for a rest."

Drummond shook his head and said, "But after Don Marco died, what was the plan then, Professor Lenhard? There was no way to retrieve the gold dust, no longer anyone who could insert it into the pipes so gold would spurt from the mouths of the lions at the appointed times. That's why you wanted Mademoiselle Trouchon to have special access, to go back in and retrieve the gold dust."

Lenhard answered by speaking directly to Graciela, using his friendly approach again. "Doctora Corzal. Never. You must believe me. I would never be involved in such a nefarious scheme."

Drummond was tired of Lenhard's ruse. Did the professor still believe he could charm her?

"Well, let's backtrack," Drummond said. "The money that went to Don Marco and the apprentices. Who did that come from?"

Montoya answered. "I believe the Capitán called it cash."

"No, actually he called it money," Drummond corrected. "There was cash, but there was also one check, and it was still there, in Don Marco's home, when he died."

"That detail will wait," said the Capitán. "That evidence belongs to this investigation."

"I must disagree," Drummond said. "The information is public. I have learned from the widow's brother that the check came from a corporation using the name Castillos, SL."

"What does that have to do with me, Inspector?" Lenhard asked. "I am simply an aficionado of the Alhambra. A loyal supporter."

The Capitán strolled to the edge of the sitting room, and Drummond took it as an indication that the financial issues were going to be fair game, so he went on. "Castillos, SL, is a company that has been buying up land around the Alhambra—land going up into the Alpujarra as well, to the cinnabar deposits near El Fuerte."

"I am at a loss," Lenhard said. "There is no reason to link me to any of this."

Drummond smiled. "We could have a Castillos board meeting right here, right now, Professor Lenhard. The company's three directors are you, Mademoiselle Trouchon and Doctor Montoya."

"It is not against the law to purchase land, Inspector," Lenhard countered without denying the facts.

"And your docents," Drummond asked, "the ones you hoped to impress?"

Lenhard explained, "The Spanish government invites purchases, even by French citizens. Global interest in Spanish assets will only result in a benefit for Spain. If the docents want to buy land, they are free to buy land."

"And if they should be presented with a theory that gold is running through that land and pouring out of the mouths of the Alhambra's famous lions? Wouldn't that make your investors more than anxious to buy land from Castillos?"

Montoya protested. "No matter what you say, I am still right about the precious quality of the Spanish earth."

Graciela suddenly stood up as if she were grilling a less than competent speaker at a conference. "Years of this nonsense about castles in Spain so that the three of you could turn these unwitting docents into investors in a company you call Castillos? Is that the logical end of your academic theory, Doctor Montoya?"

"I cannot be arrested for my academic work, even if it leads to commercial success," Montoya said. "It is the Cubano who should receive your scrutiny, Doctora. He used my digital network to break into Vatican files. I am not the criminal."

Drummond looked again at the lock on the antique box. Maybe Montoya did have a genius quality of some sort. If Montoya would not share the combination with the person he entrusted with a box of gold dust, maybe he could control the lock from a distance. Did he plan to open the box for Mademoiselle Trouchon once she was inside?

"Doctor Montoya," Drummond asked, "if you could build a significant network for the Vatican files, did you also engineer remote access to this digital lock."

"I don't know how you think I could have done something like that. I have done nothing but offer an academic theory. Nothing at all."

"But you may have set up controls months ago—around the time that el noveno returned. In fact, I'm beginning to think we should go back to a point on the hill where Ander intended to take Rubén to show him the spot where Boabdil might have left treasure. Is there an opening there, perhaps access to the pipes deep inside? Have you created a control point for the fountain right there on the hill?"

"I've done nothing but embrace a theory," Montoya said.

"You've been manipulating el noveno's flow all along, haven't you?" Drummond asked. "You've added a valve with some sort of electronic sensor so that you could control the ninth lion, make him spout at your command. That was the real cause of el noveno's behavior change."

Montoya ignored Drummond's accusations. He told his colleagues they needn't worry. He had resources, and legal help would be forthcoming. "We will be free of these ridiculous charges by nightfall."

Drummond did not want this session to end with these people being released. He continued to question Montoya. "How about the land near El Fuerte and the cinnabar veins, the patch of earth that Don Marco believed he was earning?"

"I have a good deal of land," Montoya confessed. "I could afford to make him an offer. Don Marco was inspiring the apprentices to help restore the reputation of the Alhambra. I offered him a cave—only a few hundred square meters. It had some signs of cinnabar. He was pleased when I said it could be his bonus for working extra hours. He was very pleased."

"Is there any chance that Don Marco brought his apprentices out to see the land that was going to be his?" Drummond asked.

"Only the boy who was closest to him," Montoya said. "He wanted the apprentice to see how beautiful the cinnabar glistened in the earth."

Mademoiselle Trouchon spoke for the first time. "It is all your fault, Doctor Montoya, not mine. You should not have let Don Marco take the boy out there. And the boy was making plans to bring a friend out there as well, to show him how to heat Spanish soil into gold."

"Ander wanted to take me out there?" Rubén asked. "Had he been heating cinnabar in Don Marco's cave, mixing it with the soil, trying to make gold?"

"Melting cinnabar causes mercury vapor. Even if he managed to melt a small amount, he would breathe in the vapor," Graciela said. "What Ander was doing was very dangerous."

Drummond lowered his head solemnly. "In fact, I learned only this morning that mercury vapor was detected in Ander's lungs. Perhaps that's what made him unsteady the afternoon he fell from the Alcazaba."

Mademoiselle Trouchon said, "It was not my fault. I insisted there was no option. I told Don Marco that he had no option but to stop the boy from heating cinnabar."

"That's why Don Marco had no choice." Rubén said. "Was it you who kept Ander from meeting with me?"

When Mademoiselle Trouchon did not respond, Rubén asked, "Who pushed Ander, you or Don Marco?"

At that, Lenhard stood and moved toward Mademoiselle Trouchon. The Capitán blocked him. "Return to your seat, please, Professor."

Lenhard turned to Doctora Corzal. "Doctora, I had no idea this was all going on."

Graciela looked at him, but she couldn't respond. Just a few hours earlier, Lenhard had asked her to give the French woman special access to the Alhambra.

"Please, Doctora—please understand," Lenhard pleaded. "She has not been well. Mademoiselle Trouchon has been subjected to an alarming degree of stress. Please. Continue to trust in my support for you and the Alhambra."

Coronets and drums were audible in the distance, but the procession had passed and the crowds had moved away from the Mezquita-Catedral. The street in front of the Maimonides was nearly empty.

The Capitán said he had heard enough and summoned one of the Córdoban policía, who quietly slipped nylon braided restraints onto Lenhard's wrists. Montoya was next. Madmoiselle Trouchon was still wearing hers.

"You will see." Montoya was sneering. "My attorney will make it clear that my work is theoretical. I write about the idea of gold. You cannot imprison me for my ideas."

The three were led to patrol cars waiting outside the Maimonides.

"We have some paperwork to do here," the Capitán told Graciela. "But these individuals will be transported to Granada this evening." He thanked Drummond for his investigative help. In return, Drummond thanked the Capitán for rescuing them, despite the risk he had taken traveling with a box that could have contained explosives.

"We knew what it was when we opened it earlier this morning, just after you left," the Capitán revealed.

Surprised, Graciela asked, "How did you get it open?"

"The combination. We used the four digits most likely to have been chosen by Doctor Montoya. It was not hard to guess. I also am a Granadino who remembers our history."

"Will they be prosecuted for murder?" Graciela asked.

"That is possible—both deaths are related to chemical poisoning, but the charges are likely to be somewhat less serious. Still, they will be prosecuted. They are connected to many transgressions—two deaths, fraudulent use of the Patronato identity, damage to and endangerment of a most precious national monument. And their business dealings—land purchases and their scheme to defraud the people they called their docents."

"Small compensation for a colossal crime," Rubén said, shaking his head.

"You, on the other hand, are free to carry on," the Capitán told Rubén. "You should be relieved that you are no longer a murder suspect. I presume Doctora Corzal will be resolving any issue you might have with the Vatican."

The Capitán turned to one of the policía from Granada. "Please give Dr. Torres his phone. We will need the señorita's a while longer."

"And our papers?" Rubén asked.

The Capitán told him that Judicial Magistrate Julio Villanueva would be meeting with Doctora Corzal and the Inspector. "Tomorrow afternoon in Granada. I imagine the issue of your passports will be resolved at that time."

CHAPTER THIRTY-SEVEN

Now that the Capitán had left, the story could end in the co-incidence of ideas, accidents, homicide, and greed. Crimes would be defined, cause of death determined, guilt assessed, an artifact authenticated, and a palace judged worthy of commendation. Dreams of a new Golden Age of Spain would be separated from schemes.

"The lions are authentic," Drummond told Graciela. "I believe my work here is done."

Graciela was not ready to set aside her concern. "Do you really think Montoya had the skill to control the lions from a distance?"

Drummond was sure Rubén was going to find the proof of Montoya's meddling. "Once Dr. Torres finds Montoya's mechanism and disconnects it, the fountain will be working with its natural water supply. You will see that your Wonder of the World is authentic."

"You might extend your stay," Graciela suggested and smiled.

Drummond was silent. He had an assignment waiting for him, a project in London. "I need to leave tomorrow," he explained, "after our meeting with the magistrate.

"A few more days, just to be sure?" Graciela added.

"I'll return, of course, any time you need me," Drummond said. "Is there something else?"

"Yes," she said. "There is. Some objects, which might have been sequestered and would need to be returned." She pulled her desk chair close to the couch where Ana and Rubén were now sitting. She looked directly at Rubén and spoke in a calm but deliberate voice. "Documents removed from the library must be taken back," she said. She could not be a party to the sort of investigative anarchy that Rubén was applying in his obsession with the surrender of the Alhambra. "The cost is too high."

But was it that simple? Graciela wondered. What about Rubén's intellectual curiosity? And not just Rubén's, but her own as well. And all of the people of Spain? Who could let go of a story like the one Rubén had been following? Especially if it were true.

"First, you must see what I found," Rubén said. "You must hear what the lions have been trying to tell us. I will bring you the documents. You need to see the work Ana and I have done."

Graciela knew he was right. She shouldn't be a party to the misplacement of history, even if the original crime had been committed by La Reina Isabela and the Vatican. The story was far from over. "Go," she said, "get what you need and bring it to me."

Rubén wanted Doctora Corzal to understand that his motive had been a lofty one. He hadn't had a choice. His ancestor had handed him a stake in how the history, folklore, and artifacts of the Alhambra would be understood by future generations.

He believed he needed to free the royal correspondence from the Library of the Inquisición. He also understood the Directora's rebuke had been a warning. She wouldn't be granting him any time with the documents. He wouldn't be allowed to retain them long enough to make duplicates. Even if he added a few extra minutes to the few she was allotting, he certainly couldn't copy them there in the hotel. You can't ask a desk clerk to handle fifteenth century royal dispatches as if they were common business records. His one advantage was that the Capitán had given him back his phone.

He waved the hand towel as he stood and headed toward the bedroom. Once inside, he pulled the documents from under the mattress and photographed all the papers—the ones he'd smuggled out of the library plus his copies of the two letters of surrender that he had found in Doctora Corzal's office. Now he had the proof he required. Now, as he carried everything back to the sitting room where Doctora Corzal, Drummond, and Ana were waiting, Rubén was nervous but feeling triumphant.

Ana had opened the windows. The air rising from the street below was cooler now but it still carried the scent of rosemary and the occasional faint sounds of voices. Someone had set out fixings for tea. Perhaps Doctora Corzal was less angry than Rubén had feared.

"We have connected them," Rubén said, showing the documents. "We have connected Boabdil and Luis Torres, and the Inquisitor did the work for us. Torquemada was looking for a way to accuse my grandfather of heresy, witchcraft, and the practice of magic. And I can show it."

Ana asked him to slow down and back up, to talk about the work they'd done the day before when Montoya had allowed them to use his keyword system.

"Montoya created a keyword index," Rubén said, "and we used it to search his catalogue for anything that tied Boabdil to Luis Torres. Water, fountains, Isabela, Torquemada, Solomon…"

"Torre," Ana said. "We truncated Torres to Torre. And my key phrase? Did you find the 'thousands?' The wisdom of the thousands?"

"Of course," Rubén confirmed. "Your ancestors' comparison of numbers with creation. God existed before the universal intellect, just as one came before two. When they kept on counting, it was the 'thousands' they compared to the animals."

Graciela asked if it all had come to light based on the two letters found in her office, because of the discrepancy in the two letters of surrender.

"Sí. Absolutamente," Rubén said. "The discrepancy revealed that Torres and Boabdil had worked together because they didn't want the lions moved away from the Alhambra."

Drummond asked, "And Torres, he was Jewish. Was he safe at that point?"

"He was never safe," Rubén explained, "but Isabela and Torquemada still needed him. He was the best they had. Besides, he carried papers proving he was a converso. Apparently, he was so skilled that Torquemada didn't recognize that his conversion documents were counterfeit."

"You worked as a researcher, not a grandson?" Graciela asked Rubén. "You read these with an open mind? And you told yourself no one conclusion would be better than another?"

"Look at the dates," Rubén said. "You can't forge dates. They prove my theory." Rubén quieted his voice and continued. "Torres had been summoned to the Alhambra several times during the six months before the Boabdil was ordered to clear out of the palace. And the grand inquisitor's letters showed that he knew about meetings on those dates. He had ordered Torres to transcribe those conversations. He made Torres summarize the topics for La Reina. Torres created a simple list of topics for the queen—water, the fountain, poetry, and a thousand somethings."

This was making sense to Graciela. "Zamrak's poetry, of course," she said. "Boabdil would have recited the lines on the fountain."

"And don't forget the verse I recited for you from Ibn Gabirol." Rubén stood up with the French windows open behind him and recited his favorite lines again. "'And there is a full sea, like unto Solomon's Sea, though not on oxen it stands. But there are lions… Whose bellies are wellsprings that spout forth through their mouths floods like streams.'"

Drummond put on the white gloves Rubén had set out next to the letters. He found it humorous that Rubén had carried gloves from Graciela's office, following museum protocol even while breaking into Vatican files. He read the letters again, one by one. He could track the phrases they were calling keywords, and it seemed that Rubén had uncovered a link between Torres and Boabdil that was stronger even than Graciela's secret documents had revealed. But he couldn't see a clear message about the lions.

"Look at your copy of Graciela's 1491 document," Drummond said to Rubén. "Does it actually say 'lions?'"

"Here." Rubén pointed to a line in the earlier letter of surrender that had been removed. "It actually refers to a 'thousand somethings,' which is a reference to animals, and the only animals in the courtyard are lions."

"You are proposing that Torres and Boabdil developed a code?" Drummond asked. "You're saying the lions were not directly itemized, but the 'thousand somethings' were mentioned. And this was all done to confuse the Inquisición?"

Graciela could see how the code theory could be true. "So, the two of you believe that's how the documents establish a safety net of sorts for the lions? A guarantee they will always be kept in the Alhambra?"

Ana hesitated. She didn't think it was her place to define what the Ring of Lions really meant. But when no one else spoke, she said, "Perhaps the lions are a symbol of the animal stories."

"The old stories," Rubén said. "Especially the one about different kinds of animals becoming friends and saving each other from traps and hunters."

Drummond had been studying the graceful way Rubén and Ana were slipping in and out of each other's thoughts. "And the three characters who were just hauled off by the police," he said, "didn't they claim a love for the Alhambra? Didn't they say they were friends?"

"Friendly," Rubén replied, "but not to be trusted as friends. Tricksters and hunters, that's what they are."

"They were certain the fountain could make them rich," Drummond said.

Graciela sighed. "The fountain was never about money. You have to read the writing on the basin—what Zamrak wrote on the edge. 'Silver melting... what is solid, what is fluid...'"

Rubén added, "It's the same matter...what Gabirol was talking about when he said the same matter runs through the entire universe."

"My father thought that's what the animal legends were all about," Ana explained. "In the old story, the king sent the philosopher off to find a tale about different animals joining together, becoming one."

Drummond walked over to the windows and took a deep breath of the evening air. He was thinking about Solomon. It was well known that Solomon talked to animals. Now he was wondering if it was possible that Solomon was the king in Ana's story.

"You're the storyteller," he told Ana. "What do you think?"

Ana knew the king in her story wasn't Solomon. Her stories were from the Sanskrit, the Panchatantra, translated to Arabic and retold in the letters of the Ikhwan. But Solomon would have known a similar tale. Stories are like that. Full of moments that are connected even when they do not overlap. Languages change. The characters change. Places change. Even time changes. But the stories themselves always rhyme. They glance off each other, and their echoes can never be quieted.

ACKNOWLEDGMENTS

My journey to the *Ring of Lions* follows the routes my husband Louis Branca and I often took to Spain, where we broke crisp bread, drank cold sparkling water, and felt this novel come to life. I will always be thankful for his encouragement as this story unveiled itself on the page. I am also thankful for the daily support of all of the readers, writers, editors, artists, and world builders in my family— my children Cletus Dalglish-Schommer and Natasha D'Schommer, my sister Judith Scheide, and Aimee Lopez, Jim Dalglish, and Rob Phelps.

I am deeply appreciative of the attention and care given to my fiction by my editor Gary Lindberg and by Ian Graham Leask and the entire Calumet Editions team.

I am indebted to Jane Austin Scholar Devoney Looser, who by offering context for this novel in her Foreword, has placed this fiction in very interesting company.

Special thanks for the encouragement I received from Augsburg University faculty members, students in the Augsburg MFA program, and Augsburg undergraduate creative writing majors, including Andrea Sanow who took part in an experiment that gave both of us the opportunity to begin writing our novels during the academic year.

So many colleagues were willing to read *Ring of Lions,* some of them more than once. They include scholar of languages and mythology Deb Dale Jones; prose writers and poets laureate D.E. Green and Becky Boling; novelist and short story writer George Rabasa; poet and nonfiction writer Cary Waterman; research wizard Boyd Koehler; colleague and assiduous reader of mysteries Elise Marubbio; historical nonfiction writer Jack El Hai; storyteller Neal Karlen; poet and editor Jim Cihlar; writer and editor Gordon Thomas; professor of literature Jonathon Hill; and VCFA fiction retreat authors Clint McCown and Connie May Fowler.

I am so pleased to have found the work of editors and translators including Frederick P. Bargebuhr and Peter Cole who have kept the texts of Spanish poets and philosophers available for readers; the poets and philosophers themselves—Solomon Ibn Gabirol, Abu Abd Allah Muhammad ibn Zamrak, Shalom Ibn Tzaqbel, Moses Maimonides, and many others writing in Hebrew and Arabic—along with all the craftsmen who wrote on the walls of the Alhambra.

I give thanks to César Requesens and Tatjana Portnova for inviting me to Granada Secreta; Virginia Vázquez Hernández for explaining the poem of the Puerta de Comares; Nadia Jamil and Jeremy Johns for their Ibn Zamrak translation in the Hall of Two Sisters; Francisco de Icaza for his words on the sadness of being blind in Granada; Ian Richard Netton for offering us the thoughts of the Muslim Neoplatonists; Robert Irwin for guiding us through the Alhambra; Federico Garcia Lorca for writing his poems and revealing his understanding of duende; the keepers and tellers of the stories of the Kalila wa Dimna; and Miguel de Cervantes for helping me tell my story.

It was during my first year as an undergraduate Spanish major when my advisor, Julio Castañeda, told me, "If you have not seen Granada, you have not seen anything." Of course, he told me in Spanish, "Quién no ha visto Granada, no ha visto nada." Professor Castañeda was correct.

ABOUT THE AUTHOR

Cass Dalglish is known for diving deeply into the past to bring historical figures into communication with fictional characters. Her published works include: *Sweetgrass*, Lone Oak Press, a novel, mystery; *Nin*, Spinsters Ink, a novel tracing the history of women's writing and offering an email debate between medieval women writers and misogynist male philosophers; *Humming the Blues*, Calyx Press, a jazz poetry interpretation of pictographs in the first signed document in history (2350 BCE Enheduanna). A Spanish language version of *Humming* is near completion. A kinetic interpretation, Enheduanna's Song to Inanna, is available on YouTube. Cass holds a BA in Spanish from St. Catherine University, an MFA in Creative Writing from Vermont College of Fine Arts, and a PhD in Writing with a concentration in Ancient and Archetypal Women's Literature from the Union Institute & University. Her curiosity has also led her to the study of languages, mythology, and energy practice. As a professor of English at Augsburg University in Minneapolis, Cass was lead designer and first director of Augsburg's MFA in Creative Writing. Cass studied and lived in Mexico, Chile, Colombia, and Cuba, and traveled to Andalucía to research *Ring of Lions*. She lives in Minneapolis, where she worked early in her career as a broadcast journalist.

Made in the USA
Monee, IL
19 February 2025

12255389R00177